P9-DNO-562

PRAISE FOR
SHAYLA BLACK

"Scorching, wrenching, suspenseful, Shayla Black's books are a must-read."   —Lora Leigh, #1 *New York Times* bestselling author

"Much sexy fun is had by all."
                    —Angela Knight, *New York Times* bestselling author

"Orgasmic."   —*Publishers Weekly*

"Wickedly seductive from start to finish."
                    —Jaci Burton, *New York Times* bestselling author

PRAISE FOR
RHYANNON BYRD

"Combines passion and suspense with a touch of deadly danger guaranteed to keep you reading until the very last page."
                                        —*Joyfully Reviewed*

"A fast-paced, action-packed tale starring destined mates investigating a deadly truth."   —*Midwest Book Review*

"Byrd successfully combines a haunting love story with complex world-building."   —*Publishers Weekly*

Titles by Shayla Black

The Wicked Lovers Novels

WICKED TIES

DECADENT

DELICIOUS

SURRENDER TO ME

BELONG TO ME

MINE TO HOLD

OURS TO LOVE

Anthologies

FOUR PLAY
(with Maya Banks)

HOT IN HANDCUFFS
(with Sylvia Day and Shiloh Walker)

WICKED AND DANGEROUS
(with Rhyannon Byrd)

Specials

HER FANTASY MEN

Titles by Shayla Black writing as Shelley Bradley

BOUND AND DETERMINED

STRIP SEARCH

Titles by Rhyannon Byrd

TAKE ME UNDER

WICKED

AND

DANGEROUS

SHAYLA BLACK

RHYANNON BYRD

B

BERKLEY SENSATION, NEW YORK

THE BERKLEY PUBLISHING GROUP
Published by the Penguin Group
Penguin Group (USA)
375 Hudson Street, New York, New York 10014, USA

USA I Canada I UK I Ireland I Australia I New Zealand I India I South Africa I China

Penguin Books Ltd., Registered Offices: 80 Strand, London WC2R 0RL, England
For more information about the Penguin Group, visit penguin.com.

This book is an original publication of The Berkley Publishing Group.

Copyright © 2013 by Penguin Group (USA).
"Wicked All Night" by Shayla Black copyright © 2013 by Shelley Bradley, LLC.
"Make Me Yours" by Rhyannon Byrd copyright © 2013 by Tabitha Bird.
All rights reserved. No part of this book may be reproduced, scanned, or distributed in any printed or
electronic form without permission. Please do not participate in or encourage piracy of copyrighted
materials in violation of the author's rights. Purchase only authorized editions.

Berkley Sensation Books are published by The Berkley Publishing Group.
BERKLEY SENSATION® is a registered trademark of Penguin Group (USA)
The "B" design is a trademark of Penguin Group (USA)

Library of Congress Cataloging-in-Publication Data

Wicked and dangerous / Shayla Black and Rhyannon Byrd.—Berkley Sensation trade paperback edition.
pages cm
ISBN 978-0-425-26375-4 (pbk.)
1. American fiction—21st century.   I. Black, Shayla. Wicked all night.   II. Byrd, Rhyannon.
Make me yours.   III. Title.
PS659.2.W53 2013
813'.010806—dc23   2013020743

PUBLISHING HISTORY
Berkley Sensation trade paperback edition / October 2013

PRINTED IN THE UNITED STATES OF AMERICA

10 9 8 7 6 5 4 3 2 1

Cover photo by Shutterstock.
Cover design by Jerry Todd.
Interior text design by Kristin del Rosario

This is a work of fiction. Names, characters, places, and incidents either are the product
of the author's imagination or are used fictitiously, and any resemblance to actual persons,
living or dead, business establishments, events, or locales is entirely coincidental.
The publisher does not have any control over and does not assume any responsibility for
author or third-party websites or their content.

CONTENTS

WICKED ALL NIGHT

SHAYLA BLACK

To Rhyannon Byrd
for years of friendship and laughter—
and for giving me such a fun heroine to work with.
I had a blast!

ONE

AS DECKER MCCONNELL STRODE INTO THE LOUD BAR AT HALF past nine on a Saturday night, the woman's picture burned a hole in the pocket of his black shirt. In the past six hours, he'd stared at it a hundred times. Rachel Linden, age twenty-nine. Divorced. Graduate of UCLA, summa cum laude, with a degree in education. Recent transplant from sleepy Moss Beach on the Florida coast to Louisiana. Currently employed by the Lafayette Parish school system as an elementary English teacher. Those facts might define the brunette whose dark eyes sparkled from a seemingly average oval face, but that didn't explain why just looking at her photo made him hard as hell.

"You sure this Rachel woman is going to be here?" his boss, Xander Santiago, asked, propped up against the quiet corner of the bar on his left.

"Unless she bails on her own birthday party, yep. I've got to find her before this situation goes south."

Decker sighed and surveyed the crowd through the club's flashing lights. People were getting their drink on and looking around for a nightly hookup. From what he could gather, Rachel was only here because the new neighbors and coworkers who had become her friends insisted that she celebrate her big day. Though the club was packed more tightly than meat behind cellophane, he hoped he'd spot her soon. Every minute that slid by was another minute that bad shit could happen.

And he wasn't about to let it. He was a protector by nature. If the cops weren't going to help, then he guessed it had become his job. For whatever reason—boredom, maybe?—he felt the urge to make sure she stayed safe.

Rachel's picture suggested that she possessed a shy, good-girl quality. Not usually the kind of female he gravitated to. That meant he'd probably find her in a corner somewhere, trying to blend into the wall. He'd have to fish around for some way to set her at ease before he glued himself to her side long enough to untangle this clusterfuck he'd unwittingly stepped in. As far as he was concerned, naked was the best way to keep her from harm's way because he wasn't remotely interested in being her big brother. Everything he'd been able to dig up indicated that since becoming single again, she'd lived like a nun. That was really fucking unfair to the male species. The idea of her peeling off a button-down shirt and "work-appropriate" skirt to reveal her soft curves, scantily clad in lingerie, made his cock stand up and salute.

Get your mind out of the gutter and back on business.

Decker hated that voice in his head. The gutter was way more fun.

"Are you sure about this?" Xander's brother, Javier, asked beside him.

He turned to the guy with a shrug. "No, but I don't know

what my more appealing options are. Believe me, if I hadn't run into a colossal pile of shit this afternoon looking for a cold beer and an easy lay, I wouldn't be here now, searching for a woman I've never met."

"And you tried the police?" Xander asked.

"Useless." Decker rolled his eyes. "How much evidence should I need to prove another man's intent to commit a crime? The fuckers could at least look into it."

But the lazy bastards of the Lafayette Police Department hadn't listened to a word he'd said while LSU played football. On the other hand, he probably shouldn't send a starched uniform fresh out of the backwoods police academy to do a job the CIA had trained him once upon a time to do far better.

"So you think this plan will work?" Javier asked.

"You got a better one?" He shoved Rachel's picture under the other man's nose. "Look at her. She's a school teacher. She looks sweet, for fuck's sake. I can't stand here with my thumb up my ass and let this nut job put a hole in her head."

Studying the picture, Javier sipped his tonic water. After a couple of years of supposedly being cozier with vodka than sanity, sobriety now suited him. "Of course not. I'm just saying that if she's recently divorced, she might not appreciate you romancing her for ulterior motives."

"What my brother means is that in a few short months of marriage to London, we've learned how quickly our lovely bride can hand us our balls when we've screwed up." Xander smiled. "He's thinking that you'd probably like to keep yours attached to your body."

"Exactly." Javier grinned.

"I can't tell her the truth," Decker argued. "Why would she believe a total stranger trying to convince her that someone's put a price on her head? Besides the twenty-five grand and the phone number this guy gave me, all I've got is her picture and some basic information I could have pulled off the Internet. None of that proves anything. If she actually does believe me, I'd probably scare the hell out of her." He tossed his hands up. "This asshole gave me a few days to finish the job. I'll just make the problem go away by then. Even if Rachel isn't thrilled with my method, she'll be alive."

He peered deeper into the club, ignoring the come-ons of a few girls who didn't look old enough to even be here, wearing skirts so short he could almost tell if the carpet matched the drapes. Finally, the crowd parted, and he spotted his target near the wall, just as he'd predicted. Rachel. White wine in hand. Long hair like a chocolate waterfall. Pretty profile. Thick lashes. Button nose. Full lips that would look perfect wrapped around his cock.

Damn it, he wanted to get her naked. What a shame that wasn't his first priority with her, but he hoped he could find a way to make it a close second.

She smiled as a tall, African-American woman beside her whispered in her ear. Then suddenly, Rachel whipped her gaze around and met his stare. Her little, rosy mouth opened with a gasp. Even through the smoke and over the racket of the bad country singer on the stage across the room, he could all but hear the sound. Yeah, he felt the electric zing, too. Up his spine and clear down to his toes, it engorged his cock so completely, he wanted to rip off that god-awful sensible blouse she wore, tear away her panties, and fuck her breathless in the next thirty seconds. Normally, he would, but this situation meant he had to use the head up north—at least a little. And didn't that just piss him off.

How fucking ironic that he couldn't pick her up just for the fun of it. No, he had to get close to keep her alive. Honestly,

Decker didn't like lying to her either. The hell of it was he couldn't think of another way to protect the woman he'd been hired to kill.

RACHEL LINDEN FIXED her gaze across the room at the man staring her way, standing between the two suits. Her jaw dropped before she forcibly snapped it shut. *Holy cow!* Between the alcohol and the press of bodies, she was overheated. But he made her shiver.

Military-short black hair capped off his angled face, covered by a healthy two days' growth of beard. His eyes remained hidden behind a pair of aviators that rested on top of chiseled cheekbones. His black shirt nearly busted at the shoulder seams. Under the short sleeves, his biceps bulged. The soft cotton clung to every valley and ridge of his pectorals and abdominals.

He was a man with a capital M, the sort who made a woman swallow her tongue. The kind her mother had warned her about. The type who'd starred in her fantasies. And the one she wanted sliding against her skin-to-skin now. Dark and bad, yes . . . but those big hands and muscled forearms alone said he'd be oh so good.

Just looking at him, Rachel had trouble breathing. Every inch of him was hard. If she'd had a fantasy in the flesh, he'd be it.

A tattoo—Asian writing maybe—drifted down his veined forearm. Dog tags hung from his neck. The little smile curling his lips was somewhere between an invitation and a challenge. And he was staring directly at her.

The bottom fell out of her stomach. Normally, she'd shy away from such a man. Aaron, the fifth grade social studies teacher, had asked her out a few weeks ago. He was polite and had kind brown eyes. He'd mentioned a local theater production that sounded interesting. That was her speed. This man in front of her . . .

"He looks good enough to eat. And to lick, slurp, suck . . . Damn, girl!" Shonda, one of the art teachers, murmured in her ear.

If you're going to dive into a meal after starving, why not start with the juiciest one you can find?

She glanced at Shonda's dark skin gleaming under the dim house lights and faintly flashing colored strobes. "Is it my imagination or is he staring at me?"

"Right at you, like he thinks you're a tasty snack. Go on now. Talk to him."

And say what? Hi, I haven't had sex since I divorced my ex over a year ago, and I've never had it as down and dirty and sweaty as I'll bet you could give it to me.

"Maybe he thinks I work here."

Shonda snorted. "Maybe you're insane. Jarelle is an awesome fiancé with enough freak in bed to keep me smiling, but hell . . . If I were single, I'd be all over that guy like paste on wallpaper."

Rachel laughed. Leave it to Shonda to tell it like it was. And to be right. Rachel had to admit that she'd never know what could be if she didn't try to talk to Mr. Tall, Dark, and Hot.

She turned back toward him, a welcoming smile in place. But he was already leaving behind his two friends, wearing insanely expensive suits, and walking her way. No, "walking" was the wrong word. "Approaching" was too weak. "Looming" maybe? Still not right. "Prowling," yes. "Stalking" sounded even more like it.

He tore off his sunglasses to reveal a stark pair of blue eyes, unabashedly roaming over her body with a heat that made her swallow. He kept coming at her, invading her personal space without compunction. Reflexively, she retreated. He smiled, then did it again and again—until her back hit the wall.

"Hi, beautiful."

Mercy, the low rumble of his voice was sexy. Her knees quaked.

"Hi." She breathed the word as if she couldn't quite catch her breath.

He looked her up and down, obviously scoping her out. "Hmm, you with all those curves, and me here with no breaks . . . Damn!"

OMG, was that some sort of pick-up line?

"Um . . ."

If he'd intended to flatter her, he was headed in the wrong direction. She'd write him off, except . . . The black skirt Shonda had insisted she wear tonight had seemed stupidly tight—until she saw the appreciation in his gaze. That and his line, no matter how terrible, made her think that, maybe, he actually found her sexy. And she wasn't interested in him for his conversational skills.

"Too much, huh?" he asked with a frown. "How about, there must be something wrong with my eyes because I can't take them off you."

He *was* trying to pick her up—badly—but out of a bar full of pretty girls, he'd zeroed in on her. Would wonders never cease?

Maybe if she stopped focusing on her ex-husband's litany of critical comments and started to believe that some men might like her as she was, curves and all, it wouldn't seem so weird.

"Definitely too much." She gave him a smile that she hoped looked sophisticated and wry, rather than giggly and excited.

"Oh, you like subtle. I got it." He leaned closer and leered. "Hey, baby, you come here often?"

The most obvious pick-up line ever, and when he delivered it with a grin, she laughed. If this was his idea of starting a conversation, she wasn't sure whether she should be annoyed or charmed against her will. But she was definitely leaning toward the latter.

"Never. This is my first time," she admitted. "You?"

"Same. I was thinking that I hated places like this until I saw you. You're better than a broom because you swept me off my feet."

Rachel couldn't help but laugh. "Right . . ."

"No lie, beautiful." He winked at her. "Tell me, what's your sign?"

Yield. If she were holding a sign, that's probably what it would say because that's kind of what she wanted to do for him. Oh, but she guessed that wasn't what he meant.

"Libra," she said finally. "Today is my birthday. And I'll only keep talking to you if you stop with the pick-up lines."

"Happy birthday! You mean I can't ask you for a Band-Aid?"

She frowned. How had they gone from pick-up lines to Band-Aids? "I'm sorry?"

"I need one because I scraped my knees falling for you."

Rachel tossed her hands up, shaking her head, and giggled. "Does this sort of thing usually work for you?"

He shrugged. "Don't know. I never tried. You wanna tell me come morning?"

"My mama has a word for men like you. 'Incorrigible.' "

Mock horror crossed his face. "I've given you the impression that I'm a bad boy with no manners. Okay, maybe that's not too far off. How about we start over? Decker."

He held out his hand for a friendly shake, and she hesitated only an instant before she slipped hers inside. A quick sizzle between them nearly made her shiver. It traveled up her arm and

through her body as his hand—warm, calloused, and huge—
engulfed hers. Dark hair dusted his forearms. Veins stood out.
Decker was obviously strong, but he touched her gently. When
he smiled, the light inside reached his eyes.

"I'm Rachel."

Slowly, he released her, and she was almost disappointed when
he did. "So, Rachel the birthday girl, can I buy you a drink?"

She shook her head. "I've already had two. That's my limit. I
still have to drive home."

"How about a dance?"

As if the cosmos knew exactly what Decker had planned, the
twangy singer suddenly took a break and the deejay played something slow and sexy—the kind of music that made people want
to drop their clothes and get horizontal.

"I'm not much of a dancer," she demurred.

Because if she pressed up against him and swayed to the music, she might get ideas about taking him for a test drive, at least
for the night.

Wasn't that half the point of coming here?

She'd allowed Shonda and a few of the others to drag her to
this dive to not only celebrate her big two-nine, but to see if,
maybe, she could find a hot guy to spend the night with. She
hadn't been touched since well before her divorce, and she wanted
to be kissed, experience some serious skin-on-skin contact, then
cuddle afterward. Decker didn't necessarily look like he special-
ized in cuddling, but he seemed more than capable of making her
scream. A definite bonus since giving orgasms had never been
Owen's strong suit.

"Good thing for you I am, then. C'mon . . . One little dance
won't hurt. It's either that or I give you more bad pick-up lines
until you agree."

"You have more?"

"Oh yeah!" He grinned. "Can I have your picture so I can show Santa what I want for Christmas?"

"That's months away."

"Good point. I don't want to wait that long." He thought for a moment, then grinned again. "Are you a parking ticket? Because you've got 'fine' written all over you."

"Oh my—Where do you find this stuff?"

"Thank the great people at Google."

"You looked that up on purpose?"

"Yep. I'm sure my mom would be super proud."

She slapped her hand to her forehead. When was the last time she'd laughed this much around a man? Never. Owen possessed zero sense of humor. Decker was totally different—and a welcome change.

Swallowing back her usual caution, Rachel nodded at him. "One dance."

"Great!" He grabbed her hand and tugged her onto the floor.

As he dragged her past her friends, she turned to see Shonda give her a thumbs-up, her neon pink nail polish glowing in the dim lighting. Beside her, the office aide, Alicia, laughed at something a guy at the next table said. Every man talked to Alicia. Blond and stacked and sweet as the day was long, it was a miracle that she was still single at the ripe age of twenty-four. Rachel was sure that some smart guy would come along soon and rectify that.

"Ah ah, eyes here, birthday girl." Decker gave a little tug on her arm, and she fell right against him. He settled his arms loosely around her waist, his big hands laying claim to the small of her back. His fingers dipped a little bit lower. His blue eyes flared with wicked heat. "Now I've got you where I want you. But I might have a problem."

She gave him a wary frown. "What's that?"

"I hope you know CPR because you take my breath away."

A laugh spilled out before she could stop it. She gave his shoulder a playful hit. "Stop. Tell me something about you, other than your affinity for looking up crazy things on Google. Where are you from? What do you do?"

"I'm from all over. Military brat who eventually went into the military, too. I've been out a few years. Then I did some work for Uncle Sam. Now I work for S.I. Industries in security."

The military fit. Working for the government? She doubted very much he'd pushed pencils for the IRS, but she didn't pry. Security made sense, too. With his ridiculously bulging shoulders and air of strength, he looked more than capable of being a protector.

"S.I. Industries?" she asked. "Was that Javier and Xander Santiago you were talking to?"

Since moving to Lafayette over the summer, she'd read their names and seen their pictures repeatedly in the local rag. The brothers were only slightly better known for their prestigious, growing company and the jobs it was bringing to the area as they were for the rumors they shared a wife.

"Yes. I've worked for Xander for a few years. Until he got married, I did nothing but bail him out of scrapes. Now I devote my spare time to whatever makes mischief." He winked. "How about you?"

"I'm a school teacher. Fifth grade English."

Decker gave her a long, slow smile. "I got a whole bunch of naughty teacher fantasies."

"*I've* got," she corrected automatically.

"You, too?" He pretended to misunderstand. "Awesome! You know, if you were my homework, I'd be doing you on my desk."

"You did not just say that," she scolded.

"I totally did." He flashed her a grin. "Google really is helpful. I have more."

"Stop, please." Rachel laughed. "I'm raising the white flag."

"Not yet. I have one more you need to hear." Decker curled his arms more tightly around her.

The breath of air between them disappeared as he fitted her against his body. Rachel gasped. He was hard all over. Her palms slid up his biceps and over his shoulders, both like rocks. His chest was like a hot slab of concrete. The ridges of his abdomen led her to believe there'd be at least a six-pack under there. But lower . . . He bent his knees a fraction and notched his erection against the vulnerable V between her legs. And oh, all that thickness and length couldn't be him, could it?

"Yes?" she moaned as he rolled his hips against her and hit one really pleasurable spot that . . . wow.

"That's a nice dress you're wearing," he murmured in her ear, then brushed his lips up the side of her neck until she trembled and closed her eyes.

"It's a skirt and blouse."

"Whatever. It would look better on the floor next to my bed."

Rachel's breath caught. He was propositioning her. Guys like him never found her attractive. They usually liked Alicia. On the one hand, her libido definitely wanted to say yes. She found everything about him made her heart rev. Her common sense might be hesitating, but every cell in her body clamored for her to rub against him and grab whatever pleasure he was willing to give her. But the more cautious part of her just wouldn't be shushed.

"How do I know you're not a crazed killer?"

He cocked his head. "You have any Taliban or drug cartel affiliations?"

"Um . . ." Rachel reared back a bit in his arms. "No. I can safely say that I don't."

"Then we'll have no problems. The only thing I want to massacre is your desire to say no."

Decker might have phrased it like a joke, but he looked dead serious. Was she actually considering this? Was she really thinking of going home with a man she'd met ten minutes ago and opening her body to him?

Well, sunshine, if you want sex with a hot guy, it's not like Magnolia Elementary school is a hotbed of gorgeous, single men. You're going to have to step out on a limb.

Ugh, she hated that little devil on her shoulder, always urging her to do something she probably shouldn't.

Rachel opened her mouth to politely decline when the voice blared in her ear again.

Think about this. Who talked you into marrying the poster child for bedroom boredom, even knowing he was way more versed in physics than pleasure?

The voice had a really good point. Besides, he worked for a good company and had friends who were upstanding financial pillars of the community now. How bad could he be?

She peered up at Decker, curling her arms just a bit tighter around his neck. "Do you know anything about physics?"

He raised a dark brow. "Would that turn you on?"

"No." Not at all.

"Then you'll be happy to know I failed eleventh grade science."

"Thrilled." She sent him her most dazzling smile.

"Is that a yes?" Decker pulled her closer, his face going straight into the crook of her neck, his whiskers awakening her skin with gentle abrasion.

How would it feel if he dragged his face up her body? Between her thighs? He drew his lips to the soft skin of her ear. Rachel caught her breath.

He nipped, tugged on her sensitive lobe. "Please say that's a yes. You're so fucking beautiful, you made me forget my next pick-up line."

She shivered at the rough whisper in her ear. The musky scent of his male flesh surrounded her completely. Hard, demanding, unyielding . . . he made her blood rush and parts of her surprisingly damp. What *if* she said yes?

"I want to be in charge," she breathed out, then nodded, finding her voice again. "Of everything. I want to say where and when and how."

He pulled back enough to cup her face. Surprise glowed in his deep blue eyes. "Is that how you usually roll, beautiful?"

With a nervous shake of her head, she forced herself to meet his gaze head on—and not think about the fact that his lips hovered just above her own. "No. But I need that now. I want to tell you what I want."

A grin creased his face, and he relaxed. "You should always be able to tell a man what you want. If his little ego is offended, he doesn't have much of one in the first place. And I can guarantee you, his mind isn't the only thing about him that's small."

Rachel laughed, but he wasn't wrong. Every suggestion she'd ever made in the bedroom, no matter how gentle, Owen had taken as criticism. He'd always gotten stiff—and she didn't mean his, um . . . member, which hadn't been at all big.

"I don't want any surprises. I don't want to feel out of control." She'd spent so much time turning herself inside out, trying to please Owen, only to constantly fall short. She'd never known when she was going to encounter a bad mood, the cold shoulder, or a completely unsatisfying quickie. He hadn't seemed to care how any of that made her feel, and she refused to repeat that experience.

"All right. If that's the way you want it, I'm game. You lead the way, and I'll follow."

She sighed with relief. "My place. Now."

Even saying the words made a little shiver curl up her spine. His answering grin suggested lots of screaming fun in her future. What could go wrong?

DECKER HAD TO work to hold in his surprise. If she enjoyed being in charge in the bedroom, he'd change his name to Bugs Bunny. But he'd deal with that when they hit the sheets. As soon as he'd absolved her of the notion that she had an ounce of Dominant blood in her veins, he'd send her into an orgasm-induced stupor. *Then* he'd get to work. But he didn't think he could focus on business for long before he took care of pleasure because her curves were killing his concentration.

His first order of business, unrelated to partaking of her sweetness he couldn't wait to corrupt, would be to take a quick trek through her e-mails, Facebook, and texts. He'd look for anything that might give him some clue about who would want her dead and why, see how they fit with the asshole who'd sat next to him at the bar earlier today. Frankly, his money was on the ex-husband. Nothing like divorce to make someone want a fatal bullet full of revenge. No idea what Rachel had done to "deserve" it, and he didn't care. He wasn't letting the scumbag who'd solicited him to commit murder succeed.

He grinned at her. "Your place, huh? Let's go."

"I've got to grab my purse." She turned away and took his

hand, leading him back to her table. "I must be out of my mind." He heard her mutter to herself.

Nice to know that she didn't make a habit of picking up guys in bars, but it didn't matter. He had a stash of condoms and a mission to accomplish. Rachel's personal life otherwise was none of his business.

As they reached the table, he noticed that most of her party had left in the past few minutes. Or hooked up with others and dispersed. But the tall woman with the chocolate skin was staring at her phone with wide eyes.

"I've got to go!" She grabbed her coat and looked at Rachel anxiously. "My little brother has been in a car accident. The ambulance is rushing him to the hospital."

Shock hit Rachel's face. "Go!"

"Alicia . . ."

"I'll take her home."

The woman's dark eyes slid over Rachel holding his hand. "You're busy . . ."

"You're having an emergency. I can pause for ten minutes to take Alicia home. Go!"

The statuesque woman nodded, then hugged Rachel. "Thanks."

"Do you need me at the hospital?"

The woman hesitated, but looked like she wanted to say yes. "I'll call you."

Well, hell . . . Here might be a fly in his ointment. Decker winced. He'd look like a grade-A ass for insisting they fuck while some kid might be fighting for his life. "Do you need to take a rain check, beautiful?"

She hesitated. "I have to take another friend home first."

"And your mind is going to be on her brother." He nodded

after the black woman with the outrageous shoes currently scurrying to the door.

Rachel bit her lip. "Probably. I'm really sorry . . ."

She was loyal to her friends, and he admired that. Knowing that she cared about the people around her made him feel even more protective.

Boohoo. Next thing he knew, he'd be crying at greeting card commercials. Even if she'd been the douchiest bitch from hell, he wouldn't condone her ex or some random ass-hat trying to do her in.

"Don't worry about it. How about I give you my number, and you see if you feel like calling me tomorrow?" He hated leaving the ball in her court. It seriously went against his grain, but he couldn't come on too strong now without making her suspicious. He'd think of something tomorrow, if necessary.

But that didn't mean he intended to leave her alone tonight.

"Really?"

Those big, dark eyes of hers widened in surprise. Hell, those were going to be the undoing of all his bad intentions. One of those expressions, and he felt like he was contemplating seducing Little Bo Peep, for fuck's sake.

"Of course. As much as I'd like to spend tonight with you, I can be patient. If you're still interested tomorrow, I'm yours. Don't get me wrong, I'm fighting the urge to make you the happiest woman on the planet tonight." He grinned, and she bestowed that gorgeous smile on him with the dimple in her left cheek that somehow made him harder. "But I suppose I can make you doubly happy tomorrow."

"I'd like that," she murmured.

And Decker believed that she meant it. *Hot damn!*

He scribbled the number of the new disposable phone he'd

picked up before coming here on the back of the bar's napkin and wrote his first name, then handed it to her. Rachel took it with a smile.

"It was good to meet you. I'm going to get out of here and take Alicia home, but . . . really, thanks for making me smile."

"You deserve a great birthday, beautiful. I hope your friend's brother is all right."

Just in case he'd misread her and she didn't intend to call, then he'd have to barge his way into her life in a less seductive fashion. That would suck. He wanted her taste on his tongue at least this once. He could be satisfied with one kiss, right?

TWO

DECKER TOOK HOLD OF HER SOFT CHEEKS AND TILTED HER lips under his, pressing a kiss to her mouth. Pliant, moist, velvety. *Holy shit.* Her sweetness absolutely flattened him.

No way he'd ever be satisfied with just one kiss.

Without another thought, he charged in, taking possession of her mouth and demanding more. In his arms, Rachel stiffened. Crap, he had to dial back the urgency and the impulse to crush those sweet lips under his own and take control. But this girl was like sinking into his most sugary-spun fantasy. He could kiss her for the next two days and not get enough. The idea of owning her lips for his use by his mouth, by his cock . . . Hell, he was about to bust out of his jeans.

Under him, Rachel suddenly whimpered, and Decker braced himself for her to push him away. Instead, she threw her arms around him, latched on like she was drowning, and pressed those plump breasts against his chest. He didn't need more green light than that.

Decker gripped her tighter, dove in deeper, caressing his way down her back and grabbing a handful of her pert ass, settling in for a really atomic lip lock. He tangled his tongue with hers, shared her breath, and rocked against her. She shouldn't have to guess what he wanted or how badly he ached for it. Rachel stood on her tiptoes and melted against him even more.

Until the jerk at the next table shoved his chair back, straight into them. Then she gasped and wriggled away. *Damn it to hell . . .*

He wanted to yank her back against him, wrap her legs around his waist, and fuck her into next week. But he'd promised to give her control. If he wanted more of her later, he had to live up to his word and let her go now.

Decker couldn't resist brushing her sultry lips with his own one last time, then reluctantly he forced himself to release her. "I really hope you call."

Rachel smiled, her cheeks a flushed pink discernible even in the dim light. He would bet every dime in his bank account that she didn't have a whole lot of sexual experience. And he'd be happy as hell to broaden her horizons.

Decker turned away and maneuvered through the crowd to the front of the club, then shoved the door open. Stepping out into the balmy October evening, he strode to his bike and ripped the chin strap of his helmet off the highway peg before shoving the damn thing on his head. Annoyance chafed. Of course he wanted to fuck her. But it went against his instincts to leave her alone right now for even a minute. Decker took a deep breath. He had to hope that whoever wanted her dead would give him the promised few days to complete the job before sending some-one else.

Straddling his Ducati, he settled back onto the leather seat.

Sure enough, a few minutes later, Rachel rushed out of the night-club, keys in hand, and headed to her car, her blond friend swaying drunkenly behind her. She unlocked a sturdy little white Toyota with her key fob. Halfway across the parking lot, she fished in her purse for her phone, completely ignoring her surroundings. Absently, she dialed someone and spoke to the trailing blonde, still not paying any attention to potential danger. Decker made a mental note to teach her to stay alert before he squashed this murder-for-hire plot and moved on. And once she admitted that she wasn't any sort of Domme, he might even blister her ass a little for this episode, just for fun.

The thought made him smile.

Rachel piled her inebriated friend into the passenger's seat, then hustled around the car before climbing in. Decker took that as his cue to start his bike and follow. He kept a respectable distance—not that she was paying a lick of attention—and followed her to the other woman's place, watching Rachel help her up the stairs and into her little cookie-cutter apartment. Then she raced back to her car, on the fucking phone again, and drove off. God, if he'd wanted to kill her, he could have done it twenty times by now before she ever realized she was dead.

Next stop was the hospital. The parking lot was lit decently, and the emergency room was hopping. But this many strangers this close to her made him nervous. He parked his bike and followed discreetly until she was safely inside, hating that he couldn't trail her any closer without being seen.

With a sigh, he waited in the shadows. Just in case the prick who'd hired him was impatient, he wasn't going to give anyone the opportunity to off her in a parking lot and make it look random.

About ninety minutes later, she emerged under the little portico outside the ER's automatic door. She and her wildly dressed friend exchanged a few words under the glaring LED lights overhead and hugged. The black woman's face was dotted with tears and smudged mascara, but she managed a relieved smile. Then Rachel darted out to her car as the other woman headed back into the hospital. Decker followed his little bundle of curves in the sinful black skirt. She never noticed.

Predictably, Rachel drove straight toward home. When she finally looked in her rearview mirror at a stoplight, he turned right onto another street, taking a gamble that she didn't have an alternate destination in mind. He raced to her darkened cottage on the quiet residential street he'd scoped out during recon earlier in the evening. Ditching his bike on the next cul-de-sac, he dashed around the block to beat Rachel. He wanted to check inside, make sure she didn't come home to any nasty surprises.

It took him all of two minutes to jimmy his way through a back window. She had zero security—another conversation they'd be having before he hit the road again. He crawled through to a guest room, figuring he had three minutes at most to scope out the place before she pulled into her little attached garage.

In less than sixty seconds, he'd crept through every room in the house, pried open closets, checked any other obvious hiding spots. The place was spotless and devoid of any life except a purring cat who curled around his ankles. He'd always been a dog person.

"Hairball . . ." he groused.

"*Meow*," the little orange tabby wailed at him, rubbing against his pant leg again.

Decker smiled, despite himself, and scratched the cat between the ears. "I'll bet she spoils you rotten and rubs you all the time, lucky thing."

The cat only purred louder.

He caught sight of her computer on a little desk in the corner of her living room. He'd check her phone as soon as she nodded off. Framed photos rested all around her place, on shelves, countertops, and the mantle. He didn't dare turn on lights now to investigate, but soon.

Finally, he heard the electronic hum of the garage door opening. He beat feet to a hiding place he'd found during his search, wedging into the guest room closet behind her winter clothes and the leaf for her dining room table. She came in and he heard her drop her keys in the little copper dish on the console table in her foyer. Her heels clicked across the hardwood, then stopped abruptly. He tensed.

"Did you have a good evening, Val? Been a good boy? Miss me?"

"*Meow.*"

"Don't look at me like that. I fed you before I left. I didn't leave you for that long." When the cat meowed again, she sighed. "Give me a minute, and we'll go to bed. Why you can't find the bed without me is a mystery."

As Decker grinned, she started across the floor again, and the click of her shoes progressed past the guest room and down the hall. In the master bedroom, he heard the smart tap of her heels stop before she dropped them on the floor and moaned in relief.

A minute later, he heard her set something on a hard surface with a gentle plop, then a door closed. The shower began to run.

Rachel was going to get naked. Fuck if that didn't turn him on all over again.

Decker yanked his brains out of his jeans and waited about sixty seconds before he crept from the closet. No sign of her. He heard the water splashing inside the stall and the sound of her singing a peppy, upbeat pop tune about someone calling her maybe. He couldn't fight the grin on his face as he made his way into her bedroom.

Here was a good place to start his search for clues. The cat lounged on the bed and raised his head with a yawn. Damn hairball got to sleep with Rachel tonight. Hell yeah, he was jealous.

Hustling across the room, he found her phone on her nightstand. No password protection. He shook his head and accessed her texts. It didn't take long to scroll through them. A message from Shonda earlier in the day detailing her party at the nightclub. Her mother asking whether she'd be coming home for Thanksgiving. Her neighbor begging her to cat-sit. Decker yawned until he came to Owen. It didn't take him long to surmise that this was the name of her ex-barfbag, and didn't he sound like a real fun guy.

Did you take my box of books in the closet of my study when you left? I am missing several crucial texts relating to relativistic quantum fields, two-level atoms, and condensed matter.

He was a physicist? Wow, if Rachel went for the studious type, Decker figured he wouldn't last long with her. Of course she'd claimed she was thrilled he wasn't into such things . . . But from about the tenth grade on, he'd devoted himself to T&A.

After a brief stint as a juvenile delinquent, he'd graduated from high school and joined the military. His dad wasn't around to care, and his mom had been too exhausted working three jobs to say much. Since he had aptitude for fighting and sneaking around, he'd gotten into Special Ops, which eventually led to a stint with the CIA. All that had made him get his shit together, but he was never going to be a bookworm.

He glanced through Rachel's exchange with her ex. It was a lot of blah, blah, blah. Owen was on the short list for the Wolf Prize in Physics, whatever that was, and he had notes in those texts he needed. Everything was pretty civil until, after looking for the books again, Owen insisted that she must be lying. He asked sharply if she was trying to sabotage his career, hinting that she'd always resented his work.

Rachel had stopped responding at that point. Decker wished she'd told the asshole to get fucked.

Less than an hour later, Owen had texted her some stiff, stupid-ass apology, saying that he'd found his textbooks—and he didn't appreciate her impolite lack of response, but he wasn't surprised in the least.

As evidence went, it was thin. A DA would find it circumstantial at best, but the divorce, coupled with this kind of stuff, might add up to motive.

With a frown, Decker placed the phone back where he'd found it, then peeked inside her nightstand. *Well, well, well* . . . Under a wrist brace and an old copy of *Vogue*, he found a battery-operated clit stimulator, a slender vibe that would be too weak to really get her off, and an electronic reader chock-full of BDSM romances. So beautiful Miss Button-down had a naughty side. Damn if that didn't do his heart good.

With blood giving fresh life to his unflagging erection, he dashed out to the family room and scanned her e-mails in less than two minutes. Most were from family members sending jokes or the parents of her students asking questions. A quick scan of the documents saved on her hard drive only proved that she kept her checkbook in Excel and she was a good little saver. Her Facebook was squeaky clean. He uncovered nothing suspicious.

On her way through the house, Rachel had flipped on lights. Decker finally got a good look at the comfortable place, ducking into each room to scan her pictures. He didn't see anyone who resembled the guy who'd hired him to kill Rachel.

Then again, if her ex was the guilty party, she wasn't likely to keep heart-shaped photos of him lying around after the divorce.

From down the hall, he heard her cut off the shower and he ducked back into the guest room closet to wait for her to fall asleep. He wasn't keen to spend the night against a wall, shoved behind a bunch of coats, but he'd slept in worse places. Afghanistan came to mind. He'd been through a few South American jungles in his time, too. At least here he didn't have to worry about terrorists or snakes.

A moment later, the disposable phone in his pocket vibrated, and he pulled it out.

Are you still awake?—Rachel

Oh, now, this was interesting. It was just after midnight. Did she want to reach out and touch him?

Yes, beautiful. Thinking of you. What are you wearing?

Since she'd just stepped out of the shower, he'd bet it was nothing or damn close to it. He looked forward to seeing how she'd answer that.

Rachel waited a long time to reply, and he was just about to tap out a little something designed to calm her nerves when she finally sent a message back.

Feel like coming over to see?

Did he ever . . . His cock completely approved of the idea, twitching at the thought of getting deep inside her and spending most of the night. He'd been on one case after another lately, and it had been way too long since he'd had a willing female in a warm bed. The fact that he'd get to end his drought with Rachel was even sweeter. Now he'd see that lush ass under the tight skirt—and fondle it, and bite it, and . . . anything else she'd let him do. The fact that he couldn't remember the last time he'd been this into a woman he'd just met was a bonus.

Yes! Can you guess what has 142 teeth and holds back a hungry beast?

No *idea*, she sent back.

My zipper, beautiful. Text me your address and I'll show you.

Decker heard her giggle from the next room. Then her address flashed on his screen. Oh, it was on now.

I'll be there in 15.

After a little squeal, she tossed her phone down and tore into the bedroom. Music started blaring a moment later, and he heard her opening and closing the drawers and doors in the bathroom cabinet. The hair dryer flipped on. That was his cue to leave.

Slowly, Decker opened the closet door, ducking out from under the coats and setting the table leaf back in place. He eased the window open and crawled through, landing on his feet on her little back patio. Her yard was small, but she'd made it her own lush little garden with ivy and delicate flowers in white, gold, and purple. He was clueless about their species, but he'd bet that Rachel loved it out here. She'd made this her little oasis, complete with a padded wrought iron chaise in one corner where she likely got the most shade. She'd left behind an empty teacup and a magazine on the little wooden table beside it. He kind of wished that he'd get to spend time with her in this space. As she lifted her face to the sun, she would smile and glow.

And he needed to get his head out of his ass. He wouldn't have long to right this wrong. S.I. Industries always had dirty work. Defense contracting was populated with a bunch of good ol' boys whose middle names all seemed to be Greed. He didn't have an assignment at the moment, but Decker knew it wouldn't be long. Since Xander and Javier had started sharing that lush blonde they now called wife, they seemed far more intent on enjoying the honeymoon part of their marriage. Or were they on a babymoon now? After all, they would be daddies by next May. The trio seemed disgustingly happy.

Decker tried not to, but he wondered why he'd never found someone he wanted to spend more than a few hours with. Rachel had eventually moved on from Owen, but at least she'd believed herself in love enough once to roll the dice. He'd never felt much beyond his dick twitch.

Shoving aside the thought, he climbed the fence and hopped onto the little walkway outside her kitchen window. Not two minutes later, he pulled up in front of her house again. In normal circumstances, he'd bring her a bottle of wine or at least flavored condoms, but he didn't dare leave her alone long enough to retrieve them, just in case.

After a little warning roar, he parked his bike out front and stowed his helmet. He grabbed a few necessities from his saddlebags and headed to her front door, then rang the bell. A long minute passed before she flipped on the porch light and opened the door.

Light from the foyer table off to her right spilled around her dark hair. Her skin looked smooth and ivory, untouched by the sun and devoid of makeup. Her brown eyes were wide and a bit wary, framed by thick black lashes. She'd slicked a little gloss over her plump lips, and he couldn't wait to get them under his again.

Rachel stepped back to admit him. "Hi. You were quick."

"I was motivated." He stepped in, then shut and locked the door behind him with a smile.

She wore a short, silky robe in white with tiny pink flowers on it. Decker didn't know much about women's clothes, but he was pretty sure she couldn't have on much under that. Her pert nipples beaded the front. If he did this right, he could have her naked and flat on her back in five minutes.

With a nervous smile, she backed across the foyer. "Coffee?"

"I didn't come here for anything you could whip up in the kitchen, beautiful. But if you need a minute to take a deep breath and get your head together, I'll be patient."

She let out a shaky breath. "Sorry. I've never done this, invited a man I barely know over to . . ."

"Do naughty things designed to make your heart race and your throat raw from screaming?"

The sweetest little blush crept up her cheeks. "That's one way of putting it. But it's . . . um, never been like that for me."

Decker frowned. The last thing he really wanted to do now was talk about her bedroom gymnastics with the ex, especially when he felt sure there was a whole naked wonderland under that robe waiting just for him. Sadly, she'd given him an opening, and this might be the only time to gracefully dig information out of her about Owen. He had to nail down a better motive . . . or see if he could take the douche off his suspect list. It *was* possible that someone else had it in for her, though he couldn't fathom why given how sweet she was. And she wasn't going to relax until she felt more comfortable with him. Her lack of experience, while weirdly endearing, was a hindrance.

He grabbed her hand and led her from the foyer, through the kitchen, then down a couple of steps into a sunken living room area that he could finally take the time to observe since he wasn't focused on finding clues. Easing back into the beige velvet sofa, he glanced over the patterned rugs and mirrored accents that gave the room with the yellow-cream walls a light feel. Built-in shelves overflowed with books of all kinds, along with more pictures and tchotchkes. Shimmery drapes, the same tone as the walls, covered big windows that overlooked the oasis he'd seen out back earlier. Overall, the place was light, happy, homey—somewhat like her.

The few places he'd called "home" over the years had been mostly shitholes, barracks, or transient motels. He'd usually gone wherever duty called, without any thought to putting down roots or building a future, but now . . . Xander and Javier had obviously planted themselves in Lafayette to play house with London, so he suspected he was here for the duration. Other than the humidity in the summer, here actually wasn't bad. He'd grown used to the freeways and skyscrapers of Los Angeles over the last few years, but Decker was thinking that he could kind of get used to a place like this, even having a home for once. The faint scent of vanilla lingered, like Rachel had baked or burned candles or something equally feminine. He liked it.

He liked her.

With a tug on her hand, Decker prevented her from sitting beside him. Instead, he pulled her onto his lap. She wriggled, as if trying to find a comfortable spot. Her lush ass rooting around on his cock nearly had him groaning and tearing into her clothes like a beast, but he managed to refrain.

"I can't wait to get this robe off of you and do things to your delectable body that are probably only legal in foreign countries." Decker winked, then stroked his knuckles along her exposed skin beside the lapel of her robe, over the swell of her breast. "But when you tell me it's never been really good for you, I want to know what disappointed you in the past. Tell me about the last time you had sex."

THREE

RACHEL'S BIG, DARK EYES WIDENED WITH SHOCK, AND SHE shook her head. "I'd rather not. You're going to let me 'steer,' so it won't be an issue."

As she moved in to kiss him, Decker turned his head just enough to graze the soft skin of her neck with his lips, then he rested them on her lobe. "Even so, you need to give me a little information so I understand what you don't like."

She eased back and met his stare, then tried to wriggle off his lap. He tightened his arms around her, and finally, she sighed.

"It was with my ex-husband," she murmured, looking away. "Owen was always just so . . . serious. I don't know how to put it. It seemed like something he tolerated more than loved."

"Which made you feel somehow responsible, so you didn't enjoy it either?"

Her gaze bounced back up to his, as if he'd surprised her with his perception. It didn't take a rocket scientist . . . but that deduction was apparently beyond a physicist. Go figure.

"Yes." She nodded, and he saw a sweet little flush spread across her cheeks. "He didn't ever want to talk about it."

Then Owen deserved lousy sex. *Dumbass.* "Anything else?"

"It's water under the bridge." She squirmed uncomfortably.

"I don't think so. Your last time in the sack sucked. Communication is key. We've got to have some if you want me to give you a better time. Besides, how are you going to tell me what you want when we're naked if you can't say it now?"

She chewed on that plump little lip for a moment. "All right. I don't think he knew where I was . . . um, sensitive."

That didn't surprise Decker, but he had to rein in a laugh at her delicate phrasing. "You mean he didn't have a clue where your clit was and you wished like hell he did?"

Her blush deepened. "Are you always this direct?"

"I don't see any sense in beating around the bush." He grinned. "Especially yours. It sounds like you'd be pretty happy if I could shake it once or twice."

Though her jaw dropped and she smacked his shoulder, she was smiling. "That's crude!"

"But honest. How was the rest of your relationship?"

"Well, not too good or we wouldn't be divorced."

Oh, sass. How much fun would it be to silence her bratty mouth with a kiss that made her toes curl before he turned her into a pile of goo? "Are you two still civil or did it end too ugly?"

"It's mostly polite. Owen sometimes loses his temper. I just ignore him."

And that might really be pissing the ex off. Definitely, he wanted to keep digging here, but couldn't go too deep now without making her suspicious. When he got a free moment, he'd look up the asswipe and see if his face matched the guy who'd solicited him to commit murder. Until then, he had to tread lightly with the questions about her ex—except sexually. Rachel hid a wealth of repressed desire.

"Did he ever do *anything* in bed that you liked?"

"Not really. You're probably wondering why I married him. My friends back in Florida, where I'm from, asked me that all the time. Owen is eight years older than me, and at first I liked how knowledgeable he seemed, but that didn't extend to sex. It took me years to realize that he liked to hear himself talk more than listen. When the topic was something he couldn't pontificate about, he changed it." She cocked her head and stared. "Do you psychoanalyze every woman before you sleep with her?"

Decker figured that was his cue to shut up. "You said you want a man who listens. I'm trying. How do you think I can give you what you want if I don't understand you even a little? Do *you* know what you want?"

Rachel reared back. A million thoughts flitted across her face. She looked angry, then sad, then downright confused. Decker held her tighter. She didn't have a clue what her true desires were, but he'd show her as soon as she got over this ridiculous notion of being in charge.

"It's orgasm. It shouldn't be this difficult."

Was she saying that a man had never given her one? The idea of being the first to succeed damn near made him salivate. Yes, it was probably stupid and unnecessarily territorial, but attraction wasn't logical. And he didn't think it was logic she needed as much as a hot, ripe, raunchy fucking. And then to be held.

He smiled. "That depends on you. If you really know what flips your switch and can express it clearly, we've got no worries. If you don't, you may not enjoy sex with anyone until you figure it out."

"What about you?" she challenged. "You seem like you don't have any problems just . . . blurting what you want."

He didn't blurt, just usually commanded. That wasn't relevant to the conversation now. She was getting worked up and worried. Time to calm her down.

Brushing his knuckles over the soft swell of her breast again, he watched with satisfaction as goose bumps raised on her arms and legs. "Men are simple. We're almost always ready. We don't have swells and folds. Our most sensitive nerve endings aren't hidden. You pay attention to a guy's cock, and I guarantee he's going to like it."

Rachel pressed her lips together and tried not to giggle, but she failed. "The way you put things . . . My mama would positively expire."

Decker grinned at her sweet, if exaggerated, Southern accent. "I'm not interested in your mama."

She smiled but didn't quite meet his gaze. "Kiss me."

"Yes, ma'am." That was one demand he didn't mind giving in to.

DECKER BARELY PUT his hands on her, and she began to tremble. Everything about him was so strong and masculine and called to the female inside her. Nestled on his lap, she sat just a tad shorter than him. And his wide shoulders made her sigh. He seemed to surround her, make her feel delicate. Though she'd tried so hard to be independent and stand on her own two feet since the divorce, Rachel admitted that she liked feeling tiny in his arms. She wasn't sure what she'd done to snag his attention, but she would just be grateful to spend the night of her birthday with someone as gorgeous as him and hope there was an orgasm or two in her future. He looked more than capable.

His rough hand gently cradled the crown of her head, strong

fingers burrowing into the strands of her hair. With a little tug, he tilted her head back. His mouth hung a breath over hers. She blinked up at him, pulled into his hungry blue eyes with their thick fringe of black lashes. What would his lips feel like on her skin? What would those brawny hands do to her body?

"Tell me how you want me to kiss you," he whispered.

Rachel frowned. She had to explain it?

"Passionately."

"Slow? Fast? Deep? Teasing?" he challenged. "You want me to seduce or tongue-fuck that pretty mouth?"

Her stomach clenched. Her sex pulsed. His words alone aroused her.

She gripped his big shoulders, her breath coming fast. "All of it."

A knowing smile spread across his face. "What do you want after that, beautiful? If you had to spell it out in excruciating detail, tell me what you'd say?"

Mind racing, she stared at him. Mercy, she'd assumed she had a hundred ideas, but when she tried to imagine perfect lovemaking . . . she just pictured herself writhing in ecstasy under him. That wasn't very specific, and sort of proved his point. She'd read hundreds of fabulous descriptions of earth-shattering sex, but she didn't know exactly what would feel good to *her*. Still, she wasn't ready to put the control of her pleasure in another man's hands, even if he seemed more competent than Owen, not until she'd explored and gained some confidence.

"Can we experiment?"

He shrugged. "Sure. So you want to start with that kiss now?"

Decker was teasing her, dragging it out, making her wait. She wriggled on his lap, seeking relief for the sweet pressure building between her legs. "Yes."

His grip in her hair tightened. He readjusted her body so that she straddled his hips. Then he swooped down, his mouth covering hers, at the same time he wrapped his free arm around her waist and jerked her flush against him. Rachel had no idea how many teeth were actually in his zipper. But when his steely erection rubbed against her tender folds, sending tingles scattering through her, she had no trouble believing that it caged a hungry beast.

As he nudged her lips apart, Decker swept inside like he knew exactly how to make a woman moan. He ravished her mouth as if she made him desperate. A passionate moan escaped her throat, and he greedily swallowed the sound. Heat rolled through her body, into her peaking nipples, drifting right between her legs, as he moaned and crushed her against him.

With a twist of his fingers, he forced her to slant her head so he could sink deeper into the kiss. She should protest at the way he was taking over. But all those BDSM romances on her e-reader had introduced her to the idea of a very alpha male—something Owen would never be. Those Dominant men very nearly read a woman's mind so that they could unravel her and give her the ultimate pleasure. She'd assumed that was just fiction. But the way Decker took her mouth, prowling every recess, tasting and luring her closer only to pull back, nip at her lips, pause and stare, then kiss her again like he couldn't stand a moment of separation between them made her rethink her assumptions.

They shared breaths. She tasted the spicy flavor of Decker's kiss. Instead of sating her, she only craved more. The way his mouth took hers . . . It was as if he owned her. Why did she like that idea so much? They were strangers, and he'd probably be gone in a few hours. Tonight was just a fantasy.

"God, you taste so fucking sweet. I want to devour all of you, but I can't stand to stop kissing you. Jesus . . ."

A thrill of feminine pride filled her. She'd never really been truly wanted. Owen hadn't been demonstrative. He hadn't really even liked kissing. Too many germs. Sure she'd had a few dates in high school, but they'd been with boys. Decker was a *man*.

Rachel felt herself melting into him, wanting just a few moments of his strong, sure embrace. With every breathless kiss, their lips met more urgently. Dizzying arousal swam headily through her veins like a drug he used to keep her lips his captive. The liquid pleasure spread, and it overtook through her veins. He was everything she'd ached for—and more.

"I want this damn robe off," he growled against her lips before he seized them again, plundering deep. He gave her only a moment's respite to process his words before he eased back with another snarl. "Now, Rachel. I want to see your pretty nipples. I want them in my mouth. I want them hard on my tongue. They're mine tonight, and you're going to give them to me."

With his gruff demand, her stomach plunged to her toes. The stiff points tightened, and she could feel them chafing against the silk as if pointing their way to Decker. In that moment, she wanted to give in so, so badly. Could he feel how damp her panties were?

Even if he could, she still had to be responsible for her own pleasure. Sure, she could let him do what he liked. She'd probably even love it. Likely, there would be multiple orgasms in her future. But wanting to explore sex wasn't just about reaching nirvana. It also meant growing her confidence and figuring out who she was sexually. At twenty-nine, she didn't know what made her blood sing or what made her feel most like a woman. She also didn't know much about giving pleasure. Owen hadn't been big into foreplay.

"Eventually, I will," she promised, blinking up at him. "But I'm in control, remember? You promised."

His eyes narrowed, and his fingers tightened in her hair. The hunger in his eyes gnawed at her composure. Everything about that look made her want to rip off her robe and offer herself up to him.

"All right. What do you want, beautiful?"

"You naked. Let me look at you," she whispered. Though she couldn't wait to see him, Rachel wished her answer sounded more certain. Why couldn't she be more vixen and less wallflower? And crap, when would she stop blushing?

"All right. I'm all yours." Decker spread his arms wide like he couldn't wait to flash her.

This was going to be good.

Rachel unbuttoned his black shirt and peeled away the material clinging to his broad shoulders with strained seams. She shoved it down his arms, revealing biceps that bulged and rippled as he helped her by shrugging out of the garment and tossing it to the floor. His dog tags rattled, then pinged against his hard chest, where he was muscled from the firm pectorals half covered by a patch of dark hair and some sort of military tattoo to the eight-pack of abs that disappeared into low-slung denim.

Her jaw dropped. She almost swore that she could glimpse something shadowy and male just below that black and silver buckle helping his pants cling to his hips.

Decker grinned as he stared back at her with sexual challenge. "You want me more naked than this?"

"Yes." *Please.*

"You got it." He lifted her off his lap, copping a feel of her thigh and trying to brush her robe away.

Rachel wagged a finger at him. "You're awfully pushy."

"Probably why I'm in trouble a lot." He grinned. "But let's see if I can make you forget that."

Decker opened his belt buckle with a clink and released every one of the teeth holding back his waiting erection. Then he dropped his pants into a careful puddle on the floor and stood, totally naked.

Holy mother of all that's . . . whoa! He'd been commando. No pesky underwear to bother with. Just another tattoo that looked like an eagle talon on his hip and inch after imposing inch of his massive erection.

She swallowed.

"If you work for the post office, I'll let you inspect my package." He sauntered the two steps back to the sofa and stood over her. "Hell, I might even let you if you don't."

The pick-up line barely registered with his thick male flesh bobbing in her face, its big plum head nearly purple. She had to scrape her jaw off the floor when he wrapped his hand around the stiff column and stroked slowly, visually teasing her. *So sexy.* What would he feel like in her palm? The musky scent of him rising toward her seemed more concentrated and mysterious between his legs. His testicles were big and heavy.

She was desperate to touch him.

After watching the slow, hypnotic motion of his thick fingers sliding up and down his sensitive sex, Rachel ached to do that to Decker and make him feel good.

With a fortifying breath, she forced down her nervousness, shoved his hand out of her way, and gripped the hot, hard stalk of flesh. Her fingers didn't quite meet when she encircled him. Slowly, she stroked up, swiping her thumb over the head. He clenched his teeth and hissed in a breath, hardening even more in her hand.

A tremor of need shook her. Her folds became more than a little damp.

"Damn, beautiful. That's so good. Unless you're looking to finish me off with your hand, I wouldn't do that for much longer."

Eventually, she might want that with a lover, but now she wanted to be with Decker more than simply watch him.

"Not what I had in mind." She shook her head.

"Then what are you going to do with me?"

His words ended with a moan, and the sound went straight between her legs.

Good question. Exactly what did she want? She frowned, coming up blank. The truth was, she didn't know.

The obvious was to put his big, silky shaft in her mouth and suck. She'd heard men liked that. It sounded exciting . . . a little forbidden—at least to her. She'd never done it. Owen thought fifteen minutes for sex was too long, so they'd never lingered. As much as she wished for the confidence to just wrap her lips around him, she wasn't the sort to climb all over a guy. And she had no idea what Decker would truly like or enjoy. A vague shame overtook her that she hadn't asked even once. Sex was supposed to be a two-way street. Hadn't Owen's lack of communication taught her that?

"What are your suggestions?" Rachel hoped he had plenty. Clearly, she was clueless and lost now that her big take-charge plan didn't seem to be working.

"That you let me show you." When she opened her mouth to argue, he knelt and put a finger to her lips. "I know you want to experience new things. I'm guessing you haven't had many lovers."

"Just Owen."

Understanding softened his face. Rachel didn't know how someone so angular and male could look so gentle.

"How are you supposed to know what turns you on most if you've never experienced it? We'll still experiment, but let's turn this around. Give me control. If you don't like something, you just tell me. We'll try something else."

"But I let Owen control everything, and it was a disaster."

"I'm not your ex-idiot."

No, but . . . "I can't be upset that sex is never what I want if I don't play an active role."

"You will, and it's hot that you want to. But to start, I think your active role should be to tell me what you like. For instance, you can tell me if you'd rather have your nipples caressed, pinched, or something else. Maybe you're not even sensitive there, but we'll find out. Then you can tell me if you like my mouth on your pussy, if you like to be kissed while I fuck you, or if you enjoy bondage."

Rachel felt her eyes widen. And her body begin to overheat.

"Yes, we're going to do all that and more." He cupped her thigh. "You're assuming I'm as inept as Owen. I promise, beautiful, that I won't let you down. I know we just met a few hours ago, but I'm about to become your lover. If we're going to make that work, you've got to trust me with your body or this is going nowhere."

A really good point . . .

"It's not that I don't trust you."

"Oh?" He grinned. "Well, if it's not that, then you're just naturally a control freak?"

She felt heat flood her cheeks. "I'll . . . um, plead the fifth."

With a lopsided smile, he stood, unfolding every inch of that mouthwateringly male body. The slightest inhalation made his abs ripple. His biceps flexed when he held out his hand to her. "Come with me."

How the devil was she supposed to say no to that?

Rachel put her hand in his, and he squeezed it. "Lead the way." *Show me what to do.*

He hesitated. "Is your bedroom down the hall?"

"Yes." She smiled faintly. "I actually feel so comfortable with you that I'd forgotten you don't know where anything is. Come with me, then you can take over."

Decker linked their fingers, then bent to scoop up his pants. She led him past the darkened rooms lining the hallway, then into her shadowy bedroom. She debated flipping on the lamp sitting on her nightstand. Did he want to see her? Would he rather be in the dark?

"You're thinking and not communicating," he pointed out as he set the jeans aside and drew her into his arms, against him.

"One of the perils of being a teacher. I can't say everything I think in a classroom."

"I'll bet." He kissed her nose playfully, then her cheek, moving toward her ear. "Trust, remember?"

"Yeah. Got it."

"You're nervous."

Why deny the obvious? "It's been almost two years, since just before Owen and I separated."

"A beautiful woman should be pleasured well and often. But I don't think that's the only issue. *I* make you nervous."

He didn't ask; he knew. "There were prettier girls at the bar."

"No." He shook his head. "There were easier girls at the bar. When you're twenty-one, yeah, that's great. A few drinks, a joke or two, and you'll probably get lucky. By the time a guy is thirty, he's looking for some substance along with a girl's great rack. By then, he's figured out that he likes a little conversation afterward, too."

Rachel rolled her eyes, but felt a smile crease her face. "So how old are you?"

"Old enough to enjoy talking to you," he drawled, nipping at her earlobe. "Later . . ."

Which probably meant he was over thirty. If not, he'd be with someone named Barbie or Tawny having much less conversation. But the answer didn't really matter now, especially not when he brushed his lips over her throat. Goodness, that sent an electric shiver through her body.

"I don't know anything about you," she protested.

"Do you want to know my date of birth and blood type or do you want to know what I feel like when I'm fucking my way deep inside your aching pussy?"

FOUR

DECKER'S QUESTION TURNED HER SHIVER INTO A SHUDDER. Rachel's breath caught. Heat slid through her. Blood rushed to her nipples. "Th-the latter."

"That's what I thought. We'll talk soon about why you seem to want to analyze everything. It's chemistry, beautiful. Let it burn." He curled his fingers around the belt of her little silk robe and tugged. "Now I want to see those hard nipples all naked and ready for my mouth. Drop the robe."

A thrill curled through her belly, even as hesitation strangled it. She ached to be everything he wanted. She wished she could be wanton enough to just enjoy the moment. But . . .

"What is it? Talk to me." He cupped her cheek.

"I'm . . . lost. Owen never liked to be totally naked for sex. Too earthy for him."

"*What?* Did he actually like sex?"

She shrugged. "Since he always had orgasms, I assumed he had a good time."

"I'm not so sure." He scoffed.

"Owen always wanted me to shower first, then come to bed dressed in something like this." Rachel tugged on her robe.

Decker snorted. "Then he told you to get in bed, climbed on top of you in the dark, and the sex was over in three minutes before he told you to shower again and come to bed? A week or two later, he'd repeat the process?"

She gaped at him. "How did you guess?"

"I'm getting a picture here. No wonder you're repressed and confused if you've never known anything else. What a douche bag."

"He's just . . . His brain revolves around science. He's not really into 'typical' stuff. He hates TV, cocktail parties, shopping. He thinks romance is trite and—"

"Sex is a bodily function that should be performed in the minimum amount of time?"

"Something like that."

"Then he didn't care about your feelings." Decker pressed flush against her, his erection a thick ridge prodding her belly, and took her face in his hands. "I'm going to show you how it should be. I'm not going to put my cock anywhere near your pussy until you're dripping wet and beyond ready. That's a promise."

His wicked words made her fluttery inside, like a horde of butterflies were break dancing. "Thank you for understanding. Most guys would have given up long ago, I'll bet."

He stroked her cheek. "It's just you and me. I don't care what any other guy would do, especially Owen. So if you're ready to move on and have sex instead of talking . . ."

As Decker yanked at the belt of her robe, she looked up at him through the shadows, then over at the little lamp on her nightstand.

He planted a hand in her hair and tugged. "Focus on me. If I want the lamp on, I'll take care of it. Right now, I don't give a damn about the setting. I care about pleasing you. I can't do it if you're half clothed and overthinking. You're nervous. You don't know me well. You've never done this with anyone who knows how to make you feel good. You're having a hard time letting go. I get all that. But you've got to let me try."

Rachel squeezed her eyes shut. Decker was utterly, totally right. She had to get out of her head and stop thinking about what she was used to. He'd shown her in every way that he wanted to be here with her, and had the experience and patience to give her pleasure.

With a nod, she shoved the lid on all her insecurities and worked the knot of her belt loose. She parted the silk a sliver, watching Decker watch her. He looked so sexy—intent male ready to conquer. His desire wrapped around her and caressed her skin. Her breath came hard, fast.

She peeled the robe from her shoulders. With only a whisper of sound, it slithered to the carpet beneath her feet. She stood before a man she hadn't known when she'd eaten dinner tonight, wearing nothing more than a tiny pair of black panties. Only very damp lace separated him from her secret flesh. He stared, his blue eyes darkening with hunger in the shadowed room. A shiver of thrill went through her when she thought about his reaction to what he hadn't yet seen.

"Fuck," he muttered, lifting his hand to her. "You're beyond beautiful."

"Really?"

Shut up! Rachel cursed her own uncertainty. Owen had called her chubby and chided her for her love of Italian food and an occasional piece of chocolate. Decker seemed to like the way she was put together. His warm fingers cradled her breast, his thumb brushing so close to her nipple . . . She dragged in a shuddering breath as heat burned through her.

"Gorgeous. Voluptuous." He bent and nuzzled her neck, pressing his lips to her. "So innocent looking. Every time you bat your lashes at me, I get hard. When I feel you tremble in my arms, it takes everything I have not to toss you to the bed and have my wicked way with you."

His fingers tightened just a fraction on her breast before he cursed softly. Then he gripped her neck and positioned her directly under him as his lips crashed over hers. The sensation jolted her, an immediate zing of desire. Rachel melted against Decker and opened to him entirely, meeting every possessive thrust and teasing retreat. She whimpered into his kiss, wrapped her arms around his neck, all but purring at the feel of his hot skin plastered against her.

Then he backed her toward the bed, his persistent kiss flavored with impatience and demand. Already, he was unraveling her. Less than thirty seconds and Rachel felt herself turning to putty.

Arousal. She'd read about it, even felt little tremors of it when she self-pleasured. But Decker was unleashing an earthquake of need inside her. It was rocking her every notion about sex, along with her world.

He helped her onto the bed, his mouth still on hers as he crawled after her. His huge, hard body covered her own, blasting heat through her as he gently abraded her nipples with the fine hair across his chest. More dusted his legs, and as he pressed them against her inner thighs to open her wide for his invasion, the sensation was so foreign . . . amazing. Her vocabulary was almost inadequate to describe the awakening of every nerve and cell in her body, the tingling of her skin, the pounding of her heart, the rightness flowing through her body.

A year shy of thirty, and she'd never quite understood what it meant to be a woman taken by a man. As Decker ravaged her lips with yet another deep kiss, taking everything she gave while plying her with more pleasure, she began to grasp the concept. Pure sensation wrapped her up—and finally she comprehended just how two lovers shared sex. Heartbeats and breaths mingled as they touched palm-to-palm. They exchanged an entire wealth of longing with a stare, without uttering a word. And that was before they joined bodies.

How was it possible that she felt closer and more in tune with the stranger she'd met hours ago than the man she'd been married to for nearly four years?

Rachel didn't know, but she was done questioning it. She bent her knees around his hips, letting him deeper into the cradle of her body, and held on for dear life as a joy way beyond pleasure flowed through her.

Decker's rough palms skimmed down her side, anchoring his hand on her hip. "I want inside you so bad. But I want to show you what you've been missing more."

She had almost no time to process what those shiver-worthy words meant before he worked his way down her body. His mouth hovered just above her nipples, his hot breath caressing them. The blood strained into the hard tips until they felt tight and tingly.

"Tell me what feels good so I can send you soaring."

She gave him a shaky nod, raking her fingers through the inky strands of his dark hair. "All right."

He didn't waste any more time or words. Instead, Decker just fastened his lips around her left nipple. Soft, slow, sleek . . . the touch was part exploration, part torment. Rachel arched up into his mouth with a little cry of need.

"You like that?"

"Hmm . . . yes."

Her hips moved restlessly, and she filtered her fingers through his hair again, reveling in its softness and wishing it was long enough to wrap in her fist and make him taste her nipple once more. Thankfully, she didn't have to prompt him again to pay attention to her breasts. He lapped at their tips, nipped, teased . . . tormented. Every lick and suck became its own form of torture. Ecstasy. Agony. A need for more burst through her, igniting her blood.

Decker eased back for a moment and stared at her nipples unabashedly. Under his scrutiny, they seemed to fill and tighten even more, as if eager to display themselves for him.

"So damn pretty," he whispered over the distended peak, thumbing the other. "So lush."

Rachel whimpered. *So ready for more . . .*

"You feel it, don't you?"

She nodded frantically.

"You're wet for me, aren't you?"

"Yes." *Almost embarrassingly so.*

A smile creased his face. He turned to rub his whiskered cheek against her swelling breast, her sensitive nipple. The scratchy-soft abrasion added another level of sensation, and she arched, grabbing at him.

"Sensitive." His voice rang with approval.

"I never thought so. I mean, I've never . . ."

"Responded to having your nipples stimulated?"

She frowned until he set his mouth over them again. "No one's ever really touched . . . I can't think when you do that."

"Good. Just feel. I want you to let me have my fill of your nipples. I want you to get so wet for me that when I put my mouth on your pussy, I'll have a feast that will take me a long time to devour. I want you so close, ready, and eager that when I start fucking you, you won't be able to stop screaming."

His words alone took her desire higher. The tight beat of need under her clit became an incessant throb. A few hours ago, she would have doubted that he—or anyone else—could make her feel this way. But Decker, whose last name she hadn't even asked, knew exactly how to give her body everything she'd ever fantasized about.

She was going to end her birthday a really happy woman.

"Hurry!" she panted.

But he took his sweet time tonguing his way around her areola, then brushing his fingers over the damp flesh. He came closer and closer to the aching tips until he finally sucked them in deep. The sensation darted straight between her legs again and again like a live wire. She shuddered in his arms with the jolt of desire.

"Hurrying defeats the purpose, and you're not making the demands here. You're lying back and taking everything I give you and waiting eagerly for more."

Holding in a whimper, Rachel stared up at him, blinking, breathless . . . captivated. Everything about his strong face and the desire tightening it screamed powerful male. Beyond aroused now, she ached to feel Decker deep inside her.

His bare hands gripped her hips with possessive fervor and seared her flesh. She sighed raggedly and closed her eyes, basking in the sensations piling on top of her, one after the other, until she swore she was about to combust. Or beg. This much pleasure was beyond her experience or comprehension, and she didn't for one moment believe she'd handled all he could dish out.

A hot flush rolled through her body. Rachel breathed in the musky scent of his skin and couldn't look away from his cocky smile, complete with a flash of white teeth that she found beyond sexy. She dug her fingers into his shoulders and lifted her hips to him, willing him to ease the empty ache coiling between her restless legs.

"You look good all flushed and sweet. Innocent." He breathed over her nipples, still toying, arousing, owning them. "I'll fix that."

Rachel assumed he was kidding, but Decker didn't smile or wink. *Mercy* . . . Remembering the feel of him, steely and sizzling in her palm, made her skin tingle with anticipation as she imagined just exactly how good he would feel stretching and filling her—helping her finally understand the give and take of lovers straining for the common purpose of sharing wrenching, clawing pleasure.

"Please . . ."

"Ah, begging. Always sweet, but especially tempting coming from you. I think I'm going to want more. Let me see what I can do." His smile was predatory and pleased, but somehow still set her at ease. "Take off the panties."

Rachel wanted to—really. Once she did, she'd be one step closer to fulfillment. But she had a surprise . . .

"Let me up for one second. I want to show you something."

Decker hesitated. He didn't want to. As easygoing as he'd been at the bar, that was how forceful he seemed now. And she might be in over her head, but that didn't stop Rachel from wanting him.

"A second, no longer." He eased off the bed with obvious reluctance. His hands didn't leave her bare skin until he stood too far away to touch her.

Scooting off the bed, she brushed past him with a pounding heart, full of yearning and apprehension.

Finally, Rachel inched past him just far enough for him to view her backside, then glanced over her shoulder at him, only to find his stare glued to her butt.

"Holy shit," he muttered. "That's gorgeous."

Remembering the big, silky black bow that played peekaboo with her pale cheeks, she smiled. His approval spiked bliss inside her. She'd always liked helping and doing for others, but this . . . was different. This sense of thrill was more personal.

Of course when she'd bought these panties from a catalog about six months ago, she'd been pretty sure that madness had finally overtaken her. Now she was glad she'd succumbed to the impulse. His bulging stare and damn near speechless reaction felt so sweetly fabulous.

"Do you want to unwrap me?" Rachel whispered, watching him from under lowered lashes as she wiggled her hips just slightly.

He cocked a dark brow and dragged his gaze to her face. "If I tug on this ribbon, these will come off?"

That possibility obviously excited him. Impatience pinged off of him—and boosted her confidence.

With a coy look, she batted her lashes. "Why don't you find out?"

Anchoring a hand on her thigh, Decker stepped up behind her, his hot breath on her neck. With the other hand, he grabbed one of the floppy bow's loose ends and gave a little tug. It unraveled, and the silken material slipped to hang low on her hips. With big hands, he tugged the panties down her thighs, leaving them both as naked as the day they'd been born.

With a moan of appreciation, Decker palmed her backside, his lips sliding over her shoulder. With his big body pumping out heat like a furnace, he chased away the slight chill in the room and suffused her with warmth. She tossed her head back to rest on the hard bulge of his shoulder, her hair sliding over his skin erotically.

He bit into her lobe. "You're teasing me, beautiful."

"Is that going to get me in trouble?" Where was this inner vixen coming from? It was as if knowing that she truly aroused him had allowed her to relax and engage in the sort of banter that often shaped her fantasies. He seemed more than willing to play along.

"No," he murmured in her ear. "It's going to get you fucked. Long and hard and relentlessly."

Good gravy. As dirty as his words were, they sounded not just sexual, but seductive. Decker wouldn't be mechanical. He wouldn't be merely willing—but happy—to do whatever made her come apart for him. Rachel couldn't find words to reply, so she just whimpered.

"Now." Decker bent and lifted her into his arms, cradling her against his chest. She shrieked. He tossed her onto the bed, then followed her down as she bounced on the mattress. He flattened her with his body, covering her completely as he dragged her mouth under his and claimed it with a wild kiss that left her hot and gasping under him.

This was what she'd always envisioned—racing hearts, desire, earnest need, the anticipation of pleasure so explosive . . .

Raising up on his haunches for a long moment, Decker took in the sight of her naked and flushed. "Damn, you're more lush and gorgeous than I imagined."

The appreciation on his face spoke a million praises. Unlike Owen, he was here not because sex was one of those tiresome marital exchanges he had to contend with. Decker was here because he wanted to be. Because he wanted her.

The hunger in his eyes made her nipples harden again. Her skin tingled as she waited impatiently to feel his hands all over her again, his thick erection buried deep within her.

"You imagined me?"

"Looking across the bar at you, yeah. I couldn't wait to see these." He cupped her breasts. "Get my mouth on them."

Then he was tasting her nipples again. A lick, a nip, a strong suck, and she moaned. Goodness, what he could do with his mouth . . . That direct line of sensation pulsed between her breasts and her slick female flesh below, and she writhed impatiently.

"But now . . ." He pinned her with a hot blue stare that made her quake. "I'm trying to decide how to make you come first. So many choices, and we'll get to them all eventually. Should I start with my fingers?"

Decker rolled slightly away and used one of his legs to pull hers apart. Then he stared straight down at her sex, now wet and pouting and aching. Automatically, she reached down to cover herself. Owen had said that vaginas were messy and unpleasant to look at, so she'd always kept hers shielded from him with a robe or flowing nightie.

Covering herself only seemed to displease Decker. He manacled her wrists in his grip and transferred them to one big hand before he pinned them to the bed above her head. "Don't move."

Rachel pressed against his hold experimentally. It was solid. She wasn't getting up until he let her. That should probably have alarmed her, but the ease with which he restrained her in his grip reminded her how small she was compared with him, almost helpless. That wasn't a feeling she liked in *any* other area of her life, but under Decker as he touched her . . . Everything about the moment was sublimely erotic.

With her hands trapped, cool air blew across her slick folds. She shivered. "You w-want to look at me?"

"Damn straight. Tonight, that's my pussy. I'm going to look at it, touch it, taste it . . . violate it in every way I can think of."

She blushed, the words coming from Decker's mouth rousing a tight heat inside her. Then nothing else mattered when he lowered his free hand between her legs, parted her folds with expert fingers, and dragged two of them directly over her most sensitive flesh. Pleasure tingled and burned from that spot, radiating outward for a glorious moment.

She writhed, moaned, all but begging without words.

"Like that?" he whispered against the side of her breast before he kissed the swell of flesh again, then took her turgid nipple in his mouth once more, sucking it to the roof.

"Yes!" she shrieked.

"You won't try to keep me from your sweet pussy, will you?"

Though he phrased his words like a question, Rachel knew quite well that it wasn't. She looked up at him, licking her lips and parting them, anticipation amping her up. "No."

"That's what I wanted to hear."

With one hand, he pinned her to the bed, with the other, he plumped and pinched her clitoris, so throbbing and hungry for his touch. In between, he worked his voracious mouth over her nipple. Blood raced through her body. Pleasure climbed inside her. Her senses awakened to him, so attuned. She craved more of the rough feel of his fingers, the scent of his mysterious musk rising between them, his demanding stare promising her more.

"Now. Please now." Rachel didn't care if she was pleading.

"I'm still debating the best way to give you your first orgasm. Doing it with my fingers is fun and easy." He toyed with the little pink pearl of nerves, a slow, circular drag of his fingertips over and over. "I can feel you hardening and swelling for me. Your body is tensing. I have total control of your reactions, and you look so fucking sexy flushing and begging. That prim exterior is gone, and the woman underneath . . . no other man has ever seen her. She's mine."

Rachel knew they were probably nothing more than pretty words, but she appreciated them—except that every moment he talked, he prolonged her torment. But nothing would make him move faster. Something about being utterly at his mercy made her need burn even hotter. She bit her lip.

Decker gave her a long, slow smile. "You're getting close, aren't you?

She nodded frantically.

"Fighting the urge to beg?"

Rachel nodded again. But not begging wasn't working, so she gave up. "I don't care how you do it, just please . . ."

"I care."

Decker whispered those words against her lips. Then he took her mouth in another long kiss of wrenching desire that made her dizzy and hot. She tried to curl her arms around him, but he held her hands firmly pinned to the bed.

He began her suffering again, his fingertips fondling her clitoris in long, unhurried drags. Her sizzling, slick nerves ignited. Pleasure coiled. Breathing took a backseat to anticipating his next touch. The need swelled to something far bigger and better than she'd ever given herself. Rachel writhed. *So* close . . .

"You like my fingers?" he baited.

"Yes." The breathy cry sounded an awful lot like a plea.

"I think you'll like this even more."

He prowled down the length of her body, his lips grazing her abdomen and laving her hip, before he settled between her thighs. With big palms, he pushed her legs wider apart. Then, with a deep breath, he inhaled. His eyes closed as if savoring her scent. His hot blue stare zipped up her body and captured her gaze. The electric arc between them was like a shockwave to her chest. She gasped.

Impatiently, Decker lowered his head toward her drenched folds. Rachel felt her eyes go saucer round. Would he? Sure, he'd talked about it, but . . .

Decker fell hungrily on her pouting, aching sex. He lapped at her clit with his tongue. *Oh goodness, he would.* She couldn't decide whether to squirm out of her skin or simply melt. She'd never even imagined anything like the hot, wet oven of his mouth. He sucked her in, gently grazing her sensitive tip with his tongue, then his teeth, lavishing her. Devouring her.

As she thrashed on the bed, a cry trapped at the back of her throat sprang free and echoed off the walls. The muscles in her thighs stiffened. The rest of her body followed. The precipice of pleasure rushed up to her. She could see right over the edge. Decker dangled her there—a lazy swipe of his tongue here, a starved suckling there. A frustrating nip at her inner thighs and a long, heated glance up her body later, she nearly howled with demand.

But he seemed to know exactly what she wanted and delighted in making her ache.

"Do you want to come like this?" he asked.

Rachel didn't trust that sly voice. No matter what she said, he was going to do exactly what he wanted. He wouldn't be cajoled or rushed or persuaded, even if she was about to lose her sanity.

Forget leaving her hands where he'd told her to. She thrust her fingers into the inky softness of his short hair and tried to press his mouth deeper over the heart of her need.

So, of course, Decker pulled away. "Be good or I'll make you wait for it."

"No!" she wailed, knowing it wouldn't do a damn bit of good.

Decker just smiled as he eased off of her and stood at the edge of the bed, staring. "Your pussy looks so pretty when it's pouting, beautiful." He licked his lips. "You're scrumptious."

"Why are you tormenting me?" she demanded, then bit her lip. Her lack of orgasm for the last decade wasn't his fault, just the last hour. "What else can I say to convince you?"

"That you need to come?" He shrugged. "I'll know when it's time. Now you stay here. I'll be back in a minute."

With that, he turned and searched the room. She couldn't see really well in the darkness, but the backside filling her vision was taut and firm, supported by a pair of thighs that rippled with muscle every time he took a step. Rachel sighed.

She really had hit the jackpot.

Just thinking about what might come next, her entire body throbbed, and a satisfaction that would have been so complete and mind-twisting had been right at hand . . . then he'd left the bed? When he stooped down, Rachel frowned. What was he doing?

She shook her head. He'd be back to her. While she wasn't usually confident about her sex appeal, one thing she did know? Men couldn't fake erections, and Decker had been hard since the moment he'd barged through her front door.

Still, he'd left her alone and needy. Wasn't he due a little teasing?

Smiling, Rachel lowered her hand between her legs, determined to put on a show. But when she dragged her fingers over her clitoris, just like Decker had, she hissed and arched her back. It wouldn't take much at all to push her over the edge. Another few seconds and . . .

"Fingers out of your pussy." Decker's sharp voice resonated through the room as he stood again, fist curled around something. "That orgasm is mine to give you."

"I wasn't going to—"

"You say that now, but in thirty seconds? Two minutes? Five?" *Okay, so maybe he had a point.* "You've left me aching."

"And I'll make it better," he promised, dumping a few condoms on her nightstand.

Decker held up one and tore the foil open with his teeth. He wasted no time rolling it over his huge erection and sliding onto the bed again, right between her legs. Without warning, he scooped her thighs up in his arms, lifted them around his head, and dropped his mouth back to her clit. The intense suction and almost punishing nip made her scream—and her body jolt in a hot-blooded race for satisfaction.

As she flew even closer to blissful explosion than before, a damp sweat covered her body. She strained to get closer, lifting up to the heavenly touch of his tongue. Her breath hitched, then left her lips in a broken cry. Blood zipped by the bucketful south, filling the responsive little nub he played with. Rachel felt herself swelling, the pressure building, the burn scorching. *Just another second or two . . .*

He eased his lips away.

Before she had time to moan in protest, he trapped her body beneath his own with a growl. The lust in that feral sound nearly undid her. Full staff in hand, he aligned himself against her slick, vulnerable opening, probing, feeding her the head in shallow strokes before backing out to rub her clit with his rigid stalk.

The need to take him deep, feel him stroking her walls, had her tossing her head back, breathing hard, a frantic cry on her lips. "Decker . . ."

"Tell me you want me to fuck you."

Her blood boiled, burning away any semblance of pride. "Yes. Please. I do. Now."

"Tell me you want me to fuck you until you can't take a moment more."

Even the image had her squirming beneath him and crying out again. "Yes!"

The word hadn't even finished clearing her lips before he thrust deep inside her. She gasped. Her eyes went wide with panic and pain. She couldn't take another inch of him.

Stiffening, Rachel tried discreetly to wriggle and displace him, put some distance between them.

"Does that hurt?"

"A little."

"Shh. Relax." He grabbed her hips in his hands, easing back. Rachel sighed in relief.

But he wasn't absent for long. He only put enough distance between them to work a pair of fingers inside her and stretch her. His clever digits found a sensitive spot inside her, and she arched her back, spreading wide for him until she accommodated another finger. Then another.

When she was mewling, Decker withdrew, then nudged his staff against her opening again.

His nostrils flared, his eyes narrowing. "Now you should be more comfortable. Tell me if you're not, and I'll work you open slowly. But you won't get away from me, Rachel."

As if she wanted to . . .

Then he reared back and thrust into her roughly, deeper, working against the swollen, constricting flesh of her sex. But his fingers had worked some magic. The discomfort was gone.

He groaned. "That's right. That's good. Let me in."

Wasn't he already in?

Lifting her hips up to him, Decker pressed down into her body with another shallow stroke. Then he withdrew slowly. The friction of his flesh over nerve endings she hadn't known she possessed caused her to cry out.

"I'm getting deeper, beautiful. Yes . . . You're so sweet and tight. I'm going to make you come for me. You want that. I want to feel it. Just take all of me."

She still hadn't?

Rachel moaned. Decker ground into her clit again with his hard length, then shifted down, rooting at her opening once more. With one heavy push, he grunted, then seared his way into her body, up, up, up, filling every corner and recess of her with his thick possession, stretching her almost beyond her limit.

Mercy . . .

He rubbed a sensitive spot so deep inside her that Rachel felt herself swell even more. He drew back and kindled all those nerves again. And again. The flames licking her body turned incendiary. She bucked under him, cried out for him, clenched her fists and begged. His bared teeth and determined face told her that nothing would stop him from giving this pleasure to her.

Holy cow! Rachel had known he would be every bit as good as her fantasies, but never had she imagined this sort of ecstasy.

Relentlessly, he pushed in and out of her, hitting that spot so deep and shocking with every last plunge. She closed her eyes, struggling to breathe. Her thighs tightened. She wanted her arms around him, but he held her pinned to the bed and drove into her again and again.

"Open your eyes."

She squeezed them even more tightly shut, so focused on the sensations that stacked on top of her restraint, crushing it. Her clit burned. He shocked the end of her passage with every forceful thrust.

"Fucking open your eyes and look at me."

Something about his deep growl forced her to obey. His face hovered just above hers, and he fused their stares together. A jolt, a zing, an electric sizzle—they lit her up. The forces in her body swirled together, spinning faster and faster, taking her down with them like a whirlpool sucking away her ability to breathe, to care about anything but the ecstasy about to sear across her soul.

"Decker," she whispered almost soundlessly, out of breath.

Using all the power of his muscled arms and thighs, he fucked his way even harder inside her. His stare penetrated deeper. This didn't feel like a one-night stand. Decker utterly possessed her, from their linked fingers above her head, to their locked stares, all the way to their joined bodies.

The uproar of tingles and aches throbbing with need all compounded to overload her, but they had nothing on the sudden fervor that seized her heart.

All the sensations inside her melded, conjoined, rose dangerously. Then her body combusted. Her sex clamped down on him, womb clenching, as pleasure spilled over in a lush melding of wonder, ecstasy, and thrill.

Above her, Decker pounded into her mercilessly, jaw tensing, eyes raging, breath sawing in and out of his chest with effort, with excitement. He crushed her lips under his own and gripped her hands fiercely. Then his entire body tensed as he submerged himself completely inside her, setting off another storm of astonishing pleasure. As she screamed into his kiss and held on for dear life, Rachel wondered if she'd be able to forget this night or this man—ever.

FIVE

TEN MINUTES LATER, RACHEL WAS CURLED AGAINST HIS SIDE, hand brushing up and down his chest. The room was still mostly dark, broken only by a nightlight coming from the bathroom and a twinkle from the silvery moon streaming through the window. He'd disposed of the condom and caught his breath. Even on the comfy mattress wrapped in soft sheets and what had to be homemade quilts, Decker couldn't relax. His brain wouldn't downshift to a gear other than sex. Over and over, one thought plagued his head: *What the hell had happened between them?*

They hadn't just fucked. She hadn't merely been aroused. He hadn't simply wanted her. What they'd done here had been . . . something more.

That made no fucking sense. He didn't really know this girl. But the very first time he'd clapped eyes on her picture had been a visceral blow to his chest. Touching her shook him even more. Filling her tight cunt had been absolutely earthshaking. Despite an orgasm that had all but fractured his restraint and sent him rocketing into a pleasure so surreal, he still felt stunned and dazed; he still hadn't managed to unleash all the lust broiling inside him.

It didn't add up. She wouldn't be capable of the same sexual gymnastics as that girl from Moscow. She'd never be as freaky as those twins from Mexico City. She probably didn't give a mind-bending blow job like the show dancer he'd hooked up with in Rio. But Rachel had something none of those women possessed, a quality he couldn't put his finger on that made him want to bury his cock inside her again and stay for a sweet long while. She drew him in. He liked her mix of vulnerability and sweet teasing. Her intelligence probably ranked higher than most women he'd taken to bed. The soft chime of her laughter made him smile. She was truly a terrible dancer, but she cared about the people in her life. And she trusted in a way none of the jaded women he'd met could. Hell, more than he ever had. She deserved to be protected, adored, cherished.

How fucking crazy was it that he was wondering if he could be the man for the job?

One thing at a time. First, he had to keep her safe, figure out who wanted her dead, *then* he could decide if he was actually capable of sharing his picket fence with any woman, let alone this one.

At his side, Rachel sighed, caressing him with a leisurely sweep of her hand up and down his torso. The thought of her drifting off in his arms made him smile. On the corner of the bed, the orange tabby yawned and looked at him like an unwelcome interloper. As far as Decker could tell, the cat had remained planted on his little corner of the mattress the whole time he and Rachel had rocked it. The hairball was seemingly far less annoyed that Decker had violated his mistress than he was about having his nocturnal beauty rest disturbed.

"*Meow.*" The cat's tone made it clear he was registering a complaint.

Rachel smiled against Decker's chest, then propped her chin on him to look at the cat. "Be a nice kitten, Val."

Kitten? That thing had to weigh fifteen pounds.

"Is he possessive?" Decker sank his fingers into her plush dark hair. It was so fucking soft, not weighed down by a ton of goop or hair spray. It wasn't coarse, and she didn't have extensions. It was just naturally beautiful. Kind of like her.

Shit, now he sounded like some sappy jewelry commercial.

"Not really. He's my cat, for sure. He typically doesn't like other people. He *hated* Owen. It was mutual, however. And Owen swore that Florida was a little bit safer when we moved here because I'd removed the 'beast.' The fact that Val hasn't attacked or run off means he's at least willing to tolerate you. Since he's a better judge of men than I apparently am, I take it as a good sign." She flashed a tired but teasing grin in the shadowy room. "Isn't that right, Valentino?"

Rachel stretched across the bed to pet the little hairball between his perky ears. The move exposed her breasts, and that's all it took for his cock to go from half-awake to aching for action again. Wincing, he dragged in a calming breath. He had to give her pussy a break after he'd pounded her like a madman. Besides, while she was soft and sweet and sated would be a good time to ask her questions that might help him. Any information would be better than grasping in the dark.

"Valentino?" he asked. "Like the famous actor?"

"Yes. Like his namesake, Val seems to be well liked by the female felines in the neighborhood. The males . . . they turn their tails up at him. Val is also a little bit of a diva and likes his way. That's a cat thing, but it's even more of a Val thing. I found him as a stray when he was just a baby kitten. I was married to Owen, and he threw a fit. But I just couldn't resist Val."

That soft heart of hers again. Of course she'd take in a little runt with big green eyes that purred and rubbed against her leg. Rachel's sweetness was part of her charm.

When had he last spent any time with a woman who had this kind of goodness? Probably during the Clinton administration. What did he know about family pets, nice girls, and comfortable beds? Jack squat. He needed to get his head on straight and do the job he'd come to do before he contemplated anything else. But what was there to think about? It wouldn't be long before Xander and duty called, whisking him away. Rachel needed to fall for a great guy who would be there for her day in, day out. Not one who'd be jaunting off to another continent at a moment's notice to stop the spread of industrial espionage or whatever shit S.I. Industries faced.

Even with all that running through his head, he couldn't stop himself from pressing Rachel against him, kissing her forehead, then settling her face onto his shoulder. Her sigh of contentment made him harder.

"So, is Val the only friend who came with you from Florida?"

"Yes. After the divorce, Owen and I had a few ugly fights. My family lived nearby, and he tried to drag them into our dispute once. I didn't love the principal of the school I worked for, and I couldn't afford to stay in the house my ex-husband and I had bought together, so I started applying to schools all over the South. Lafayette Parish hired me."

So if Owen lived in Florida, how could he have been in a bar in Lafayette yesterday, soliciting murder? It was possible. But likely?

But if he ruled the ex out, how many other suspects did he have? Zilch.

"It's nice that you've made some friends here."

She smiled. "Shonda has been great. I'm so glad that her brother is going to be all right. A couple of broken bones and a mild concussion, but he'll heal up."

"Good news." He paused, brushing his fingers through her silky sable hair again. "You seem like such a kind person. I'll bet you don't have any enemies."

Rachel lifted her head to look down at him and paused. "Not that I know of. I'm generally on better footing with Owen now. My family says he's got a new girlfriend and that Carly has been good for him. I can't think of anyone else I've exchanged any cross words with."

"Know if his girlfriend's jealous of you?"

"Why should she be?" Rachel shrugged. "I'm out of his life and have *no* interest in returning."

Even if it didn't seem likely, the sexually inept ex still remained his only suspect. Not that Decker wouldn't love to nail his ass to the wall, but he worried that pinning this murder for hire on Owen might be a bit too easy, like saying the butler did it. If the guy lived in Florida, it would be awfully inconvenient to travel to Lafayette simply to solicit a murder. And obvious, too. Then again, maybe he'd simply called a sympathetic friend and convinced him to hire out this dirty work. Hard to know . . . Better to keep digging.

"I'll bet you're an expert at handling agitated parents," he praised. "And your students must love you."

"I've only been teaching here for a few months, but my interactions have been largely positive. Most of my parents are really involved in their kids' lives, so that makes the partnering great."

"You haven't had any trouble with them?"

"No."

"Like all your new neighbors?"

"The few I know, yeah. It's a neighborhood of mostly young professionals, so everyone is busy doing their own thing."

So unless she had some secret or silent hater, had seen something she shouldn't have, or was the target of some random freak, Decker didn't have any better suspects than Owen. Damn it, he had to get to a computer and find a picture of the guy, check his current whereabouts, see if that's who'd plopped his hateful ass down on the barstool beside his and offered him mid-five figures to kill Rachel.

"What about you?" she asked, cutting into his thoughts.

Decker opened his mouth to give her a bullshit reply, but paused. He was already lying to her about his reason for being at that bar, his reason for going home with her, his reason for staying. For some damn reason, he didn't want to lie about this, too.

"I don't have many friends beyond Xander and Javier. A few of their local buddies are cool. I've spent a lot of time on tours and missions all over the world. A lot of the guys I considered friends didn't make it home. I've got my share of enemies. I've got a ruthless streak. If anyone fucks with me or mine, we're going to have problems."

Rachel pulled back a bit. He drew her close again and held in a curse.

Oops, probably too much. Likely, he'd scared the hell out of her. He tried to laugh it off and hoped she bought it.

"God, that made me sound like I live in a cave, eat raw game, and beat my chest."

She giggled, at ease once more. He let out a relieved breath.

"Maybe a little. I was trying to ask you why you're in Lafayette. Is this a temporary stop?" she asked.

"Maybe." He shrugged. "That depends some on the Santiago brothers. I've been here a few months, and I'll be here at least another few days. That's the longest I've stayed in one place since I was a kid."

Her gaze slid away, and he didn't have to guess that she was telling herself right now not to get attached to him, not to see any sort of future. Normally, he'd applaud that insight. Now, for some reason it absolutely pissed him off.

"But I like Lafayette well enough. Xander and Javier seem really content to cozy up to their new bride and wait for their baby to come. I don't see them leaving her side anytime soon, and she likes it here, so I might be here a lot longer."

"So they really share a wife?" she whispered, sounding a bit scandalized.

Crap, he'd seen shit that would shock her to her pretty pink toes. Probably done a few things that would incite the same reaction.

"Yep. They're fairly open about it among their friends. Her mother wasn't keen on the idea at first, but she's come around. You probably would have thought Xander was an ass before London. Javier was a fucking train wreck. They both need her, and she's got a heart big enough for two."

"I'll bet they scandalize their neighbors."

Since Xander had been really persistent about seducing London in their backyard over the summer, and she and Javier had almost been caught fucking in the car in their driveway a few weeks ago? "No doubt."

Rachel smiled and braced her chin on his chest again. "You're easy to talk to."

"You are, too," he answered honestly. "Sorry if I got a little, um . . . demanding earlier. I promise I won't drag you off by your hair—at least not often."

"Did you hear me complaining?"

"Hmm . . ." He pretended to cock his head in thought. "Unless 'please, don't stop' is some new code for 'no,' then I guess not."

Even in the dim light, he could see a faint flush crawl up her cheeks. "In fact, it was . . . wow."

He cupped her chin and brushed a thumb over her slightly swollen lip. "It was pretty 'wow' for me, too, beautiful."

And he meant that. It wasn't because of her spectacular technique or her deviant sexual kink. It definitely wasn't because she dressed as scantily as a Hollywood Boulevard hooker. It wasn't at all because she knew how to seduce a man in sixty seconds or less. It was precisely because none of those things were true about Rachel.

She had permanence stamped all over her, and he wasn't a staying sort of man. He was going to have to be careful not to hurt her if—no, when—he left. Why lie to himself? This cozy feeling would pass, right? Probably, but . . . he didn't want to know why the idea of parting ways with her made him somewhere between grumpy and enraged.

"Tired?" she asked with a smile.

"No."

"Hungry or thirsty?"

"No." He grinned. "Ask me if I'm horny."

She wrinkled her nose. "I hate that word."

"Ask me if I want to fuck you again."

Rachel hesitated, then with an impish smile, she lifted the blanket covering them both and tried to peer down at his cock, but it had to be too dark for her to see. To make sure she didn't miss even an inch of his cock throbbing for her, Decker threw back the soft sheets and handmade quilt and took himself in hand.

She gasped. "I don't think I need to ask."

Her voice suddenly sounded throaty, and it turned him on even more.

"I want you again, Rachel." He lifted her hand from his chest and eased it down to his hard cock.

He died a small, shuddering death when she wrapped her fingers around him and stroked softly, down and up his sensitive length, then brushed over the tingling head. When she bent to kiss his shoulder, his chest, another tremor wracked his body.

It didn't make sense. He'd spent three days in bed with a Victoria's Secret model last time he'd been in Manhattan. Besides being gorgeous, Mandy was experienced, voracious, and unapologetic. She never expected anything more than an orgasm. Normally, she was his kind of girl.

The fine trembling in Rachel's fingers told Decker that touching him meant something to her and that it was important to her to give him pleasure. And that was revving up his libido more effectively than skimpy lingerie.

Was he getting older and going traditional? Or had he crossed from sentimental right into sappy? It hadn't escaped Decker that Rachel trusted him with her body when she hadn't trusted any other man but her husband. He was as moved by her nervousness, her care, and her goodness as he was by her lush tits—and that was saying something. She had a great rack.

He felt . . . stuck on this woman and had every intention of staying by her side, not only to protect her, but until he could figure out why being with her smacked him with the force of a two-by-four to the forehead.

"I want you, too." In the dark, she closed her eyes and smiled a bit shyly.

Instead of annoying him or making him wish they could just skip to the fucking, Decker found an answering smile stretching his lips. So sweet. So honest in her every response. He felt a bit guilty for lying to her about his reasons for picking her up at the bar, for being here with her now. But he couldn't apologize for wanting to shield her from a potentially ugly fate and keep her safe. Until this played out, he'd thoroughly enjoy her goodness.

"I want to suck . . ." She glanced down and swallowed, watching her fingers slowly move over his aching dick.

His breath caught. *Holy fuck!* Even the hint that she wanted her mouth on him made him harder than steel-reinforced concrete.

"My cock?"

"I'm not used to that word." Her voice trembled, and her hand shook. "But yes."

He thrust his hands in her hair and led her down to his waiting erection. "Be my guest."

Her back stiffened, and she tensed against him. "Don't laugh at me, but I don't know how."

Dumbass Owen hadn't ever sank in between those luscious lips? Given what Rachel had said about her ex, Decker wondered if the moron had even tried or had he found that a time-consuming waste, too? Owen's loss was absolutely his gain.

"There's no right or wrong way. Open wide, suck deep, and do what feels natural."

"All right." She looked adorably nervous, and he loved the idea that he would be the first inside her plump, pink lips. Yes, it was caveman of him. So fucking what?

Rachel didn't hesitate or study the situation. She had a lot of gumption when she wanted to; he was learning that already. In fact, he liked her for it.

Then her lips closed around the head of his cock, and he wasn't thinking anything anymore.

She had to stretch wide to fit her lips around the swollen mushroom head, and the sight of it sent a hot rush of blood south, engorging him even more. He'd had plenty of blow jobs in his life, but this one was different.

Because she was different. No denying that.

If he hadn't been solicited to kill Rachel and had simply run into her in a bar, he would have taken a long look at her, licked his lips, and kept walking. She was attractive, no doubt. As well as warm and kind—two things he would have sworn he didn't need in a sexual partner.

But at his age, maybe it was time to realize that life really was about more than the next adrenaline rush of danger and getting laid.

Hell, listen to him, all mature and shit. Decker rolled his eyes. Actually, they rolled into the back of his head as Rachel sighed, sucked back up his length with a flat, wide tongue, then opened around his girth to take him even deeper. God, she wasn't spectacular at it, and that didn't fucking matter at all. Knowing that she was trying, that she was trusting him, that she was giving him something she'd never given anyone . . . all of that turned him on. If she'd been insanely good at it, too, he would probably—

Oh hell, he'd thought too soon. Suddenly, she found a coordinated rhythm, a steady up-down that encompassed most of his shaft, paid extra attention to the head, then—*fuck!*—she cupped his balls. Now *that* was beyond stunning.

And if she did this for very long, he'd be totally done for.

"Rachel, beautiful . . ." He slid his fingers deeper into her hair and curled them into fists, gently tugging on her hair. "Baby, slowly. You don't want to—Oh, shit!" He hissed in a long breath, then tensed and shuddered. She might be a novice, but she'd quickly conquered that inexpert thing. That had to be one of the shortest learning curves in history.

"I'm doing it right?" she murmured, then licked the head like a damn ice cream cone, over and over and . . .

Jesus, she was killing him.

"Oh, yeah," he gasped. "And then some."

She giggled. "You sound distressed."

No shit. "That is *not* funny."

"Maybe not to you . . ." Rachel flashed a coy smile at him, clearly happy with herself, before she set back to her task.

Decker closed his eyes and let the slow, burning heat of her mouth surround him. An intense suction that made him shudder came next. He jolted under her leisurely bobbing head. When her tongue lapped around the sensitive head, then a tender drag of her teeth followed, he groaned aloud and nearly hit the roof.

He'd had better in his life . . . maybe. He couldn't really remember right now. But no woman had ever paid so much attention to his reactions, adjusted so quickly, all to so obviously please him. That reality set him ablaze.

Swallowing back another groan of pleasure clawing up from his chest, he tried to nudge her away. Of course, his hips had other ideas, thrusting up into her sweet, pouty mouth and making his cock right at home.

"Rachel, you need to stop."

"Why?"

He focused in on her sparkling eyes and swollen lips before she engulfed him again. With a groan, he closed his eyes and indulged for a moment, shafting her lips with his steely length for a few sublime seconds. Then he tugged on her hair just enough to bring her away from his cock and sat up.

"If I have to pick where I'm coming next, it's going to be deep inside that tight pussy again, beautiful. Lie back for me." Decker rose to his knees and nudged her to her back. "Spread your legs."

"But I was having fun," she protested, not complying with his demand.

"I promise you can have more fun later." Because there was no way he didn't want to immerse himself between her silken lips again.

Then he didn't give her another opportunity to talk. With his own body, he urged her back, eclipsing her. Decker looked down at her, tousled dark curls, rosy cheeks, sweet lips, pleading eyes. Christ, he wanted this woman.

When he'd first heard that some ass-hat wanted her dead, he had felt an undeniable urge to keep her alive. When he'd seen her picture, the itch to have her under him had broken out across his body like allover hives he knew he'd have to scratch away. Now that he'd seen her, met her, talked to her, fucked her . . . maybe a few nights with her might not be enough, after all.

Well, wasn't this quite a U-turn from his attitude the previous afternoon? But damn it, he was always packing up, moving on, setting out for the next "big adventure." Color him cynical, but adventure often wound up with him chasing trigger-happy dirt-bags in third-world shitholes and either freezing his ass off, sweating to death, or picking sand out of some really uncomfortable places. At thirty-three, wasn't it time to stop playing the grown-up version of cops and robbers and latch on to something real? Wasn't it time to stop settling for Ms. Right-now?

Rachel was looking pretty damn real and right for him. He wanted to lay her out, fuck her, exhaust her, wake her up, and do it again until she was happily spent and clinging to him. Yeah, that sounded like an awesome version of paradise.

Tearing into a fresh condom, Decker rolled it down the desperate flesh of his cock. He didn't waste time with niceties except to check that she was wet and ready. The pair of fingers encountered slick, swollen flesh. Oh yeah, they were a go. She wasn't just wet, but juicy. Perfect.

Lining himself up, he pushed in one inch at a time, checking for discomfort. Her body had quickly adjusted to his size because she didn't have any difficulty taking every bit of him on the first agonizing thrust. But slow and steady had won that race. The urge to sprint to the finish now was strong—because when didn't coming inside a gorgeous woman feel good?—but he wanted to see her go off like a fireworks show first.

Buried in as deep as he could be, Decker flexed his hips and pushed a bit more. She hissed, then her eyes flew open and met his stare. He could happily dive into their chocolate depths and stay for a sweet, long while.

He stilled for a moment, feeling her tight walls engulf him, sucking him in deeper. He shuddered, his spine stiff, his body seized by the need to experience her in every way possible. The first time had been good. Already Decker could tell the second time was going to be even fucking better. *Yee-haw!*

Gathering her against his chest, Decker lifted her lush hips and eased out of her snug pussy before he stroked deep again. She felt electric around him, squeezing him as she gasped, jolting him with another sizzle of need. Jesus, what was it about this woman?

Rachel wrapped her legs around his hips and rocked with him, thrusting to his rhythm, her little cries driving him higher and higher. Frantically, she kissed her way across his shoulder, to his jaw. Then he claimed her mouth, his tongue plunging as deep as his dick. He wanted all of her every way he could get her. Her nails dug into his back, and she went wild underneath him, urging him on silently to give her every fucking thing.

After that, containing himself . . . impossible. His hips moved like they had a mind of their own, hammering her with long, rapid strokes. Tingles burned in his balls, danced through his body.

He grabbed her tighter, somehow managing to sink even farther into her body, deeper than he swore he'd ever been inside any woman. Blood raced, his heart chugged. Fuck, this was going to be good.

"Mine," he growled.

She'd probably question that statement later. He ought to as well. But now, what they shared felt damn good. Right. Like he'd willingly fight any man to the death who wanted to touch her. That shit wasn't happening—at all. In this moment, for this night, she was absolutely, unquestionably his.

And the thought turned him on even more. Fuck, at this rate he wasn't going to last long, which blew his mind. Orgasm number two didn't usually happen for a long while, and he could really lay thick pleasure on a woman while he took the time finding his own. This was completely different. Damn it, he intended to make sure she climaxed before this growing need blew off the top of his head.

As pleasure surged, his heartbeat roared, mixing with the deafening sounds of her mewls. As she screamed, arching up to him, Decker surged deep, filling her one final time. Blinding heat seared him. Her pussy constricted, pulsing, caressing the length of his cock and annihilating his restraint. As she shuddered through her orgasm, his seed spewed with the force of C4, detonating everything inside him.

Damn, at this rate, she was going to kill him. But he'd die happy.

With a groan, he stumbled from the bed, damn near dizzy, and disposed of the condom. She looked so gorgeous all flushed and damp, lying across her bed. He snagged a towel from the bathroom, ran warm water over a corner, then returned to clean her up.

"I'll do it." She reached for the terrycloth, still panting.

Decker edged away. "*I'll* do it. You'll lie there and look pretty so I can contemplate all the other ways I can sully you."

With a tired laugh, Rachel rested back against the mattress. She was a bit stiff, a little self-conscious as he wiped her clean, but he was relieved to see that she trusted him enough to allow this intimacy.

Once he tossed the towel back in the bathroom, he crawled over her body and hunkered down beside her, nudging her to her side so she lay against him, her thigh tossed over his. The ceiling fan churned anemically overhead, fighting ineffectually against the humidity, sweat, and blazing sexual heat in the room.

He didn't think he'd make it until dawn before he'd want inside her again. As she pressed against him, lips caressing his chest, her breasts cupping his ribs, he mentally revised that to an hour. Maybe less.

"So that's what sex is supposed to be like?" she whispered.

Decker hesitated. "Really fantastic sex. This was above and beyond for me, too."

Rachel sighed happily. "I'm glad you came over tonight."

"Yeah." And if she thought for one minute that he was about to get up and leave, he had a big surprise for her. With someone out to get her, he wasn't budging. After that . . . well, he was starting to think that maybe he wouldn't budge then, either.

SUNLIGHT STREAMED THROUGH the window, despite the blinds slanting up. Decker cracked an eye open and found Rachel draped across him, still completely naked, her dark hair cascading over his shoulder and down his arm. He raised his head a fraction. Her eyes remained closed, dark lashes feathering gentle half-circles on smooth cheeks. In the morning light, he saw a little spill of freckles on her nose. Her fingers splayed across his chest. Her breathing remained deep and even. So trusting.

She made him hard as hell. Again. Still.

After waking her at two and four thirty to slide into those sweet curves and possess her again, he should be sated and totally exhausted. But at just before eight a.m., even with shaky legs and an empty stomach, he was contemplating another go-round.

Yep, this woman totally flipped every switch.

And if he wanted to keep her alive long enough to see where this was leading, he needed to stop mooning over her and figure out who might be trying to kill her. Item one on the agenda: Dig up a picture of the illustrious ex and see if Owen was a match for the ass-hat in the bar. Preferably before Rachel awoke and wondered what the hell he was up to.

Slowly, he rose from bed and grimaced. He felt grimy, and couldn't remember the last time he'd actually slept over with a woman. And he'd gotten soft since a damn toothbrush was pretty high on his list of must-haves.

Tossing on his jeans and the pistol he'd hidden beneath, he headed to the guest bathroom down the hall.

Inside, he flipped on the light. Bless Rachel. She'd thought of everything to make a guest comfortable. The vanity held a new toothbrush, fluffy towels, shampoo, and soap.

Decker made quick use of them, then wrapped the beige ter-rycloth around his hips. As he cracked the bathroom door, he heard a crash in the kitchen. His heartbeat kicked into high gear. Adrenaline ratcheted up, and he charged out, pistol in hand, ready to fight whoever had come for her.

As he sneaked down the hall, his back hugging the wall, he heard a feminine cry, then another crash. Fuck, what was going on?

Heart pounding, he forced himself to stay calm and crept closer, finger on the trigger, promising that any motherfucker who wanted to hurt her was going to find himself minus a head.

Fighting for calm, Decker clung to shadows until he rounded the corner and had a straight sightline into the kitchen. But he didn't see anyone attacking Rachel. Rather, she attacked a plastic bin of flour and a couple of eggs while wrestling with a stainless steel bowl. A can of nonstick cooking spray rolled down the counter. She slammed down a wooden spoon, looking beyond frustrated.

Actually, it was kind of adorable.

Until she emerged from behind the tall counter and he realized she was wearing a frilly red apron, a pair of black stilettos—and nothing else.

He wanted to fuck her right now.

Darting back into the bathroom, he grabbed his jeans and flipped them over his pistol, hiding the piece, then sauntered down the hall and set everything down within easy reach—just in case—on the adjacent kitchen table.

"That looks mighty good," he drawled.

She blinked up at him, flushed and flustered. "Pancakes will be ready soon."

"I meant you, beautiful. Forget food right now. I'd rather fuck you."

And he didn't take no for an answer; snagging one arm around her waist and dragging her against his body, he dropped a hard kiss across her lips. Jesus, she smelled sweet. She'd brushed her teeth and pulled her artless curls into some half-up, half-down 'do that made him want to mess it up with his fingers.

He claimed her lips, sinking into her mouth and delivering a long, slow kiss of good morning. Rachel melted against him, opened wide to let him in, and gave as good as she got. Hmm, he could get used to this . . .

When he pulled back and sent her a steamy stare that suggested they get busy, she blushed a pretty pink.

With a laugh, he glanced down her body. "In fact, you look good enough to eat, beautiful. Did you dress up just for me?"

The blush deepened. "Maybe a little."

"I like it. I'd like the shoes better if they were up around my ears, but . . ."

She rolled her eyes. "Is that supposed to be another pick-up line you found on Google?"

"Nope. That's all me. Impressed?" He winked and found that he really liked teasing her. He adored the way she looked down demurely while giving him a flirtatious smile with a hint of the devil.

"Decker, you're a wicked man."

"You ain't seen nothin' yet," he promised, then pulled her in for another kiss.

Sweet. Always so damn sweet. She didn't taste like danger, betrayal, or another man, as the other women he'd taken to bed for the last decade did. She was warm and real and . . .

Shit, he sounded like some poetry-writing pussy. But it was all true.

With an arm around her waist, he didn't have any trouble finding the big bow at the small of her waist and untying her apron. She barely had a chance to sputter a little protest before he yanked it over her head and tossed it to the ground, then silenced her with another kiss. A moment later, Rachel threw her arms around his neck and pressed herself close, rubbing against his nagging cock.

Decker thrust his hands in her hair, no longer giving a shit about her pretty curls arranged away from her face and all around her shoulders. "You keep doing that and you're definitely going to get fucked."

She gave a throaty laugh. "Promise?"

Fitting his hands around her ribs, under her arms, he lifted her onto the white tile of the kitchen counter. She gasped when her bare ass made contact with the cold surface. Rachel squirmed and tried to get comfortable. He just smiled. "Yes. Right here. Right now. Spread your legs and brace your heels on the edge of the counter."

She blinked, looking so gratifyingly shocked, but she complied. "Just . . . like this?"

"Exactly like that," he confirmed. "You make me ache for you every time."

A fresh blush bloomed over her whole body.

"You ever had sex outside the bedroom?"

She shook her head, biting her lip and casting her gaze down again. "No."

"Oh, beautiful . . . We're going to have so much fun." He grabbed her ankles and spread them wider, helping her anchor her heels on the edge of the counter, toes pointed down, leaving her pretty cunt completely open for his stare, his tongue, his cock.

Best breakfast ever, and he couldn't wait to dive in. He was on his last condom, but after this, he'd somehow manage to drag himself out of her pussy long enough to feed her and run by the drugstore. After that, all bets were off.

Ready for a feast, he ran a finger down the inside of her thigh, skirting ever closer to her sensitive, swollen center. How fascinating to watch her folds grow slick and flush and pouty for his attention. Every part of her was beautiful.

He dropped his towel and took a few sidesteps over to his jeans, carefully removing the condom without disturbing the gun. Rachel watched, her breathing rapid, her lids heavy, her lips rosy and parted, her legs spread wide. When had he ever seen a sight more gorgeous? No doubt, he was a lucky son of a bitch that she was all his, at least for now.

And the thought crept back in that if he played his cards right, she could be his forever.

His teasing mien fell away. The inner caveman roared, wanting to break free, to claim, to take, to mark. He'd never, ever felt anything like this, but he wasn't about to fight something that felt so right.

Decker stuck the condom wrapper between his teeth, ready to tear it open, roll it on, and sink so deeply inside her that she'd never think about walking away.

The thought was spinning in his head. Her heavy breaths, his pounding heart, the gravity of the moment—it was all broken by the ringing of a doorbell.

SIX

RACHEL GASPED AND STIFFENED, THEN SCRAMBLED OFF THE counter. Decker snagged his towel from the hardwood floor and blocked her. No way was she answering that door or talking to anyone unless it was someone's ninety-year-old grandma. And even then, he intended to frisk her for weapons.

"Are you answering the door in nothing but high heels?"

Panic flitted across her face, then she cursed. "No."

"Go put some clothes on. I got it."

"You don't have any clothes either," she screeched.

Decker pointed to his jeans on the table, then turned her toward the hall, urging her back toward the bedroom with a little slap. "Go. You expecting anyone?"

"No." She jogged down the hall, carrying her shoes. "No one ever rings my doorbell, especially this early on a Sunday morning."

Frowning, he watched her disappear into her room, then snagged his gun and jeans, putting the latter on and palming the former. He shoved the condom in his pocket again. Whoever stood on the other side of the door was going to get his nuts blown off if Decker deemed him unfriendly.

All kinds of pissed off for being cockblocked, he stalked down the hall. "This better be nothing."

When he reached the door, he tore it open to find a man of average height with hazel eyes behind round glasses, a checkered shirt, and khakis. He had nondescript shoes and an even more blah cut of hair in an unremarkable color somewhere between blond and light brown. The only thing worth mentioning was the scowl on his face.

"Who are you?" the stranger asked.

Decker slanted him a menacing glare. "Who are you?"

The scholarly, sharp face told him the guy was a few years older. The hint of paunch suggested this dude was more sedentary. The permanent vertical furrow between his brows said to Decker that the stranger scowled a lot. He lacked a coat, so it wasn't like he could hide a shoulder holster. The piece might be tucked into the small of his back, but . . . The man's hands looked too soft to be lethal.

Whoever this was, Decker didn't think he was threatening. Annoying? That he already believed.

"I'm here to see Rachel." The other guy tried to look down his nose at Decker, but that had to be hard when he had to look up a few inches and through glasses to meet his stare.

"She's . . . busy." Decker flashed a tight smile and hoped the dude got the right idea. Whoever he was, no way was he homing in on Rachel.

Mr. Glasses straightened his rims and glanced down Decker's body, rolling his eyes at the tattoos and hard abs. Then his stare bulged when he spotted the gun pinned to his thigh.

"What are you doing with that?" he backed away a step. "I hope you're a policeman."

Not exactly, but close enough. "Something like that."

"Are you hurting her?"

"Would I be answering the door if I was?" Decker rolled his eyes.

"Are you taking advantage of her?" Though nervous, the stranger looked ready to dress him down.

Decker tried not to laugh. Taking advantage of her? *Every chance I get . . .*

"None of your business. Who the hell are you and why are you standing on her porch when you weren't invited?"

If it was possible, the guy got even more uptight, and some suspicions about his identity took root. And if this was who he thought, that would really fuck up everything.

Before he could say another word, Rachel came skidding around the corner and into the foyer. She stopped at the door with a gasp. "Owen, what are you doing here?"

Yep, that confirmed his suspicions. *Damn it.* While it seemed awfully convenient that Four-eyes was in town when Decker had been solicited to kill her, the truth was Owen hadn't been the guy on the next barstool, offering him twenty-five thousand down and another twenty-five when the job was done. Yes, Owen could have hired someone to employ him. But why? Rachel's ex looked more like the sort who would protest violence, not create it. With a curse, Decker surreptitiously tucked his pistol in the small of his back before Rachel could spot it, and leaned against the wall.

If Owen hadn't solicited him to commit murder, then he was back to square one, trying to figure out who had.

WEARING LITTLE MORE than a frilly robe with her hair in disarray, Rachel stared at her ex-husband, who gave Decker a derisive glare, then sent her a look filled with scorn. She bristled. He'd moved on with his life. Hers was none of his business now.

"I'm here to talk to you," Owen said stiffly. "I didn't realize you were occupied. New boyfriend?"

"We just met," she admitted softly.

But Decker talked over her, throwing an arm around her shoulders. "Yes. I'm possessive, too."

Rachel nudged Decker, wondering what the devil was wrong with him. Then she tugged him away from the door, pulling it open. "Come in, Owen."

Val had other ideas. The fat orange tabby pranced to the door, sniffed at Owen, and hissed. Beside her, Decker laughed.

"You've still got that beast?"

"Of course."

"Hmm . . . And now you've added another." He shot Decker another disdainful stare.

Annoyance flared through Rachel. Who was Owen to judge? She hadn't met his new girlfriend, Carly, but she sounded like she could be a bimbo. So she'd gone for the hot guy who was good in bed this time. So what? She was entitled.

Except Decker was way more than that. When she'd met him at the bar, then texted him for what amounted to a booty call, she hadn't expected anything beyond a good time. Instead, he'd put her at ease while challenging her notions of herself and sex. He'd been patient, understanding, willing to listen, and ardent in bed. If he wasn't a one-night stand, he might be everything she wanted.

"Can you make him put a shirt on first?" Owen sounded nothing less than acerbic.

Suddenly, Decker dragged her closer. "Only if you stop being a judgmental asshole. If you want to talk, you can wait while we put on some clothes, which I'm opposed to by the way."

Rachel gaped at him. "Decker . . ."

"Hey, I offered to get dressed. After what he interrupted, I think that's pretty magnanimous of me."

She felt a furious blush creep up her cheeks. Why not just take out a billboard announcing that they were having sex. "Would you—Shh!"

"I think he could have guessed what we were up to, beautiful." He grinned at her, and damn it, there was no way she could stay mad at him. Mercy, she must be out of her mind.

She turned back to Owen, doing her best to stand tall and look prim, despite wearing a robe designed for seduction, with her hair a wild tangle all around her. "The living room is straight to the back of the house. If you need coffee, I'll make you a cup quickly before I—"

"No, you won't." Decker picked her up, lifting her against his chest. "He'll survive without caffeine for five minutes." He sniffed her and nuzzled her neck. "Or thirty."

She gasped. "Decker!"

"I am not amused, Rachel." Owen glowered.

He never was. She tried not to sigh.

Decker got in his face. "You came over here unannounced and uninvited early on a Sunday morning. Don't expect her to just drop everything for you. You should have had the common courtesy to call first, but you didn't because you're either an inconsiderate bastard or you wanted to see if she'd be alone. Either way, that makes you a prick. If you're just rude, then shut the fuck up and stop acting like you're the most important person here. If you hoped to find her still alone, sorry to burst your little bubble. Rachel is far too gorgeous and kind to spend her life without someone who knows how great she is. You've moved on, and she's doing the same. If that's too much for you to handle, then scoot your annoying ass down the road. If you're staying, then I expect to hear some courtesy and respect for her, especially since you knocked on *her* door. I've heard all the asshole I'm going to take from you. Are we clear?"

Rachel pressed her lips together to hold in a gasp—and a cheer. Decker had just defended her in the most beautiful way possible. She wanted to hug him, kiss him, tell him how grateful she was. Not only was he funny and great between the sheets, he was protective and kind in his brutish way. Everything she'd always wanted and never gotten from her ex. She melted inside, especially when Owen had the good grace to look contrite.

"Yes," he mumbled. "I . . . You just startled me."

Decker didn't look like he believed Owen, but he let it pass. "Like I said, you can wait for us in the living room. We'll be out soon."

"I need to talk to Rachel alone," her ex-husband protested.

She wanted nothing less than to spend quality one-on-one time with Owen.

"Not going to happen. If you have something to say, you can say it with me in the room," Decker answered for her. Normally, she'd hate that, but if it kept her ex's visit brief, then she'd agree to anything.

Owen adjusted his glasses, bristling. "It's quite private."

"Too bad. If you want to talk to her, that's the deal. I don't have to negotiate."

Owen's hands curled into fists and he pinned them to his hips. "This is ludicrous. What exactly do you think I'm going to do to her?"

"I don't know, but this craptastic attitude of yours isn't giving me a warm fuzzy. If you want to talk to Rachel, we'll be out shortly. If you want to leave, don't let the door hit your ass on the way out. That's the deal."

Without waiting for a reply, Decker turned and carried her through the foyer and down the hall. Shock still pinged through her. What the hell was he up to? Why did he give a rip about Owen wanting to talk to her? Even with the uncertainty, she couldn't hold in a smile.

He wandered back to the bedroom and set her on her feet. Rachel's head raced as she shut the door and whirled on him. "I don't know whether to thank you from the bottom of my heart or ask you if you're psycho. Do you have any idea how long I've wanted to set Owen on his butt?"

"I'm sure a while. It's obviously long overdue, since the prick seems to think that you should ask, 'How high?' whenever he tells you to jump." He cocked his head. "You did that for years, didn't you?"

She frowned. "Probably longer than I should have."

"Then he deserved what he got. You're no longer his, and you don't have to do a damn thing he says."

"But I'm not yours, either." And that was the confusing part. She didn't really expect him to care about her problems with Owen, but he'd made sure that her demanding ex didn't walk all over her. "You didn't have to stick your neck out there."

"Yeah, I did. You're too good for him. I wasn't about to let him treat you that way."

Those words made her liquefy into a puddle of goo. Who was she kidding? It made her want to fling aside her robe and plaster her naked body to his. "Thanks. That means a lot. Asserting myself with him is something I've struggled with for years. I know I should. I just don't like confrontation."

And every time she'd tried, Owen had done his best to make her feel petty and regret it.

"Then I'll take care of it for you."

His words took her aback. "I-I don't expect you to stay and listen to whatever Owen is droning on about. It will be long and dull and probably sanctimonious. If you want to take a rain check on the pancakes, I'll let you off easy."

Decker clenched his jaw. "I'm not in a hurry to leave, Rachel. And I'm not thrilled with the idea of leaving you alone with a man who doesn't know how to draw the line between you two, much less be polite. I'll blend into the background if you want, but I'd like to stay. One of the truths about being a protector for a living is that your instincts are well honed. I don't like him being here. Why isn't he in Florida?"

What did Decker think Owen would do to her? He was annoying, but harmless.

"I have no idea."

"Let's put some clothes on and find out." He gave her a hot, lingering stare. "Or take them off and deal with him a lot later."

Rachel sent him a playful swat. He was good for her ego, but she shouldn't keep Owen waiting. Not only was it rude, but he'd make her pay for it eventually, when Decker had gone for good.

Within minutes, Rachel found undergarments, jeans, and a red, scoop-neck T-shirt in her closet at the back of her bathroom and dressed. She ran a brush through her hair and applied a little lip gloss. She wasn't getting prettier than this without makeup, and that would take too long.

Emerging back into her bedroom, she saw Decker fully dressed in last night's clothes. His five o'clock shadow had grown thicker, darker, making him look more disreputable. Dangerous. She shivered. That shouldn't turn her on. She'd never been attracted to the bad boy.

Rachel couldn't deny that she'd made an exception for him.

"Let's go." She smiled at him and found herself blushing as she remembered everything they'd done last night.

As if he could read her mind, Decker grinned back. "And get this over with so we can come back to bed."

Hand in hand, they made their way down the hall, Decker leading her through the narrow corridor. She had no idea why he hadn't bailed when she'd given him the opportunity, much less why he'd stayed and seemed determined to stake his claim in front of Owen. It was kind of unnerving . . . but it was mostly nice. He'd defended her and was now standing by her side during what she feared wasn't going to be a fun conversation. Not at all what she'd imagined when she'd invited Decker over last night, but she had to admit that she was pleasantly surprised. This was her first one-night stand, and she didn't know the etiquette, but something told her this might last longer than a few hot, sweaty hours.

Back in the living room, Decker took a seat on the sofa and immediately began staring down Owen. She escaped to the kitchen and made coffee for all and tidied up, prolonging the moment she had to face her ex. A few minutes later, she brought out the steaming mugs, along with sugar and cream, and some homemade cookies she'd baked the other night out of boredom. They were still soft and fresh, and she didn't think she could face Owen without something in her stomach. Even if his attitude might make her want to throw it all back up.

After she set the tray of everything on the table, Decker wrapped his arm around her and pulled her back onto the sofa with him. Then he leaned in and made coffee for her.

"Sugar and cream?" he asked.

"Please." She wondered how he'd guessed. "Do you still like yours with cream Owen?"

He watched them stiffly. "Yes."

When Rachel scooted forward to help Decker, he shook his head. "I've got it."

Minutes later, he handed her a mug of morning goodness and an oatmeal raisin cookie. A moment later, Decker slid Owen's across the coffee table to him. She couldn't see his face, but his body language beside her was tense with a not-quite-friendly warning. Then he poured his own brew and drank it black, snatching up one of the cookies and groaning as he took a bite.

Decker was noisy and intrusive, and she had a feeling he intended Owen to be very aware of his presence. He was almost overly protective, and she probably ought to be annoyed, but she smiled a bit.

"So what brings you to Lafayette?" she asked her ex politely. "I assume you came here from Florida to see me for a specific reason."

Owen sipped at his coffee, obviously savoring it. "You still make some of the best coffee. I need to remember to put some cinnamon in mine." He set the cup on the saucer, then adjusted both to the little side table beside his chair. "Since you're . . . occupied, I'll make this brief."

"Smart man," Decker mumbled beside her.

Rachel elbowed him. "I'm listening. Go ahead."

"As you might have heard, I'm dating someone now. Her name is Carly. She's an aide at the university. Very bright woman."

"I did hear. That's wonderful. I hope you're happy."

Owen hesitated. "I've come here for her."

Rachel cocked her head and frowned. Owen thought visiting his ex-wife would somehow make his current girlfriend happy? "I don't understand."

He sighed, rubbing his hands together and humming. Owen did that when he was uncomfortable. "Carly's brother lives here in Lafayette. She had plans to come see him, and I didn't want to spend these few days without her."

What? Owen had never wanted to leave work. Missing her would have been the last reason he'd have torn himself away from everything he considered vital.

"We've been dating about eight months, you see. We started slowly at first. But we—" Owen slanted an annoyed stare at Decker. "Is it necessary to have this conversation with him in the room?"

"We've covered this. I'm not leaving." Decker leaned into the sofa and threw an arm around her, sending him a tight smile. Technically, he didn't bare teeth, but he might as well have. "So if you want to talk to her, I'm staying."

Rachel tossed Decker a questioning stare. Wasn't the morning after when the hot guy usually walked out and never returned the lonely girl's calls? Instead, he looked not just protective, but possessive—a bit like he wanted to stake a claim so her ex would understand.

Owen looked ready to launch into one of his logical tirades where she felt reduced to an inch tall, even though he never raised his voice. He just talked in hundred dollar words and used analogies only a physicist could understand to make her feel dumb.

"I'm not asking my guest to leave for you, Owen. You and I aren't together anymore, and I don't owe you anything. If you want to talk, I'm listening."

"As you wish." He didn't sound pleased as he glared at Decker. "I'd appreciate if you'd butt out."

Decker held up his hands. "Hey, if this is about your love life, as long as it's got nothing to do with Rachel, you and I have no problems."

"I've no idea how you can like this muscle-bound Neanderthal, but . . . Back to Carly. I see a future with her. I would like that very much. But . . . we've run into a snag. You know me, Rachel. I'm uncomfortable with feelings."

The understatement of the millennium. "Go on."

"She's convinced that I need more closure with you before I'll be ready to move on. She is adamant that until I understand my part in what went wrong between us, I can't really embrace another relationship."

Rachel sucked in a breath. The last thing she wanted to do was talk about her past in front of her current squeeze, even though they had almost no likelihood of sharing a future. She'd love it if there were possibilities for her and Decker; last night had been incredible—everything she'd fantasized about and more. He was still something like a dream this morning. But real life wasn't a fairy tale, and she wasn't expecting happily ever after.

"Owen, I think we've said everything important between us."

"No." He swallowed. "Tell me . . . Was I truly insensitive to your feelings?"

What a catch-22. If she said no, Owen would know she was lying. If she said yes, it would spark an unpleasant discussion. Good gravy, sometimes she hated her pathological need to do the right thing.

"Yes. We discussed this at the end, if you'll remember."

"I didn't understand. Explain it again."

Rachel heaved a sigh. "You were always very absorbed with your work, Owen. Before I even left the room, you were already pondering atomic particles or quantum entanglement or whatever the project of the moment was. When I entered a room, most of the time, I wasn't even sure you knew I was there."

Owen inhaled stiffly. "Of course I knew. I'm sorry if you thought otherwise. Not everyone understands my work. But Carly does. She finds it as engrossing as I do."

Then she ought to be a regular barrel of fun. "Great. Maybe you two have more in common than we did and—"

"Let's cut to the chase," Decker interrupted. "If Carly wants you to understand how you fucked up the first time, let me clue you in. You were self-absorbed, dumbass. Dude, it's not always about you." Decker scowled across the room at Owen. "You didn't care if you gave Rachel pleasure or made her feel loved. You were more interested in your job than your wife, and that's never going to make any woman with a drop of passion in her blood or an ounce of love in her heart happy."

Owen sputtered angrily, then gaped at her with his face full of betrayal. "You've spoken to him about us?"

"You've spoken to Carly about our marriage," she pointed out.

Adjusting his shirt, Owen stiffened righteously. "Yes, but we've been dating for some time now. We're contemplating a future together. If I'm not mistaken, you can measure the time you've known this obnoxious lothario in hours. Rachel, I don't know what you're thinking, but he's using you for sex. Then he'll leave you. I thought you respected yourself more than to act like a . . . cheap floozy for someone like him."

She reared back as if he'd slapped her in the face. In a way, he had. "I was thinking about experiencing all the orgasms I never got when I was married to you. And Decker might not have phrased it nicely, but he's absolutely right. I didn't feel valued, Owen. I don't think you ever truly loved me. If you came here for advice, I'll give it to you. Start by caring about something besides work. Romance is important. Sex is more than a bodily function. Don't make her feel like an interruption or your dirty necessity. You did that to me all the time, you . . . jerk."

The enormity of what she'd just said hit her. She gasped. Had that really just spewed from her mouth? Her mama had taught her that if she didn't have anything nice to say, she shouldn't say anything at all. But if he'd come here for the truth, why not give it to him? Clearly Decker was rubbing off on her . . .

"What she said," he added with a proud smile.

"I'm speechless," Owen admitted, looking stupefied. "I didn't know you felt that strongly about frivolous things like flowers and intercourse. I married you because I thought you were far too sensible to care much for such inane things."

"You didn't ask. And honestly, you wouldn't have cared how I felt, Owen. And I'll tell you the truth. Carly probably cares about those things, too, because she's a woman, not a robot. If you want to keep her, you need to figure out how to meet her halfway."

"I never meant to hurt you," he offered.

Too little, too late. Rachel sighed. "I know. It's water under the bridge. I just hope you're ready to be a better man and partner with Carly."

Owen didn't answer. He simply sat there, looking disoriented and lost in thought. Rachel had never seen that expression on his face. He was actually worried about losing Carly. The woman mattered to him.

Amazing. Maybe she should have been more honest with Owen while they were married. Instead, she'd done her best to be understanding. The minute he'd started taking her for granted, she should have said something. But the few times she'd tried, Owen hadn't understood or hadn't thought it important. His dismissive attitude, as if her feelings were nowhere nearly as important to him as subatomic particles traveling faster than the speed of light at CERN, had really hurt. In the grand scheme of the universe, of course his work was important. But at the time, she'd wondered why she hadn't mattered, too. He'd been far too interested in chasing what Einstein had never been able to prove.

In fact, when she'd said she wanted a divorce, his long sigh of irritation—with nary a word of protest—told her they were never meant to be. If she'd faced that sooner, she could have saved herself a few years and a lot of heartache.

"You've gotten what you came here for, pal. Thanks for stopping by." Decker stood and rounded the coffee table to stand over Owen expectantly.

"I . . ." He looked at Rachel. "That's so much to contemplate. You're talking about changing the way I do everything, the way I approach life. Sex is actually important to women?"

"Yes, Owen. I know it's a lot, but—"

"Look, this girl is either important to you or she isn't," Decker cut in. "If she is and you want to keep her, then use your head. There's a reason she sent you to talk to Rachel. Women don't usually want their man talking to an ex unless they're at the end of their rope. And when did you get the stupid-ass idea that sex wasn't important to women?"

Owen frowned, gaping. "I know it's important to most men, but . . . I assumed women were less interested in such things."

"The amount of pleasure you give her is a direct statement about how important she is to you, ass-hat. If you can't make the effort to make her feel good when she's yielding her time and body to you, then how can she feel valued?" Decker shook his head. "Didn't you ever learn to kiss and sweet-talk girls in high school out of their bras and into their panties?"

A red flush swept up Owen's face. "No. I let beer in college do that for me."

Which probably explained why he'd kept a few bottles of good wine in the house when they'd been married and given her a glass or two when he'd been "in the mood."

"Well, now you know that females like conversation with their orgasms. They like to feel special." Decker dragged Owen to his feet, and her ex stood as if in a daze. "Try that with Carly. Ask her what she likes and listen. Put a smile on her face. And fucking call next time you're thinking of dropping by to see Rachel."

He managed to scoot her ex out of the room, down the hall, and out the front door without a protest from Owen. The way Decker had handled her ex had been nothing short of brilliant.

The second Decker shut the door behind Owen, he locked it and flashed her a sharkish grin.

"Decker?" She backed away.

"Beautiful . . ." He urged her against the foyer wall, kissing her absolutely breathless. A girl could get used to this . . .

Too bad he wouldn't be around.

Rachel broke the kiss. The thought that he would soon leave and she would probably never see him again bothered her way more than it should. It was a good idea to part ways soon, before she started losing her heart to Decker. Or maybe it was already too late?

"Do you want those pancakes now? I really do know how to make them. I don't want to send you off hungry." She tried to wink and tease and not let on that his imminent departure was breaking her heart more than it probably should.

She expected him to agree, maybe share a casual breakfast with her. Then she supposed he'd smile, offer some thanks, along with a kiss or two, then climb on that gleaming motorcycle of his and leave. The last thing Rachel had ever imagined was for his face to thunder over, for his blue eyes to penetrate her bravado, and for him to press every inch of his hard body into her possessively.

"If you want pancakes, fine. If you don't want to send me away hungry, then let's skip the kitchen and go back to bed. I'm famished for you."

SEVEN

DECKER HELD RACHEL, NAKED AND WARM, CLOSE TO HIM IN postcoital bliss, and eyed Val meowing on the far side of the bed. No doubt, they were both hungry, but that wasn't his biggest problem.

Fighting down a mild panic, he dropped a kiss on Rachel's brow as she slept, then he covered her up. Away from the bed, he stepped into his jeans and tucked the gun into the small of his back before making his way to the kitchen. As he did, he jammed his hand in his pocket, searching for his phone. Val followed, and he kind of wanted to high-five the cat for hissing at Owen.

Rachel's diva pet turned cheetah and ran straight for the pantry. In the cheerful white kitchen, Decker flipped on the lights and opened the door. The cat purred and rubbed up against his bag of dry food, then looked at him with a plaintive wail.

No wonder Rachel was a sucker for Val. He'd nearly perfected crying like a baby to get his way.

With a faint grin, Decker scooped some dry food into Val's

bowl. The feline immediately darted to his dish and dived in, dismissing him.

"Lucky thing." Decker only wished he could solve his own problems that easily, but he was going to have to make a call to even start in that direction.

Peeking down the hall, glad that Rachel hadn't stirred from bed, he called Xander, who answered just before the fourth ring, sounding distinctly pissed off. "This better be good."

Which meant that he'd caught his boss having a little nookie with London.

"Hang up!" Javier snarled on the other end, clearly near his brother.

Which meant they were both having a little nookie with London.

Talk about bad timing . . .

"Don't need me for a few days. I still can't figure out who's trying to off Rachel. She's not safe alone." And he hated lying to her about why he'd picked her up at that dive bar, but the truth would scare the hell out of her. He would stay for a while, protect her, make this asshole go away . . . then decide what to do with his life. He'd have to come clean with her eventually, but what they had was too new. She might not understand or believe him. If he was still seeing forever with her after the danger had passed, then he'd sit her down, spew the truth, and they'd hash it all out.

"Got it. I won't call you unless the world is ending. If you promise from now on not to call on a Sunday morning," Xander growled.

"No problem."

Without another word, Xander ended the call. The man was almost as devoted to the operation of S.I. Industries, the family business he ran with Javier, as he was to London's pleasure. Almost, but not quite . . .

With that, Decker pocketed the phone, then helped himself to Rachel's laptop. In less than ten minutes, he figured out that Owen and Carly had flown into Lafayette on Saturday about noon, not necessarily enough time to have made it to the bar by two to solicit him to commit murder. That would explain why he might have hired a go-between. And provide Owen a great alibi if suspicion ever turned his way. They were scheduled to fly home tomorrow evening.

Another interesting tidbit jumped out at him. Owen and Carly had applied for a marriage license. They'd blown past the three-day waiting period. In fact, they hadn't married in the sixty days since applying. The license had expired. What was that about? Had Carly gotten cold feet? Had that been the bump in their relationship Owen had alluded to?

To compound Decker's problems, Rachel clearly expected him to leave anytime now. She'd probably wake up from their latest round of breath-stealing, eye-crossing sex, try to feed him, and assume he wanted to go. He had to put a stop to that shit now so he could fix everything else. Time was ticking, and whoever wanted Rachel dead was expecting a call to confirm completion of the job any minute now. What was he going to do once Monday morning rolled around and she wanted to go into work? Tie her to the bed?

The idea had delicious possibilities, but only with her consent. Somehow, he didn't think she'd agree to miss school for just about any reason. *Fuck.*

His thoughts racing, he strode to the pantry. He was no Chef Ramsey but he got by. Pulling out a loaf of bread and retrieving some eggs from the refrigerator, Decker managed to scrape together something that looked like sustenance within ten minutes. By that time, Val was happily purring around his ankles and meowing his thanks.

Plating everything onto the first dish he found in the cabinet, he tossed on a banana from the counter, grabbed a couple of forks, and poured them each a glass of juice. As he made his way down the hall, he heard Rachel stirring. Val darted to his mistress, and by the time Decker entered the bedroom, she was cuddling with the little fur ball.

She looked up at Decker with sleepy dark eyes and rosy cheeks. A little smile played at her lips. Barely concealed by the sheet, Rachel looked a bit rumpled and a lot sated. She was probably the most beautiful woman he'd seen, not because she was perfect or belonged in a magazine. Because he had put that look on her face. Because she looked like his.

Oh fuck, he was in deep.

"Did you cook?"

"Just for you. I did my very best to make it edible, too."

"You mean it won't taste like something the school cafeteria sells?"

He hesitated. "I can't promise that. It might be worse, since I don't really cook. But I get points for effort, right?"

"Sure." She smiled at him, looking really happy. And what did it say that seeing that expression on her face gratified him?

"Good. I can trade those points in on . . . favors, can't I?"

"Like?" She flirted coyly from under her lashes.

He set the plate on her nightstand and bent to nuzzle her neck. "Hmm, suck your nipples like candy. Or spend lunch between your legs. Feeling your mouth all around my cock? I know, how about spending the afternoon inside you."

"For that, I'll give you lots of points." Then she shifted her

gaze away. "I'd love for you to spend a little more time with me
if you've got it. And you want to."

Decker kissed her cheek and handed her the plate. Here's
where he had to lie to Rachel again. And fuck all if he didn't hate
that. Maybe he should tell her the truth. It was her life, after all.
But he hated to take away her upbeat attitude about the world.
He didn't want to be the one to make her afraid. His role was to
protect her, shelter her. He might not be Mr. Happily-ever-after,
but by damned, keeping her safe and unaware of the danger was
a job he could do well.

"I'd love to, beautiful. In fact, I'd love to spend a lot more time
with you today, especially since you probably have to return to
work tomorrow."

If he hadn't managed to solve this by tomorrow morning, no
fucking way was she stepping foot outside this house without
him. He'd think of something to keep her near him.

"Actually, I've got next week off for fall break. I've been looking forward to this time to finish unpacking my boxes and get my
garden ready for the winter before the weather turns cold. I have
a feeling this Florida girl might find the chillier winter here a bit
of a shock." She popped a bite of egg into her mouth and moaned.
"I don't even know if this is good, but I'm so hungry, I'll say it's
delicious. Aren't you going to eat?"

He plopped down beside her, relieved as hell. She was off for
another week. With any luck, he'd have this wrapped up pronto.
After that . . . well, he'd have to decide what came next. Somehow,
he didn't picture wanting to walk away from her. Which meant
that someday he was going to have to come clean about his lies
and pray she didn't hate him.

Plucking the toast off the plate, he took a bite and washed it down with juice. The shit wasn't half bad. Nice to know he hadn't poisoned her with his lousy cooking.

He hoped his next lie went over half as well . . .

"Well, as soon as I move my stuff from the Santiagos's place into a motel, I'll come back and take you to dinner. How's that?"

"Sure." She frowned. "Why aren't you going to stay with your friends?"

"They're newlyweds, and I'm in their way. I need to find a place of my own since it looks like they might put roots down here for a while. While I look, there's a motel down the road . . ." He rattled off the name of a flea-infested, rent-by-the-hour place he'd passed a few times.

Rachel looked appropriately horrified. "That's murder central. I haven't been in Lafayette that long, but it's mentioned all the time on the news. Lots of body bags."

"Really?" He shrugged. "I'm a big boy. I can take care of myself."

"Why not somewhere else? There are much better places . . ."

"If there's a bed and a shower, that's all that matters to me. It's just for a few days, tops."

Biting her lip, Rachel looked at him uncertainly. "Why don't you stay with me until then? No pressure," she blurted. "I'll understand if you say no. You might feel awkward, but—"

"I'd like that. If you're going to be free, I want to be here with you. I like waking up next to you, beautiful."

She'd taken the bait well. Now, he could settle in and investigate. If he had to wait out this fucker for a few days, he didn't have to let her out of his sight. It was perfect.

Rachel took his hand. "That settles it, then. Do you need to grab anything from the Santiagos's place?"

"Yeah. It won't take long. I'll take you to lunch . . . then we can see about working off all those brownie points."

And somewhere in the middle of that, he was going to have to figure out a plan of attack. It wasn't acceptable that he didn't know who was trying to kill his woman. Decker meant to solve that fast.

AN HOUR LATER, they'd finished their meager breakfast, showered, then straddled the back of his motorcycle. Rachel had been adorably anxious about riding one. Apparently, he'd be responsible for another first for her. That made Decker smile.

She'd relaxed quickly, learned to lean into the turns with him gently, and stay fluid the rest of the time. It felt right having her behind him with her arms wrapped around his middle and her cheek between his shoulder blades.

It didn't take too long to cross town on a lazy Sunday before noon. The new day was still in its golden infancy, shining through the branches of the green trees that Decker suspected would soon lose their leaves to the coming winter. Though the town's population was well over 100,000 people, it functioned a lot like a small town. It was both typically Southern and possessed an interesting, laid-back charm.

Rachel seemed at home here, too.

Wondering where the hell his head was when it should be on the fucker who wanted her dead, he focused, coming up with a rough plan as the bike ate up the couple of miles of road to his destination.

A few minutes later, they pulled up in front of the sprawling house the Santiagos were renting until their own was built. He had a key for security purposes, and his stuff was in the guesthouse out back, but for this ruse to fly, he needed to put on a show. And he needed the guys to play along.

As he stepped off the bike, Rachel did the same, tugging off his helmet and trying to finger-comb her hair back into something less tangled. While that occupied her, he surreptitiously pulled his phone from his pocket and sent Xander a quick text.

Here. Play along. Got plan.

Then he headed for the door. Halfway up the stairs, Xander sent a reply text with his agreement. Then Decker was ringing the doorbell. To his surprise, it wasn't his longtime boss and friend who opened the door, but the wife he shared with his brother. London smiled and glowed, pale hair framing her angelic face, her plump cheeks rosy. She wore a loose-fitting blue cotton shirt that hid any baby bump she might have and matching polka-dotted pajama pants. He was pretty sure that was the most clothing London had worn in the house since their wedding.

"Morning, Decker. Come in," she greeted warmly.

He hesitated in the doorway. "Am I interrupting anything?"

"That was earlier, when you called, asshole," Xander quipped as he approached, wearing hastily donned jeans and a collared shirt inside out. Standing behind London, he planted a kiss on the back of her neck.

"Stop giving him a hard time and let him in," Javier called, suddenly coming around the hall from the bedroom and stepping into view. The elder brother wore a gray bathrobe and probably not a damn stitch more. A morning shadow covered his lean cheeks and cleft chin, but no missing the relaxed mien full of lazy satiation. "He didn't actually come by while we were busy, so give him credit for that."

Decker smiled. This couldn't be more perfect if he'd scripted it. When London and Xander stepped back, Decker entered, holding Rachel's hand and bringing her with him into the airy, barrel-ceilinged foyer of the elaborate house.

As the door shut behind them, Decker grinned. "Thanks for getting out of bed for me. I'm going to get my things and vacate, like I promised." He tugged on Rachel's arm and brought her to his side. "Gang, this is Rachel Linden."

The Santiago brothers both said a polite hello and shook her hand. London stepped forward with a smile and wrapped her arms around Rachel. "I hope you don't mind. I'm a hugger."

Sweet as always, Rachel hugged back. "Not at all. Me, too. It's great to meet you."

"Likewise. Have you lived here long?"

"Just a few months."

London gave a little squeal. "Same here. We should have lunch soon and talk about places to shop. I'm still making friends in town. I've only got a few, and I'd like to get out before I get too big with the baby . . ."

"You need others besides us, little one?" Javier murmured in her ear, teasing. "I'm hurt."

"You're not very good at girl talk, Javi." She tsked. "Xander is even worse."

Javier looked displeased. "I don't know whether to be happy that you think I'm better than Xander at anything or annoyed that you find me a better representation of female companionship."

"Blow it out your ass, brother." Xander grinned, then turned back to Decker.

Everyone drifted to the living room. London sat in the middle of the sofa, and the brothers took their respective places on either side of her. Javier's hand tousled their wife's long, loose hair. Xander's hand dropped to her thigh. Decker risked a glance at

Rachel on the loveseat beside him. She looked both a bit shocked and envious, and it occurred to him that she deserved to feel as desired and adored as London. Could he fulfill that need for her?

"Coffee for either of you?" the blushing blonde asked, trying really hard not to be affected by her husbands' touches and failing more than not.

"No, thanks," Rachel replied.

"None for me," seconded Decker. "We won't stay long. I'll just grab my things . . . Rachel has been kind enough to let me crash with her for a few days while I find a place of my own, so I won't interrupt your newly wedded bliss anymore."

London flushed, and when Xander laughed, she nudged her elbow right into his stomach. "We love having company . . ."

"You don't have to be polite, *belleza*. It's always nice to see you. It's even nicer to see you leave so Javi and I can be naked with our wife," Xander snickered.

Decker laughed. "You're an asshole."

Xander looked like he could care less.

Shaking his head, Decker turned to Rachel. "Will you be all right here if I gather my stuff? Shouldn't take long."

"Sure." She sent him a reassuring smile.

He squeezed her hand, then rose, sending Xander a look. His pal followed. Decker heard the girls talking animatedly and glanced back to see Javier watching them with a doting expression. Rachel would be fine here. Unless the bastard who'd hired out her murder was watching her day and night, he would have no idea where she was. Javi would keep her safe.

"What the hell is going on?" Xander muttered in his ear.

"I gave her a sob story about being in your way and needing another place to hang for a few days so I could look for some digs of my own. I can't think of another ruse that will keep me with her twenty-four/seven. I'm almost sure that Rachel's ex-husband isn't the one trying to off her. I think he's too clueless to hire a killer. I've got no other suspects, and I don't like the way any of this smells."

Xander appeared to mull his words, then nodded. "I can see that. And she has no other enemies?"

"Not that she knows of, according to her."

"Think she's being dishonest?"

They reached the guesthouse out back that Decker had been using, and he started gathering his toiletries from the granite vanity and shoving them into his duffel. "No. She can't lie worth a damn."

"Then she's not paying attention?"

"More like she could never imagine that." Decker gathered a pair of jeans and a jacket from the back of the chair in the corner and tossed them into his bag. "She gives everyone the benefit of the doubt. Her ex was a douche bag of massive proportions to her for years, and she still tried to make excuses for him and see his best. She's really . . . fucking sweet."

"You like this girl." Xander cocked his head and stared, looking oddly gratified by his observation.

Decker looked down and focused on his duffel's zipper, then paused. *Why deny it?* "Yeah. The first time I saw her picture, it was like an uppercut to the stomach. She just manages to tug at me in a way I don't understand."

"Ever been in love?"

"No."

"That's why you don't understand it. Love is a sneaky bitch. One minute your life is normal. The next you're mooning over a woman who's just mowed you down, like some tornado you didn't see coming. She's suddenly the center of your thoughts, and you don't know how it happened. It's a short trip from there to her becoming the center of your universe."

"I met Rachel less than eighteen hours ago." But hadn't he already been thinking about a future with her?

Xander shrugged. "I knew London about, oh, thirty minutes when I started to think she might be the one. Javi said it was about five minutes for him. There was just an instant click."

That made sense to Decker now. Twenty-four hours ago, he would have thought Xander was insane. "Damn."

"When you know, you just know. I've seen you with a lot of women—mostly bimbos—over the years. She's not your usual speed. You seem more . . . settled around her."

He scowled. "Just because you're married doesn't mean the rest of the world wants to be."

"You've never been the kind to bury your head in the sand. Don't start now." Crossing his arms over his chest, Xander leaned into his face. "I've never seen you stick your neck out this far for anyone. I mean, I paid you for years to get me out of scrapes."

"I'm damn good at it, too."

"The best, which is why Javi and I hired you to help with the company's security. But you wanting to protect Rachel, taking days and days to do it, practically moving in with her . . . I know damn well it's not a platonic situation. In the past, you were always a blow-and-go kind of guy. Once the orgasm was over, you were pretty much done and gone."

How was that for an unvarnished truth? Pretty exact. Decker had gone through most of his life not making too many connections or calling anyplace home. The curse of the military brat. It had carried over into adulthood. But now, he had the oddest desire to plant roots and grow them. He didn't want to be alone anymore. No, that wasn't it. Being with Rachel appealed to him, even more than he would have thought. What if he made her his, had someone to come home to every day, got married and started a family?

Decker didn't hate the idea. And that just about floored him.

"Maybe . . . things have changed," he acknowledged.

Xander grinned. "I knew it! One look at you and—"

"But it's not that simple, Xander. I'm just a fling for her." And didn't that suck? "Rachel thinks I'll be gone in a few days, tops. I doubt she'll miss me when I've gone. She's only been divorced about fourteen months. She may not be ready to hear that I'm . . . falling in love."

"She has feelings for you. It's all over her face."

"And when she finds out I lied to her about almost everything?"

"She'll forgive you." Xander clapped him on the back. "Dude, you're trying to save her life and preserve her peace of mind."

Yes, but would she believe that he'd wanted her for *her* and not just because he'd been playing the hero or fulfilling a responsibility?

"If I haven't solved this by Tuesday night, I'm going to have to tell her that someone wants her dead, that I picked her up for a reason . . . everything. I don't want to scare her, but I need to come clean with her. I'd just rather do it once I know she's safe." He blew out a ragged breath. "I don't want to lose her."

"Sounds smart. Who are your other suspects? What's your plan?"

"Some ideas have been brewing in the back of my head. I need to look into her neighbors and friends, just to make sure there's no one I should zoom in on. Her ex might not have been the one to hire me, but my gut tells me the whole damn mess has something to do with him. I've just got to prove it."

"Can I help?"

"Occupy Rachel for a few minutes and let me borrow a laptop."

"Sure. I'll shut you up in my office at the back of the house for a bit."

Decker lifted his duffel, nerves biting his belly. "Perfect."

Xander shut him into the room lined with bookshelves. A sleek laptop sat in the middle of the leather-topped monstrosity. He tried not to think that the guy had probably done the nasty with his wife here more than once and focus on his task.

A few clicks of his computer later proved that her friend Shonda had neither the money nor the motive to want Rachel dead. The woman had four hundred dollars in checking, and her rent was past due. Shonda never had so much as a parking ticket, and she'd been named teacher of the year at Magnolia Elementary last year. Saturday at noon, she'd been working on a Habitat for Humanity project about forty miles away. And the woman's brother was still in the hospital. Decker scratched her off the list of suspects.

He looked into her neighbors. The house next door to her on the east had actually been vacant for the last six weeks. On the other side lived Brian Boone, a man who traveled for a living. His girlfriend either lived there or took care of the place while he was gone because she always signed for his deliveries. According to Brian's credit card statement, he'd just dropped a hefty sum at a jewelry store Friday afternoon, then sprung for a fancy French dinner last night. Twenty bucks said the guy was engaged now. Happy people didn't usually solicit murder, especially in the middle of popping the question. Decker removed him from the list, too.

A quick scan of all the occupants on her street and the rest of her coworkers didn't turn up a single red flag. And this wasn't some random psycho killer. They usually wanted to do their own dirty work just for the thrill.

So he came back to Owen. Her ex seemed like the sort of guy who didn't want to get his hands dirty. If he was so worried about repairing his relationship, why would he bother with Rachel? Did it have something to do with that expired marriage license?

That was it. He needed to talk to Owen, man to professor, and find out what the hell was going on. While he was at it, he should meet Carly, too. Men were far more likely to murder than women, but hiring the work out was definitely a female's style. She might consider an assassin something like a life adjustment handyman.

But in order to talk to the struggling lovebirds, he would have to leave Rachel. *Damn it.*

With a sigh, he cleared the computer's cache, shut the lid, and picked up the duffel. A rough plan formed in his head. He'd no more stepped into the living room when the group shot his plan to hell.

"I'd like that," Decker heard Rachel say. "Tomorrow would be great."

"You'll like my friend Delaney. She's really kind. Just slap me if we get too deep into the baby talk. She's been through this twice, and I'm still trying to figure out what's going on with my body."

"Tomorrow for what?" Decker barked.

Rachel welcomed him back with a smile. "London asked me to meet her and her friend for lunch."

He didn't like it, but to balk might make him look controlling. Or force him to explain now. Decker took a deep breath. Rachel would be with two other women in a public place. As far as the guy who wanted her dead indicated, the job didn't have to be complete until probably the day after tomorrow. A little breathing room. Decker vowed to take precautions and do everything possible to keep her safe.

He forced a smile. "That's awesome. I'm sure you'll have a great time."

But the outing bugged the hell out of him over their early dinner. His fear for her caused him to reach for her three times during the night to make love to her, each time successively more possessive than the last. While she slept, he swiped her iCloud password and downloaded an app that allowed him to track her phone. Anxiety made him pull her into his lap over breakfast so he could hold her close. That same niggling worry urged him to hold her tight as they were walking out the door. He escorted her to her car and watched her drive off. Decker figured that she'd get angry or suspicious if he stalked her the three blocks to the restaurant. The roads were public. She'd be fine; he had to believe that.

Straddling his Ducati, he made his way over to Carly's older brother's place. Christian Adams, age thirty, hadn't been hard to track down. He was an auto mechanic with no priors. Divorced two years ago. No kids. Ho hum. Hopefully, Owen, Carly, and this dude would all be at his house, packing up and getting ready to head to the airport.

When Decker pulled up in front of the place, it looked spotless and well kept, if a bit older. Mature trees swept over the roof in the breeze. A big dog napped on the front porch.

A minute after he rang the bell, a short brunette with tousled dark hair, kind blue eyes behind a pair of studious glasses, and a kindly inquisitive expression answered the door. She wore a little sundress that hung off one shoulder and suggested that she'd donned it hastily. No evidence of a bra.

Decker's first impression was that this woman would never stoop to murder. Her capable, open air told him she'd rather deal with a situation head on.

"Hi. Is Owen here? I'd like to talk to him."

She turned wary. "You are . . . ?"

"Decker." He put out his hand. "I'm his ex-wife's . . . boyfriend."

"Oh." Her eyes widened as if startled. "I . . . yeah. He told me about you."

So he'd made an impression on Owen. Nifty.

"Are you Carly?" he asked.

"I am."

No doubt from Carly's tone, she was really confused about his reason for being here. In truth, he was now, too. If Owen hadn't wanted Rachel dead enough to hire him, and Carly wasn't that kind of woman . . . who did that leave? A few more questions, then he'd have to move on, turn his head inside out, and dig deeper to figure out who might want Rachel on a morgue slab.

"Nice to meet you." He stuck his hand out.

She took it. "Same to you. Is something wrong?"

Decker shrugged. "Just like to make sure Owen and I don't have any problem."

He had no burning urge to get along with Rachel's ex, but women usually understood everyone wanting to make nice. So he smiled and waited for her to play along.

He was surprised when she blushed. "I don't know what you and Rachel said to Owen, but he's been expressive and, um . . . really affectionate since he came back."

"That's good to hear." Decker smiled faintly. Nice to know that the good professor had listened and understood.

Carly led him into a little den and picked up a few dirty glasses on the table—then swiped a pair of her panties from the floor and shoved them behind her back pocket with an even deeper flush. "I should thank you, in fact. He told me that Rachel didn't say much, but that you really set him straight."

Which told Decker that the professor had gotten somewhere between frisky and freaky with his girl in the last few hours, and that she was really pleased.

"He seemed distraught."

Setting the dirty glasses in the adjacent kitchen, she rushed back to the den. "We've had a rough time lately. We were going to get married a few weeks ago, actually. I didn't plan anything elaborate, just a small ceremony at the Justice of the Peace. I think . . . I knew I wouldn't go through with it. I kept thinking that it takes two to tango, and Owen couldn't tell me why Rachel left him. Somehow, I just knew it was important that he understand. I think now he does. And I'm so glad." She winced. "Sorry to ramble. You don't know me from anyone, and I'm blurting out my personal life to you. Bad habit. Do you want something to drink?"

"No, thank you."

"Let me go back and find Owen. I think he's . . ." She blushed again. "I'll be back."

So Owen had been enjoying his postcoital nap when Decker had knocked on the door. Nice.

As Carly disappeared into the bedroom, Decker contemplated what the hell he could say to Rachel's ex. What if this was the dead end he suspected? Yeah, he supposed it was possible that Owen had been enraged that Carly had put a stop to their first wedding because of what she perceived to be unresolved issues with Rachel. But Owen really didn't seem like the sort to deal with anger via violence. With logic and scientific theory? Absolutely.

What the hell was he going to do next? Talk to Rachel. Why wait until Tuesday? He had to tell her everything now—and tell her that he loved her. Let the chips fall where they may. Decker raked a hand through his hair and rose, pacing the small room. He didn't know exactly when he'd lost his heart. Probably when she'd laughed at his really terrible pick-up lines. He only knew that he couldn't lose her now.

He was about to bolt for the front door when he spotted a framed photo on the wall. Obviously taken a few years ago, Carly stood in a red cap and gown, smiling wide as she held her college degree. Beside her, her parents stood, smiling proudly. But none of that caught his eye. It was the man hovering just behind her.

Carly bopped back into the room. "Owen will be out in a minute."

The toilet flushed, and the sound faded into the background. Decker's world narrowed and his heartbeat roared as he stared at the photo. "Who's this in the picture with you and your parents?"

"My brother Christian. Why?"

Decker's blood ran cold. "Where is he now?"

She shrugged. "Um, he said something about putting in a few hours at his shop before taking us to the airport."

Monday. Yeah, the guy would be at work. That fit. Decker breathed a sigh of relief because he knew now that Christian Adams had been the man who hired him to commit murder. And the asshole was occupied on the job and out of Rachel's path. No reason to think that if he wanted to hire a killer, he'd go do the work himself.

"Does your brother like Owen?"

"He's been reserved so far, but I think he'll come around now." She nodded. "Christian was pretty pissed when I called the wedding off, and I know he thought Owen was still hung up on Rachel. He just wants what's best for me, especially since our parents passed away. But Owen and I are going to be so much better now. We decided today to plan another wedding, a big one, next summer."

Good. It would be awkward with big brother in prison, because Decker intended to nail this asshole to the wall and make him pay for ever thinking about hurting Rachel. But no need to clue Carly in on that now.

"Congratulations." Decker opened his mouth to excuse himself when his phone buzzed. It was Xander.

911. London says Rachel never showed for lunch. Is she with you?

The text made his world stop on its axis.

"I've got to go."

Decker didn't wait for Carly's reply, just ran for the door. He tapped out Rachel's iCloud password to track her phone. She should have been at the restaurant twenty minutes ago, and the location of her phone indicated that she was home. Fear stabbed his heart.

Dear God, let her be safe.

He hopped onto his bike, Carly chasing him, and called 911. After sending the police to Rachel's house, he shoved his helmet on with shaking hands. Revving the motor and racing down the street, Decker prayed that he wasn't too late.

EIGHT

AT THE FIRST STOPLIGHT AWAY FROM HER PLACE, RACHEL reached over for her phone to text London that she was on her way. As she dug through her purse, she remembered leaving it on the kitchen counter to charge. With a sigh, she made a U-turn as soon as the light changed to green, then headed back to her house to grab it—just in case Decker called. Yes, he'd said he'd be back after lunch. She hoped he meant it because she wasn't ready to be without him.

Gosh, she sounded awfully attached . . . and maybe a bit in love.

Wrestling with the realization, Rachel let herself in absently and headed to the kitchen, pulling her phone from the power cord.

Suddenly, Val hissed low and loud, then let loose a cantankerous meow, snagging her attention. When she turned to find out what was troubling her high-strung feline, Rachel discovered a man of average height and build standing in her foyer with grease under his fingernails, a determined look in his eyes . . .

And a gun pointed at her head.

She froze with terror. Her brain told her to scream, but the moment was like a bad dream. She felt pinned, immobile. Useless.

Her assailant trekked closer, keeping both hands on the pistol and the barrel trained right between her eyes.

"No. Please." She hated whining pitifully, but it was instinct. "Don't."

Who was he? What did he want? How could she get out of this mess? A thousand thoughts flew through her brain.

"Shut up," he snarled, his dark, unkempt hair falling limply into his face. He wore mechanics' coveralls that proclaimed his name was Chris and an icy expression full of murder.

"M-my wallet is out in my car. You can have—"

"I don't want your money, bitch. I want you dead." He spotted the phone in her hand, then nodded at it. "Put that down and step away."

She shook so hard that as she reached toward the counter, the phone rattled out of her hand and skittered across the slick tile, plopping into the sink with a *thunk* that jolted her nerves. Though he wanted her to, Rachel couldn't bring herself to actually come closer to the violent stranger in her house. He stood between her and the front door. He'd get multiple unobstructed shots off if she tried to dart down the hall or toward the patio. He blocked her path to the front. The only place to step was deeper into the kitchen.

Rachel trembled as she veered two deep lunges into the narrow galley, near the sink and cutting boards.

And the knives.

Mercy, could she be brave enough to grab one and defend herself?

If it means the difference between life and death . . .

Good point.

"W-what do you want with me? Why kill me?"

He crept closer, still aiming that gun at her. "You're in the way of my sister's future, slut. She and her fiancé can't be happy because of you."

"I don't know who you mean." She shook her head. "You have me confused with someone else. I'm not involved with anyone—" Except Decker. Was he secretly engaged?

The man rubbed a greasy hand across his cheek. "Maybe you're not involved with him anymore, but Carly called off the wedding because she was sure that the professor was still hung up on you. My sister has been through a hell of a lot, losing our parents in the last year. If your sniveling ex-husband makes her happy, I'm going to make sure she gets him. That means you're going to die."

Understanding dawned with terrible clarity. Rachel's heart stuttered, and she shook her head frantically. "You're wrong. Owen isn't hung up on me. He loves your sister. He came to see me yesterday and told me how much he wants to make Carly happy. I don't want him back, and he doesn't want me either, I swear! You don't have to shoot me."

"My sister was worried enough a few weeks ago to call off their wedding. If you're not around . . . problem solved."

"Owen wants to marry Carly," she insisted. "And I'm in love with someone else."

Her attacker sent her a snide grin. "That slick guy with the sunglasses and the leather jacket? The one who's been in your bed since Saturday night?" He snorted. "You really are a dumb bitch. I hired him to kill you."

This time, Rachel's heart stopped altogether. "What?"

No way could she have heard that right.

Chris nodded. "I gave him twenty-five grand on Saturday to have you dead quick. But I've been watching. I guess he wanted to fuck you before he killed you. I can't wait on him anymore. If you want something done right, you've got to do it yourself."

Rachel almost couldn't process his words. Patient, passionate Decker was a contract killer? His rough-around-the-edges demeanor didn't hide a tender heart, but a brutal one? He'd intended all along to watch her gasp her last breath?

Her first instinct was to refuse to believe it. No way. Decker wasn't violent. He was protective and would never hurt her. He had feelings for her, didn't he? She would have sworn that he did.

Why was he so persistent about picking you up in the bar Saturday night? Other women were looking at him. Younger, prettier ones. More experienced ones. You wondered at the time why he focused on you. This would explain it . . .

But she'd believed that whatever he felt was real. She would have bet her life on it.

Apparently she had . . . and she'd lost.

Betrayal gashed open her chest. She felt so damn alone and frightened. Decker had seduced her, intending all along to off her? For a brief second, she closed her eyes, but when she tried to imagine him hurting her in any way, she only saw his face, his understanding, his encouragement, his blue eyes filled with caring.

It didn't add up. He'd had a hundred opportunities to kill her. He could have done it in her sleep. He could have poisoned her when he brought her breakfast. And why would he have introduced her to his friends or let her go to lunch with London if he just wanted her six feet under? Granted, she didn't really *know* everything about Decker, but she'd been sure that she had felt his heart. It had been big and kind and caring. It had called to her own.

The click, the connection, the depth of her feelings . . . She refused to believe it was all a lie. He'd shown her pleasure and consideration. Affection even. Why do that, only to kill her? Before Decker she would have never believed that she was sexy enough or special enough for him, but he'd made her see something different in herself, in her heart.

Rachel refused to doubt her feelings for another minute. Maybe this psycho had mistaken Decker's identity. Maybe he'd been watching her and lied about Decker's intentions to throw her off her game. Heck, maybe ol' Chris was just insane. Whatever the problem, it was on him. Decker wouldn't kill her.

But he also wasn't here, so if she was going to make it through this encounter, it was up to her now. She had to talk this guy off the crazy train and fend for herself somehow, because she wasn't ready to die.

"I-I'll cut off all contact with Owen. I'll change my number. I'll move and not leave a forwarding address, if you want."

But the gunman was already shaking his head. "You moved out once. That didn't pry you from his mind. In fact, not being able to find you might only make him obsess more. But knowing that you're totally beyond his reach . . . Then he'll have to move on. And my sister will be there for him. They can finally get married and she can be fucking happy. But Carly and Owen are flying home tonight." He glanced at the clock on the oven wall. "In fact, I've got to be back at my place to take them to the airport in less than an hour. By the time they land, I want her to know that she has Owen all to herself."

And he intended to leave her lying lifeless in a pool of her own blood, staining the white tile of her kitchen floor. No way was she going to let that happen.

Rachel swallowed, gathering her courage. Then she jumped

him with a growl, shoving him back toward the foyer with all her might.

He went careening back, flailing and trying to catch his balance. He reached out to brace for his inevitable fall. The pistol fell from his grip, clattering to the hardwood floor beneath him and sliding all the way to the front door as he landed on his butt with a thud.

She didn't wait for him to get his bearings, but darted back into the kitchen and grabbed her biggest knife—a huge, serrated sucker. For insurance, she grabbed the paring knife, too, and held it down by her thigh.

When he jumped to his feet and charged toward her with murder narrowing his menacing eyes and his large hands outstretched like he meant to strangle her, she was ready. Rachel knew that once he got his hands around her neck, he was too strong, and she'd be done for. She'd never see her family or friends again. Mercy, her mother . . . She'd miss Thanksgiving, Christmas, Shonda's wedding. She'd never know her future, her children, or see old age. She would never be able to tell Decker that she loved him.

Oh hell no!

As the criminal came closer, she raced toward him again, big knife stretched over her head. Rachel didn't think she could kill him. She wasn't sure she would be able to live with that, no matter how terrible he was. The idea of sinking this into his chest made her wince inwardly—but he didn't need to know that.

She darted closer, and as she expected, her assailant grabbed her wrist and tried to wrest the knife from her grip. She only had seconds and one chance to surprise him. No way was she going to screw this up.

While he clamped down on her wrist, trying to make her release the wicked blade, Rachel drove the paring knife into his thigh, seriously close to his groin. She hoped she at least nicked something vital.

He screamed and dropped his grip from the wrist above her head, cupping his leg protectively. "Bitch! I won't give you an opportunity to cut me again."

Blood dripped from the little knife and onto her fingers, onto the floor. Rachel watched in horror as he managed to hobble away and went after his gun. She was either going to have to chase him and finish him off . . . or let him shoot her dead.

She swallowed. Her heart thrummed, and fear laced her veins with ice. Her skin felt tight. Her thoughts raced. Why couldn't he just leave this alone? She could try to pick up her phone and call the police, but she'd barely finish giving the 911 operator her address before he'd be back with his gun to shoot her. Same if she tried to dart out the back door to freedom.

No choice. She was going to have to hunt him down and snuff him out before he did the same to her.

Steeling herself, she gripped both knives and rounded the corner from the kitchen, into the long walkway to the foyer.

The thug stood there, frozen and bleeding.

In front of him, Decker stood, legs akimbo, arms outstretched, a gun in each hand. "Don't move a muscle, motherfucker. If you even twitch, it will give me a lot of pleasure to put a bullet in your miserable brain."

WELL AFTER THE police had taken Christian Adams away in handcuffs for a trip to the hospital to get some stitches, Rachel sat, drinking a cup of coffee for warmth. She was fully covered, but she felt chilled to the bone. An EMT had wrapped a blanket around her after he'd checked her out and doctored a cut on her finger. He'd cautioned her about some bruising and given her something for her headache.

She had stabbed a man. In self-defense, yes. In her spinning thoughts, the moments slowed and replayed in an endless loop. More than once since, she'd tried to wash the blood from her hands, but she swore she could feel it seeping into her pores. Christian Adams hadn't given her a choice. He would have killed her if she hadn't fought back. That knowledge gave her peace of a sort. She'd finish reconciling it all later.

In the interim, the police had taken her statement. They'd taken Decker to the back of the house to get his separately, and she hadn't seen him for hours. Carly and Owen had come. Who'd called them or why, she had no clue. But her ex-husband's fiancée had been absolutely horrified at what her brother had attempted. The woman's pleading apologies ran through Rachel's brain. But nothing sank in. Vaguely, she recognized that Owen had stepped up for Carly and now seemed like the man she needed. He promised her they'd get through this together and have a big wedding whenever she was ready. The way Owen had looked at Carly, like she was his moon and stars, had made her really happy for the couple. She wished them well. It wasn't Carly's fault that Christian had taken it upon himself to think killing his sister's man's ex-wife was a good idea. Rachel hoped that Owen and his fiancée could live happily ever after now, despite the jail time Christian had coming. Someone should be happy.

The hope that it might be her looked increasingly dim.

The police told her that Christian had, in fact, hired Decker to kill her. They found the twenty-five thousand dollars and the number of a disposable phone Christian had purchased when they searched Decker's belongings. In her head, she knew that must mean everything between them had been a lie. He had likely conned her, and she'd eaten up every morsel of the bait. She would just need time to recover, get over her anger, grieve. Maybe a decade or two would be long enough to forget him.

The problem was, her own stupid heart insisted that what they'd shared was real. Even if Decker hadn't been completely honest, somewhere in the midst of his ruse, she'd seen his heart, how good and kind and genuine he could be.

"You all right?" a woman's gentle voice asked behind her. Rachel turned to find London standing at her back, her pale hair loose over her slender shoulders. London draped an arm around her with a face full of soft empathy.

Rachel wanted to crawl into a corner and lick her wounds, even as the thought pissed her off. Where the hell was Decker so she could at least have a good scream at him? How *dare* he lie to her and hurt her?

"I'll be fine," Rachel murmured, hoping that her fibbing wasn't too obvious. "You don't need to be concerned about Decker's sham. I'm sure you had nothing to do with it."

"It's not what you think," Xander insisted a moment later, hovering protectively beside his wife. "He never had any intention of hurting you."

Rachel ached to believe him. But her head kept telling her heart to stop being so damn naïve. "With all the evidence to the contrary, that's hard to buy."

Yet somehow, she sat there, waiting for Decker to emerge from his interrogation so she could catch a glimpse of him, wait for him to say *something* to her. She yearned to believe that she'd know the truth by seeing it on his face, but . . . that was another foolish notion.

Or she'd settle for someone delivering the punch line to this really awful joke. Everything seemed surreal.

"Honey . . ." London moved closer to hug her, and Rachel felt the smallest swell of the other woman's baby bump. A little jolt of envy pierced her.

She'd probably never feel a child growing in her body. Quickly on her way to thirty, divorced once, and then deceived by the man she'd probably always regard as the love of her life, she didn't see motherhood in her future. And she didn't want to swing a third strike. Maybe she was just meant to be alone. Or she should try devoting the rest of her days to a cause she could be passionate about and get lost in.

Of course nothing would ever give her the kind of mind-bending passion Decker had. Or would make her feel as special. She'd always want to believe all the wonderful words he'd spoken to her, all the pleasure he'd heaped on her, but Rachel feared nothing and no one would ever fill the void he was leaving behind in her life.

Good gravy, she sounded maudlin and woe-is-me. Because she loved Decker and knew that no other man would do. Somehow in the span of a few golden hours, she'd ended up surrendering her heart to him.

"I'll be all right." She stood and hugged London. "It'll just take time."

The pity in the woman's blue eyes made her heart lurch. Xander hovered nearby, his face grim.

"Don't give up on him yet. He's really a good guy," London murmured.

"He cares a lot about you," Xander swore.

Maybe. Maybe not. She didn't know what to think anymore.

With another hug and a squeeze of her hand, London left, clinging to Xander's arm and promising to call next week. She waved them out with a wan smile, then sat staring at the wall.

As they departed, sunlight slanted through her back windows, illuminating her house in a gorgeous glow. And yet for her, the world felt as if it were coming to an end.

Seriously, she was going to have to pull herself up by her bootstraps and stop crying in her beer.

Suddenly, the EMTs came by and took the blanket. They inquired after her again, and she sent them away. There was nothing wrong with her that first aid or a trip to the ER could fix.

Shonda texted that her brother was being discharged from the hospital. Rachel sent her a smiley face back, too exhausted and dazed to manage more. She didn't know whether thirty minutes or an eternity passed.

Finally, there was a flurry of activity at the back of her house. Men yelled. Doors shut. Someone laughed. Then a pair of uniformed officers and a detective made their way toward the front door, sparing a smile for her.

"We'll call you if we have any other questions, but otherwise you're free," the detective said. "Rest up. We'll leave a few uniforms outside so you feel safe."

"Thank you," she murmured.

"Thanks, guys. I've got it from here."

Decker.

Rachel whipped around at the sound of his voice. He stood at the opening to the hallway, still wearing yesterday's clothes. He hadn't shaved. He really hadn't slept much. And he still looked not just sexy as all get out, but so familiar and beloved that she felt her eyes tear up.

The detective nodded and shut the door behind him, closing her in the house alone with Decker.

"Why are you still here?" she asked. She didn't want the question to come out like an accusation, but it probably did.

"Because we're not done, you and I." He prowled closer, closer, until he stopped right before her. "Rachel, I don't know what Christian told you or what you believe, but if I had really wanted to kill you, beautiful, you'd be dead. I learned a thousand different ways with Delta Force and the CIA. I've used a fair number of them. I'm not a Boy Scout. But I would never, ever, for any reason hurt you."

She wanted to believe him so badly . . . "So was it some sort of sting operation and you seduced me to catch a bad guy?"

"No, I really do work for Xander and Javier now. Nothing I told you was a lie. I just didn't confess that I sought you out because, earlier on Saturday, Christian Adams approached me in a bar and mistook me for someone he'd connected with online to do a kill-for-hire job. The other guy apparently backed out, but didn't tell Christian. When he hit me up, I thought he was joking. By the time I realized he was serious, the guy was slapping down money, your picture, and giving me a few days to finish you off. I went straight to the police. I swear it, baby. They told me I didn't have enough evidence. So I decided to keep you safe myself. I didn't tell you because I didn't want to scare the hell out of you." He grimaced. "And I didn't stay out of your bed because resisting you was beyond me."

Her first instinct was to protect herself and toss his explanation back in his face. But she took a deep breath and started turning it over in her head. She could picture Decker thinking that some guy's "job opportunity" was a joke. If he'd actually done anything illegal, the police would have taken him into custody, so they must have absolved him of any wrongdoing. That meant . . . he probably had approached and seduced her because he'd ultimately meant to protect her. Was it that hard to believe that he'd wanted her, too?

After years of neglect at Owen's hands? Sadly, yes.

"How much of what we shared was pretend?" Her voice was small, and she hated asking the question, but for her peace of mind, she had to know.

"Between us in bed naked, with me deep inside you?" He crouched in front of her. "Not a damn thing."

Rachel slid her eyes shut. Her heart leapt at his words, and her mind pushed back. She hated this turmoil.

"Was I just a fling for you?" His question cut through her confusion. He sounded uncertain.

Wait. Was he actually worried that he hadn't been meaningful to her?

She opened her eyes, falling into his blue stare, wanting to stay there forever. "No."

"Thank fucking God."

Before she could respond, Decker settled his arms under her knees and behind her back, then lifted her against his chest. He began to cart her down the hall.

"Wha . . . what are you doing?" she sputtered.

"Putting an end to this bullshit."

Rachel gaped at him, her thoughts a muddle. What did he mean?

She didn't have to wonder long.

Decker carried her into her bedroom and tossed her on the bed. On her way down, she saw his suitcase in the corner of the room, wide open. Half the contents were on the floor, as if the police really had conducted a search of his stuff.

He grabbed a few things from the little duffel and scooped them into his hand, enclosing whatever he held in his fist. She didn't even have time to sit up and confront him about what in the heck he was doing. No, he lowered himself on top of her, tying her wrists to the slats in her headboard with two mismatched athletic socks he'd held.

"What the devil . . ." she demanded. "Decker!"

"The problem we're having now is trust. You don't really trust that I was protecting you from Christian. You sure as hell don't believe I fell for you. Both are the absolute truth. Beautiful, you changed something for me." He cupped her face. "No, you changed everything for me. If I'm not just a fling for you, and you're mad that I lied, that has to mean that you care about me, too. Right?"

Good gravy, how could he figure her out so easily? "Bite me."

"Love to. Where?" he grinned.

Teasing wasn't going to work. She wasn't going to fall for his sense of humor all over again, even if his warm body pinned her to the mattress, reminding her just how hard and built he was all over. How good he could make her feel.

Rachel just glared at him. "That is not funny."

"No? How about this . . ." He kissed his way up her neck and murmured in her ear. "They should suspend your driver's license because you drive me crazy."

"Ha ha." She was mad, damn it. And she wanted to stay mad until she decided otherwise. After the day she'd had, she deserved it.

"Still not moved? I'll try again." He caressed her cheek. "You must be the sun and I must be Earth, 'cause the closer we get, the hotter you get. Or maybe I should say that everything about you pulls me in."

How was she supposed to reply to that? It was part offhand joke, part compliment. The truth was, everything about him pulled her in, too.

"You cannot give me more pick-up lines and think that's going to make everything all better."

"Not even a little?" He nipped at her lobe, then started unbuttoning her blouse. "Wanna fuck? Breathe for yes; lick your elbow for no."

Seriously? With a growl, she tugged at her bonds, but Decker was good at bondage, like he was good at everything else. She wasn't going anywhere until he decided to let her go.

"Stop it!"

But he didn't. Once her blouse was open, he parted the sides and ran his hands down her lace-clad breasts, then up and under her back. He opened the clasp with a twist of his fingers, and the bra sagged away from her body. He pulled it loose and cupped her, thumbing her sensitive nipples.

Rachel bit back a moan. "Decker, I didn't say yes."

"You're breathing, aren't you?" He winked, then pulled a switchblade from his pocket. "Sorry. I'll buy you a new one."

Before she could wonder what that meant, he cut up through the straps of her bra and tossed the useless garment across the room.

"Hey!" she protested.

The only response Decker gave was to work his way down her body, pausing to kiss her nipples and stroke them with his tongue. She wanted to stay angry—really. But the way he delved into her gaze, so attentive and in tune with her, the way he touched her, like she was his everything . . .

Rachel wasn't listening to his explanation. She'd made excuses for Owen for years, and didn't want to be the same sort of stupid twice. On the other hand, could she let the best thing that ever happened to her walk out because she refused to have a conversation? No.

Then again, he didn't seem to want to talk that much . . .

Suddenly, he crouched at the end of the bed and pulled her shoes off, then nipped at her toes. "I'm having a party at your feet, beautiful. I think I should invite your pants down to join."

Despite herself, she laughed. "What if my pants are not in the mood for a party?"

Decker sent a sexy smirk her direction. "I can fix that. Wanna see?"

"What if my pants are busy?" she challenged.

"They aren't yet, but give me ten minutes."

"Incorrigible." And impossible to stay mad at. "That's what you are."

"Yep." He sent her a sly glare as he unfastened her pants, tugged at her zipper, then yanked the jeans down her thighs. Naturally, her panties followed, leaving her bare from the ankles up. "Is that what you're going to tell your mama when I meet her?"

Rachel opened her mouth to answer, but he rubbed the heel of his palm right over her sweet spot. Her breath caught. Sparks and tingles zoomed right behind her clit, and she struggled to find her brain. "Why would you be meeting my mother?"

"If I'm going to stick around, I've got to." He smiled softly at her . . . even as his hand played between her legs. "And believe me, I plan to be with you for a long time."

"It's really hard to think when you're doing that." She squeezed her eyes shut.

"Then don't. Just look at me."

The way his command caressed her, like supple velvet, had her complying. She focused on him. "What?"

"I'm not joking, and this isn't a line. I'm your Mr. Right. I want you. I love you, Rachel. Marry me."

She blinked up at him and sucked in a breath. Not a hint of a smile creased his face as he pulled off the last of her jeans and panties, then tore off his own clothing, donning a condom and crawling between her legs. He probed at her opening gently, then eased deep inside her in one long stroke that made her shudder with pleasure.

Of her own volition, her thighs parted. Her back arched. She moaned in welcome.

"Home is where the heart is, and mine is right here. Trust me. Believe me. Marry me."

Rachel moved with him, tilting to take him deeper and melting into him when he wrapped his arms around her and snagged her gaze, seized her mouth, and captured her heart for good.

He took his time, working her body with unhurried strokes and questing fingers, caressing her all over, making her feel like the most beautiful, most beloved woman in the world.

"Why?" she whispered, her stare clinging to him.

"Because I've needed you my whole life. Roots and home and love. You're all that for me and more. I know it's fast, and you don't know me well . . ." He paused to seat himself deeper and send her senses reeling with leisurely thrusts designed to steal her breath. "But I can make you love me if you'll give me time. I'll be your shelter, your protector, your . . . whatever you need."

The last of her anger and fear bled out. Only Decker and his earnest gaze remained. He'd never be easy to live with. He'd probably be really unpredictable, but she needed some of that in her life.

"I do." Rachel laid her lips across his. "Love you, that is. You made me realize how good I could feel, how sexy the right man would find me . . . the kind of caring about my feelings and my pleasure that a partner should give." She grinned at him suddenly. "Hey, are you affiliated with Google?"

He laughed and pushed into her again, the pleasure surging, rising, about to crest. "No, I just swiped a few pick-up lines from them."

"I don't know, Decker . . . You have everything I've been searching for."

Somehow, he smiled at her through a groan. "Is that a yes?"

Rachel rotated her hips beneath him, and felt ecstasy begin to tingle through her body. "Yes!"

The bliss exploded, and as she pulsed around Decker, he slammed into her, then let go of his restraint with a cry.

Her heart beat furiously, and she struggled for her breath. Decker barely let her drag in some air before he jumped off her, tossed away the used condom, and dragged her to her feet. "Let's go."

She looked at him as if he'd lost his mind. "Where?"

"Vegas. I don't want to wait until even tomorrow. We'll find a nice chapel and get married by Elvis and have something to laugh about with our grandkids."

Rachel would have giggled . . . except that he looked dead serious.

"What about your parents?"

He shrugged. "They've got a big shindig for my younger sister and her fiancé coming up in a few months. We'll send them pictures. Bet our wedding will be more fun."

"Well, my parents . . ." What? They had seen her get married in the big white gown once. Did she really want to do all that again? No. This time was just for her and Decker. "They'll enjoy the pictures, too."

Decker pulled her in tight for a hug. "That's the spirit! It's either that or I'll call the police and report you for stealing my heart."

Would she ever get used to his crazy sense of humor? A whole bunch of protective male covered it and roared when she was threatened. But she loved this side of him, too. She'd thank him later for picking her up on false pretenses and lying to her to keep her safe. Let him sweat a little. In the meantime, she couldn't wait to be his.

"Um . . ." She started giggling uncontrollably. "This is crazy! What will my last name be?"

"You still don't know, do you? That's awesome!"

"It's a little irresponsible, so put me out of my misery and cough it up, Decker."

He peered at her playfully. "Would you believe Papadopoulos?"

"Papa-doodie . . . what?" She smacked his arm. "No!"

"Pavlyuchenko?"

"No Pavlov's dogs or whatever in this house." She rolled her eyes. "Try again."

"You got me. It's Blaszczykowski."

Rachel wrapped her arms around him and laughed. "I'm going to call the police and have you arrested for stealing my sanity."

He gave her a juicy smack across the lips. "It's McConnell, honest truth."

"Much better. Do you know how difficult it would be for a bunch of fifth graders to spell Blaszczykowski?"

"I'd bet you'd get a laugh or two out of it."

She pressed her lips together to hold in a grin. "True. I'm grabbing a suitcase, I guess. I'll be Mrs. McConnell by tonight."

"Yes, you will. But I'd rather just call you mine."

ABOUT THE AUTHOR

Shayla Black (aka Shelley Bradley) is the *New York Times* and *USA Today* bestselling author of over thirty sizzling contemporary, erotic, paranormal, and historical romances for multiple print, electronic, and audio publishers. She lives in Texas with her husband, munchkin, and one very spoiled cat. In her "free" time, she enjoys reality TV, reading, and listening to an eclectic blend of music.

Shayla's work has been translated into about a dozen languages. She has also received or been nominated for the Passionate Plume, the Holt Medallion, Colorado Romance Writers Award of Excellence, and the National Readers' Choice Awards. *RT Book Reviews* has twice nominated her for best erotic romance of the year, as well as awarded her several Top Picks, and a K.I.S.S. Hero Award.

A writing risk taker, Shayla enjoys tackling writing challenges with every book.

MAKE ME YOURS

RHYANNON BYRD

For Will . . .

ONE

DRIPPING WITH SWEAT AS HE TOOK A LATE NIGHT RUN ON THE moonlit beach, Scott Ryder had a strange feeling burning through his veins, twisting its way into his bones. One that didn't have anything to do with his grueling pace or the miles of sand he'd already covered.

The feeling had been building inside him for weeks now, making him restless, leaving him in a generally shitty mood. He'd tried to shake it, but he couldn't. Damn thing just kept growing, pissing him off even more. People were starting to go out of their way to avoid him at the station, which was just as well, seeing as how he hadn't been in the mood for conversation. But tonight he'd been forced to attend the retirement party for one of the other deputies in the sheriff's department, and his nerves were still scraped raw. It wasn't that he didn't like Dwight Jones. Dwight was an all right guy who was looking forward to spending his days either out on the golf course or on his new fishing boat and he wished him luck. But Ryder's boss, Ben Hudson, had been at the party with his new wife, and for some unknown reason the sight of them had set his teeth on edge.

He didn't want the sheriff's wife for himself. Reese was more than easy on the eyes and had a killer smile, but Ben had staked his claim the moment she hit town at the beginning of the summer, so she and Ryder were friends and nothing more. But the way Ben kept looking at her during the party, as if marriage made him the luckiest bastard in the world, had made Ryder want to put his fucking fist through a wall.

He knew damn well that his reaction didn't make any sense. Christ, he wanted Ben and Reese to be happy. After everything they'd been through, they deserved it. He just couldn't stomach being near all that cozy, romantic bliss. Not when this itch in his veins wouldn't let off, his instincts constantly twitching, as if he were missing something important and needed to open his damn eyes so he could figure out what it was. He'd had the same kind of feeling before, when he'd worked black ops, and it'd saved his ass too many times to count. But he'd left that life behind. He no longer had to live in constant survival mode. There was no danger here. No one gunning for his life or the people he cared about. Which meant he needed to calm the hell down and learn to relax.

Heading into the last half mile of his run, Ryder repeated a familiar phrase in his mind. His personal mantra now that he'd settled down in the cozy little town of Moss Beach.

Nothing to run from . . .

Nothing to run to . . .

There was a peace and perfection in those simple words. They meant freedom. A new beginning. A new life.

Unfortunately, they were nothing but lies. Because while he might not have anything to run to, he was sure as hell still running *from* something. He might have decided to stay put in this

scenic little beach town on Florida's Gulf Coast, but that didn't
mean he wasn't fighting an internal battle every damn day of his
life. He'd physically stopped, but his mind was still running at
top speed, doing everything it could to forget about—

Shit. Don't even go there, he muttered to himself. And that
thought was swiftly followed by a guttural *Christ, I need a drink.*

He spent a lot of time these days telling himself what he needed
to fix his head. A drink, a woman, or *women* when he couldn't
be bothered to choose which one he wanted to take home for the
night. If he wasn't careful, he was going to develop a reputation
in town as the lawman who could screw his way through hoards
of party girls without ever losing his breath. At the age of thirty-
three, it wasn't a distinction to be proud of. It just meant that
while all the other guys were getting on with their lives, he was
still acting like an idiot who thought with his prick. Or one who
would only touch a woman if she let him tie her—*No, damn it.*
He wasn't going *there* tonight either. In his current mood, those
thoughts wouldn't lead him to any place good.

Hitting the five-mile marker, Ryder finally slowed to a walk
and pulled off his damp T-shirt, using it to wipe the sweat from
his face. He headed across the sand toward the beachfront duplex
he rented from an elderly couple who had retired there after
living in New York for the past forty years. The house was designed with an entrance to each half at the sides of the duplex,
bougainvillea-covered trellises creating two pathways that shel-
tered the entrances from the street, with matching archways in
the back that you could walk through if coming up from the
beach. The profusion of flowers was a little fanciful for Ryder's
taste, but his sister had gushed about them when she came for a
visit last month, claiming the trellises gave the house "Southern
charm."

Wondering if he'd finally be able to chill enough tonight that he could sleep, Ryder had nearly reached his front door when he sensed a slight movement to his left, in the shadows of the trellis, and he reacted before he'd even given conscious thought to the possible threat. That's what over a decade of black ops training could do to you, and despite being out of the game for a few years now, his reflexes were as lightning quick as ever. Dropping his shirt, he reached into the shadows, snagged a feminine arm, and yanked the woman into the moonlight, the shrill scream on her lips quickly shifting to an outraged snarl as she brought her other arm around to strike him across the face. He quickly blocked the move, catching her wrist and pinning both arms behind her back, while she flailed in his hold, kicking at his shins with her sandal-covered feet.

"Who are you?" he growled, quickly assessing that she wasn't a physical threat. Her hair covered her face as she struggled to free herself from his embrace. But despite her efforts, there wasn't a chance in hell she could break free. He knew how to counteract every one of her defensive moves, which only infuriated her more.

Narrowing his eyes, Ryder carried out a quick visual check on the female. She had her head down so he still couldn't see her face—but what he *could* see of her made his mouth go dry. Waves of silky strawberry blond hair. Her miniskirt and short-sleeved, button-down shirt revealed creamy skin and a body that was slight but deliciously feminine. So familiar it was almost too good to be true. She had the right shade of hair. The right frame. The right shape. The right fucking everything, ripped right out of his goddamn memory to torment him.

He could hear a roaring in his ears, drowning out the rational voice in the back of his mind shouting for him to move away from her. Instead, he continued acting purely on instinct. On the raw, powerful lust that ripped up through his insides the instant he realized he had someone who reminded him of *her* in his arms. The very woman he never allowed himself to think about, let alone fantasize. But this was like a gift from fate. The bastard had never been kind to him in the past, but at the moment Ryder just didn't give a damn. The only thing he had to worry about was convincing the little hellcat that there was something a hell of a lot better they could be doing together than fighting.

His breathing got deeper, nostrils flaring as he pulled in her light, purely feminine scent, the autumn night warm enough that the air was still sultry and damp from an earlier rainstorm. His body had already reacted to the feel of her wriggling against him, a serrated groan on his lips when her belly brushed against his erection, making her gasp. She went instantly still, but not with fear. It was more like . . . surprise, and he knew the exact instant her anger flared into lust—and he was done for. In that moment he couldn't have walked away from her if his goddamn life depended on it.

For all Ryder knew, the woman was a thief who'd been getting ready to clear his house out, but he didn't care. She smelled like Lily, had that same gorgeous hair and sexy figure, and he was too fucking starved to resist. One second they were standing on the walkway in front of his door, and in the next he had her plastered against it, wishing like hell that he'd replaced the blown bulb in the outside light so that he could get a better look at what he was tasting. His mouth had instantly settled against the base of her pale, slim throat, his tongue fluttering against her hammering pulse as he grabbed the front of her short-sleeved top and ripped. By the time Ryder could hear the shirt's buttons pinging against the ground, he already had his mouth buried between her beautiful breasts. Any concerns he might have had that she wasn't on exactly the same page as him were shattered by the low moan she gave when he ripped the silky cups of her bra down and curled his long fingers around the firm, delicate mounds, covering one of the hardened tips with his mouth. She cried out as he suckled her, her short nails digging into the bunched muscles in his shoulders, and it was like losing himself in a fever dream, her wild response to his aggression only adding fuel to the fire.

The nipple in Ryder's mouth was tight and sweet, the intoxicating taste of the woman's skin cranking his lust up to a primitive level. That irritating voice was still shouting in the back of his mind, warning him to snap back to reality and think about what he was doing—but he was too far gone, and she was too damn hot and willing. Her hands were already fisted in his hair, holding him to her as he switched to the other breast, her thigh riding his hip as she arched against him, as if she was as desperate for this as he was. And he was beyond desperate, his dick so hard he could have hammered through the fucking door with it. And the longer he touched her, the harder he got. Not that she was complaining. The woman was grinding herself against the front of his running shorts, riding the hard ridge of his cock, the husky sounds spilling from her lips the sexiest damn thing he'd ever heard.

He didn't have a condom on him, which meant he couldn't fuck her until he got her inside. He might be aching for it, but he wasn't stupid. He'd always been religious about suiting up with latex and had never screwed without it. But this hot little stranger made him damn tempted.

"We need to move this indoors," he rasped against the soft skin just under her right breast. Gripping her hips, Ryder dropped to his knees and kissed his way down her flat belly, until he'd shoved her skirt up and had his face buried against the silky front of her panties . . . then lower, between her legs. A rough, guttural sound crawled its way up from his chest as he caught the hot, mouthwatering scent of her cunt, the sexy underwear already damp with her juices. And then she had to destroy the whole goddamn thing with the soft, whispered sound of his name.

"*Scott.*"

Ah, Christ. No one fucking called him that but *her*, and it hit him like a bucket of ice water in his face.

He should have listened to his gut, to that damn voice that had been shouting in the back of his mind, because this woman didn't just *resemble* Lily Heller. She *was* Lily Heller!

No. No way. Not her. Not Lily. Couldn't be. She was just someone who reminded him of her. Someone he could still touch and get his fill of. Someone he could—

Damn it! He tried, but he couldn't do it. Couldn't buy his own bullshit. The lie had been blasted into a million tiny fragments and now he was going to have to pay the fucking price for being an idiot. No doubt with his sanity.

Jerking back to his feet, Ryder gripped her shoulders as he locked his sharp gaze on her face for the first time in three years. "*Son of a bitch,*" he grated under his breath. Big green eyes with lashes that were long and thick stared back at him. Rosy lips parted for her panting breaths. Moonlight spilling down on those firm breasts, her pink little nipples still glistening from his mouth and tongue.

Oh, God.

He was shaking so hard she was jerking in his arms, but he couldn't stop, unable to believe what was right in front of him. The girl he'd left his life and career for—the one who had been the object of his most dangerous obsession for far too long—was trapped between his body and his front door, blinking up at him with those big, bright eyes while she tried to catch her breath.

Lily Heller, daughter of his ex-boss and goddamn thorn in his side, in the flesh, staring back at him as if she could eat him alive, with her perfect tits out and her skirt hiked up around her waist. *Jesus.*

Ryder rubbed a rough hand over his mouth, wondering how he could have let things go so far. What the hell had he been thinking?

He hadn't. Which was the problem. He'd shoved rational thought to the back of his mind and focused on what he wanted. Instant gratification would screw you over every time. Damn it, he knew that. Had an IQ that said he was way too fucking smart to make that kind of mistake—but his dick had apparently failed to get the memo. And now, thanks to this royal little screwup, he would have to go through life knowing *exactly* how right it felt to have her under his hands and mouth.

"Fuck!" he ground out through his clenched teeth, shoving away from her. At six-three, he towered over her, even though she wasn't a short woman. Maybe five-six or five-seven, though she seemed more petite because of her build. She was slim, but feminine as hell, and he wanted nothing more than to take her back into his arms and—

Shit. He couldn't do it. Because if he did, it was going to goddamn destroy him when he had to walk away. And he *would* walk. He didn't have any other option. He never had where this girl was concerned. Yeah, she might be twenty-five now, but he still thought of her as the gangly, innocent teen she'd been when he first met her all those years ago.

Before he could get his mind wrapped around this new reality in which Lily Heller had suddenly popped back into his life, she shoved her skirt down, yanked the sides of her shirt closed, and glared up at him. "Do you mind telling me why you attacked me?" she snapped.

His jaw tightened. "I didn't attack you. You're the one who tried to hit *me*."

"Only after you yanked me in front of you," she shot back, as if he'd been the one at fault.

His voice was raw. "News flash, woman. That's what happens when I find someone lurking in the shadows outside my front door."

"I wasn't lurking," she argued, that bright gaze lowering to his bare chest and shoulders for a moment, before she finally lifted it back to his face. She drew in an unsteady breath, then blasted him with a sharp, "I was waiting for you to get home!"

Ryder made a low sound of frustration in the back of his throat, and this time her gaze drifted to the scar that ran from his temple to the middle of his right cheek. Something he didn't quite understand moved through those green eyes, but she didn't flinch. The last time she'd seen him the scar had been raw and fresh. It was still ugly as sin, but looked a hell of a lot better than it had then. He never even thought about it much anymore when he was with a woman, but he quickly felt himself go hot under the skin, as if he was actually embarrassed for her to see his face like this.

Fucking ironic, considering she was the reason he had the scar in the first place. Not that he'd ever tell her that. But every time Ryder looked in a mirror, he was reminded of just how dangerous his obsession with this girl could be.

"Why are you here?" he growled, his nostrils flaring with a fresh surge of fury as he stared her down. "What the hell do you want, Lily?"

She bristled with irritation. "Wow. You're just all kinds of kindness and warmth, aren't you? First you manhandle me, then you maul me, and now you're being rude. Is that any way to greet an old friend?"

"Cut the crap. You were hardly manhandled or mauled, and we were never friends. Your old man made sure of that. So what the fuck are you doing here?"

She started to pale, losing that pleasure-flush that had been in her cheeks, the angry tension that had been riding her slender frame gone as quickly as it'd come. "Believe it or not," she said quietly, licking her lips, "I'm here because I need your help."

"Bullshit," he snarled, fisting his hands at his sides so that he wouldn't do something stupid. Like reach out and grab her again. "I'm the *last* person in the world you need to get near. Go back home to your daddy and leave me alone. Whatever problem you've got, he'll take care of it."

"I . . . can't."

"Why the hell not?" he exploded.

She blinked again, and this time a tear spilled from the corner of her eye. "Because he's dead."

Ryder shook his head, thinking he must have heard her wrong. "What are you talking about?"

She took a deep breath, then exhaled in a shuddering rush. "Heller's dead, Scott. Rado killed him eight days ago."

Rado? Just the sound of that terrorist bastard's name put an icy feeling in Ryder's gut. Of all the scumbags in the world, Yuri Radovich was the one he hated the most. But the man was supposed to be a corpse. Ryder knew, because he was the one who had killed him.

"That isn't possible. Rado is dead, Lily."

A wry smile twisted her lips, the raw pain in her expression making him flinch. "Yeah, that's what my father thought. Until the monster waltzed onto our boat and slit his throat."

"Jesus." His head was starting to pound like a bitch. "You're sure it was him?"

She sniffed, and jerked her chin up in response.

A fierce scowl wove its way between his brows. "Then why the hell am I only just hearing about this? Why hasn't anyone informed the old unit?"

"Because I doubt anyone but me knows at this point, and I've been on the run," she told him, her tone tight and clipped and anything but calm. "I don't have my cell phone, but even if I did, I wouldn't have called you because who knows if your phone calls are being tapped and traced. I'm sorry for just showing up out of the blue, but it's not like I had any other choice. Even if I'd had a computer and could have e-mailed you, there's a chance he could be monitoring your account. You know what he's like—how extensive his reach is. And I didn't have time to come up with some other brilliant way to contact you because I've been doing everything I could just to make it here in one piece!"

"On the run from what?" he demanded, finally noticing how tired she looked. How shattered. "What happened, Lily? Why doesn't anyone know that Heller is dead?"

Her voice shook as she explained. "I was with my father and his girlfriend, Nancy, in the Bahamas when Rado made the hit. We were staying on Nancy's boat, moored in some cove, when he and his men found us. He killed my dad and Nancy and had them thrown overboard." Her voice started to crack, but she took another deep breath and went on. "He would have killed me, too. He actually took quite a lot of pleasure in explaining why I had to die and exactly how he and his men were going to do it. But I . . . I got lucky and managed to get away."

Ryder worked his jaw, guessing there was a hell of a lot more to the story than that . . . and dreading what he knew was coming.

"Do you understand why I'm here?" she asked, stepping toward him, those incredible eyes shimmering with too many emotions for him to name. "You're the only person I could think of who stands any kind of chance against him. The only person I trust. And I know I don't have any right to ask—I know you don't owe me anything—but I'm asking anyway."

In a flat tone, he said, "You want me to protect you."

It wasn't a question. Ryder knew damn well that's why she was there. He just didn't know what he was going to do about it. The situation was complicated as hell. One of his worst goddamn nightmares come to life.

Because while Ryder might be capable of protecting Lily Heller from Radovich, he didn't have a fucking clue how he was going to protect her from himself.

TWO

SITTING ALONE AT THE SMALL TABLE IN SCOTT RYDER'S kitchen, Lily took a moment to calm her heart and get her thoughts straight. Her body and emotions were still reeling from the way he'd touched her, not to mention the nightmare she'd been living for the past week. And then there were the three years she'd spent missing him every second of every day, even when she was pretending she didn't. She hadn't even been able to escape him in sleep, tormented too many nights by her dreams. Dreams where she'd see his rare smiles and hear his rugged, sexy-as-hell laugh.

God, she had it so bad for this man. She always had.

He'd told her to sit down and wait while he changed, and no more than a minute passed before he was walking back into the kitchen, his running shorts replaced by a pair of jeans and a black T-shirt. The hem of the shirt hung just low enough to cover his crotch, no doubt to hide any lingering evidence of the massive erection he'd been grinding against her only minutes before. What she wouldn't give to go back to that moment and just stay there, stuck in a replay loop that had him putting his hands and his mouth on her again. And again . . .

On the journey there, she'd repeatedly told herself—when she wasn't reliving those horrific moments on Nancy's boat—that she was finally over Scott Ryder. Completely. Forever. She'd tried to convince herself that she was running to him to buy as much time as she could—not because she was still the crushed-out girl who'd constantly obsessed about him, that obsession growing into heart-wrenching emotion as she'd grown older, only to be destroyed when he'd walked out of her life without so much as a *See ya.* But her delusions had been shattered the instant he'd touched her. No matter how badly she *wanted* to hate him, she . . . couldn't. Not when there was still so much raw need for this man living inside her. It'd dug itself down into her bones, like a parasite, unwilling to let go, even after he'd taken her heart and ground it into tiny little mutilated pieces three years ago. Which left her in an even more miserable situation than she'd already been in, seeing as how he'd made it more than obvious on his doorstep that he was *not* happy to see her.

Whatever imagined need or desire she'd thought she'd glimpsed in his eyes all those years ago must have been nothing more than her wishful thinking.

Really? whispered a voice inside her head. *And just whose mouth was that turning you inside out five minutes ago?*

Huh. That was true. So then what was his freaking problem?

And what are you going to do about it?

At any other point in her life, Lily might have worried about the fact that she was carrying on a silent conversation with herself. But after the hell she'd been through, she wasn't fazed by that soft voice. What threw her was the man standing across the kitchen from her, his powerful arms crossed over his chest as he leaned against one of the counters, a fierce scowl wedged between his dark brows.

It didn't seem possible, but she was even more drawn to him now than she'd been when he was one of Heller's Hellions, the nickname she'd given to her father's deadly, highly trained black ops unit. Without any conscious decision, Lily found herself thinking back to her eighteenth birthday, when Ryder had been invited up to their house to watch a game with her dad. Before his retirement, the men in her father's unit had lived in barracks on the grounds of their estate, which had been provided by the military in Northern Virginia. Not wanting to miss an opportunity to steal glances at the gorgeous soldier who her father had told her had a genius IQ that rivaled his combat skills, she'd grabbed a sketch pad and settled into a chair in the corner of the room. But that was as far as her plans had gotten, because it was Ryder who had spent most of the evening watching *her* instead of the TV. Flustered and overwhelmed with desire, she'd kept her attention focused on the blank page in her book, keenly aware of his dark eyes moving over her features, studying them individually. But why? She'd wondered if he thought she was odd, like the boys she'd gone to school with had. Or had he liked what he saw? Liked *her*? She'd wished she had the answer, but she'd had no basis for comparison. Not when her nearly nonexistent experience had been with bumbling adolescents, while he'd been . . . God. What he'd been was incredible. The most intensely sexual, potent male she'd ever set eyes on.

And he still was. Maybe even more so. And boy did that suck. Considering she wasn't getting any.

Why not? If not now, when? Your time is running out.

She didn't like to think about it, but knew that damn voice was probably right. In that instant, Lily made the decision to go "balls out," as guys said, and give his seduction her all. Hell, it's not like she had anything to lose, except maybe her pride. But it was going to hurt just as much if she lost without even trying, so the way she saw it, she might as well give it a shot. Especially when the odds were hardly in her favor of surviving more than a few weeks, at best. Ryder was good, but she had a clear understanding of exactly how evil Radovich could be. Not to mention determined. Now that she'd finally been honest with herself about why she was there, she knew there was no way she could let Ryder get caught up in her problems. She had maybe a week, tops, before Radovich tracked her down. Which meant she'd have to be gone before then, drawing him away from this man who had claimed her damn heart without even trying.

Apparently growing impatient with their silent standoff, he gripped the edge of the counter behind him and very quietly said, "Start talking, Lily."

Enjoying the chills his rough voice gave her, she leaned back in the chair she'd taken at the small table and held his stare. "What do you want me to say?"

"I want to know what happened on that boat."

"I told you what happened. My father was killed, I got away, and I have no doubt that Rado is looking for me. I need your help until I can figure out what to do."

SHE WANTED TO figure out what to do? Christ, her options were so limited he could count them on two fingers.

One: Kill Radovich before he killed her.

Two: Start a new life somewhere with a new identity and hope like hell the terrorist never tracked her down.

Both options had their dangers, and he wished to God there were a third, easier solution here. Wished Rado had just stayed dead, like he was meant to be, instead of coming back and wreaking hell on this woman's life.

Now that she was sitting under the bright kitchen lights, Ryder could see the shadow of a healing bruise on her right cheek and another along the side of her jaw. It killed him inside that she'd been hurt. That some prick had hit her . . . marked her.

Was this what had been itching at his senses for the past weeks? He wasn't a spiritual guy, but he'd spent enough time in Heller's unit to trust his survival instincts. But this feeling in his veins had been different, sharper and more vital, and he hadn't recognized it for what it was: A call to protect someone *else*, instead of his own sorry ass. If he hadn't been so goddamn determined not to think about her, would he have been able to figure it out? He didn't know—but it was probably going to be a question that hammered at him for the rest of his days.

He didn't like failing people. And no matter what he did, he always ended up feeling like that around Lily. Like he was doing it all wrong. Not getting it right. Out of his element and in over his head. Which was only part of the reason he'd known he needed to walk away.

"Obviously," she said, tucking a wayward curl behind her left ear, "we need to know what's happened since I ran. I've been completely cut off, so I have no idea if Rado has gone after anyone else, or if he's gunning straight for me. If he's hoping to stay off the government's radar and remain dead, then he'll put everything he's got into finding me. Do you stay in contact with any of your old intel sources?"

He shook his head. "Not the kind that would know anything about Rado. I left that shit behind, where it belongs."

Something that looked too much like pain flashed in her eyes. "Including me? Am I just an unwanted piece of your forgotten past?"

His fingers tightened on the counter until he could have sworn he heard the Formica groan in protest. "You weren't mine, Lily.

Don't make it sound like we had some understanding that I shit on. I never fucked you over."

She didn't say anything right away. Just stared across the small kitchen at him with those big, soul-trapping eyes. And then, very softly, she said, "But I wanted to be yours. I wanted to belong to you." She slowly shook her head, her tone chagrined. "I hoped—" She broke off with a low, pained laugh. "God, you have no idea how badly I hoped you felt the same, but you were so good at giving nothing away. If I'd known you would touch me the way you touched me tonight, I never would have been able to keep my hands off you."

His jaw went so rigid it felt like it could crack. "Did you ever stop to think that maybe I'm just not attracted to you?"

One of her slender eyebrows slowly arched. "I think the fact I'm holding my shirt closed because it's missing all its buttons says differently."

He would have argued, but it was pointless, given his actions. Score one for his dick. Now his brain had a hell of a lot of catching up to do. Desperate to retake the ground that he'd lost, he said, "What happened tonight was a product of circumstance."

The look in her eyes turned laser sharp, making him flinch, as if he'd been pinned under a microscope. "So you're saying that you were willing to fuck me when you didn't have a clue who I was? When I was just some random stranger lurking in the shadows? But once you realized it was me, you're now no longer interested?"

He gave a jerky nod.

"Bullshit."

"Whatever you think, it shouldn't have happened."

Her chin shot up a notch, making his insides cramp. He'd seen that stubborn look on her face too many times to count when she'd been living with her father. But he'd never had it directed right at him. "I wanted it to happen a long time ago," she said, all but laying the words down like a challenge.

His own words were raw. "It's not happening again."

Her eyes narrowed. "Why?"

"Because you're practically a child," he growled.

She looked stunned. "Excuse me?"

"I'm eight fucking years older than you are," he muttered.

"So?"

"So . . . I've known you forever. Your dad was my fucking friend."

Her brow knitted with confusion. "And that was why you always treated me as a friend, but never anything more? Because you think I'm too young for you?"

He didn't say anything. He just stared, hard, warning her to quit with his look. But the little fool just wouldn't shut up.

"You know, sometimes . . . sometimes I would catch what I thought was a glimpse of interest in your eyes. Something that you didn't hide quite in time when I would turn unexpectedly and look your way." She moved to her feet and took two steps toward him, before his wrathful expression stopped her. "Do you have any idea what those looks would do to me? How badly I wished you would just do something . . . *anything*? How terrified I was that I was just imagining it? Whatever you wanted from me, I would have been more than willing to give you, Scott."

"Christ, Lily. You don't even know me. You don't know what I'm—"

"You're wrong," she whispered, cutting him off. "I know all about you."

He gave a gritty laugh under his breath. "Right."

She took another step toward him and lowered her lashes. "Would you like it better if you gagged me? Tied me up? Slapped some handcuffs on me? Because if that's what it takes to get you off, then I'm willing. I trust you."

It was the strangest sensation, the way all the blood in his body turned ice cold, while his skin burned with heat. Releasing his grip on the counter, he flexed his hands at his sides. "What the fuck did you just say?"

Her gaze flicked up to his, and caught, locked in the fury of his glare. But she didn't back down and cower. Instead, she licked her lips and said, "I know all about your sexual . . . whatever you want to call it. I know you're into the bondage scene. My father made sure he did his research thoroughly on every one of his men before they came to work for him, as well as *while* they were under his command." There was a brief pause where she bit her lip, and then she murmured, "Your file was fairly extensive."

He was so furious he was shaking. "You read my fucking file?"

She narrowed her eyes again. "Front to back. I memorized the damn thing."

His lungs seized so tight he couldn't even draw his next breath. He didn't think it was possible, but he went even colder inside. "You know about my mother?"

Her head cocked a bit to the side, her gaze questioning. "I know she was a single mother. That she raised you without your dad. But that's all."

He scraped out a low curse, not looking at her. But he could feel the force of her sudden uneasiness blasting against him. "Scott," she said hesitantly. "What's wrong?"

What was wrong? Jesus. He choked back a humorless laugh, not trusting what it might turn into. She hadn't been back in his life twenty minutes, and already he felt stripped down like a live wire, all his raw parts torn and exposed, getting prodded by every fucking word that came out of her mouth.

"I don't like the look on your face," she whispered. "You know you can talk to me, right? Is there something about your mother you don't want me to know?"

He scrubbed his hands down his face, then dropped his arms to his sides and forced himself to look her in the eye. "We're not talking about my mother, Lily. And before you think you can just loop back to your original topic, we're sure as shit not talking about my sex life."

"Why?" she pressed softly, clearly not knowing when to quit. "Does it scare you to know that I'm okay with what you like from women? Is that what bothers you about our age difference? You think I won't understand?"

Completely ignoring her questions, he bit his words out. "Did you or did you not come to me claiming that Rado is trying to kill you?"

"It's not a claim. It's the truth."

"Then maybe you should stop playing games you can't finish and tell me what the fuck happened."

He could tell from the look in her eyes that his attitude was getting to her. "I've already told you what happened."

He slowly shook his head. "Not how you got away."

"What does that have to do with anything?"

Nothing. Not really. Except that it was driving him out of his damn mind, wondering what those bastards had done to her.

Her lashes lowered, concealing something in her eyes that she didn't want him to see. "I got away, Scott. That's all that matters."

Fuck it. He'd let her keep her silence. For the moment. "I'll protect you," he muttered, crossing his arms back over his chest, "but I won't take any of your shit, Lily. You'll have to follow my orders. Do you think you can do that?"

Her little chin went up again. "Why do you think I can't?"

He gave a sarcastic snort. "I remember what you were like. Always defying every order you were given."

A low, tight laugh slipped from her lips. "That was a long time ago. I didn't like being treated like one of my dad's soldiers and I acted out. It doesn't mean I have a death wish."

"You could have fooled me." She might have been innocent when it came to sex back then, but she'd had more than enough backbone to defy her father in every other aspect of her life. "You were reckless as hell."

Her head tilted a bit to the side again. "What are you talking about?"

"That skydiving instructor you let take you up had shit for brains."

For a few seconds, she just stared at him in confusion. Then realization slowly dawned, her expression caught somewhere between fascination and shock. "Ohmygod. That was *you*? You're the one who scared him off ever taking me up for another jump?"

He jerked his shoulder in a stiff roll. "All I did was talk to him."

"And make him nearly piss his pants! He thought you were going to kill him."

Choking back a satisfied laugh, he said, "That's a little dramatic. I just told him I would kick his ass if he ever came within twenty miles of you again."

She placed her fingers over her lips, still looking dazed. "He apparently thought that meant the same thing when coming from you."

"Yeah, well, you know me better than that."

"I thought I did. But then I also thought you weren't coward enough to sneak off in the dead of night without a word."

Jesus, she just wouldn't let up. "Don't start, Lily. Leave the past in the past, where it belongs."

"So because I liked to skydive when I was younger, you think I'm . . . what? Reckless? Stupid?"

"It wasn't just the skydiving. It was the rock-climbing, the whitewater kayaking, the fucking bungee jumping from bridges only an idiot would have jumped off of. You treated every school break like a chance to finally find a way to kill yourself!"

Color burned beneath her pale skin. "So I liked to push my limits. What's the big deal? At least I wasn't doing it with drugs and sex."

A muscle started to pulse at the side of his jaw. "You were headed there."

"That's a lie and you know it," she snapped. "But it's good to know that you were worried enough to stick around and make sure I was okay."

"Topic, Lily. For once let's try to stay on fucking topic."

She was breathing too hard to say anything for a moment, those green eyes flashing with anger. "Fine. Is there anyone local who can help us if we need it? Or are we on our own?"

Pushing his hands in his pockets, he said, "There's Ben. But I don't know if that would be a good idea."

"Who's Ben?"

"My boss."

She studied his expression, no doubt seeing more than he wanted her to. But she simply said, "Dad told me you were working down here as a deputy. So Ben's the sheriff?"

"Yeah."

"You trust him?"

"I trust him," he replied, then immediately frowned. "But it's going to be complicated, seeing as how he's . . ."

"He's what?"

"In love." He winced, feeling like a damn idiot. "He just got married and all that shit."

"Oh." She shook her head. "Um, I'm failing to see the point. Why does his being in love and married make this complicated?"

Taking a hand from his pocket, he shoved it back through his shaggy hair and grimaced. "Because the guy's walking around with fucking stars in his eyes 24/7 these days. He's going to take one look at you and start playing matchmaker." Ben never had before, but something in Ryder's gut told him this time it would be different. There was too much crackling tension in the air between him and Lily. The kind anyone could pick up on and mistake for something sexual.

With wide eyes, she asked, "Does he do that often? For you?"

"I'm not answering that," he muttered, shoving his hand back in his pocket.

"Why not?"

"Because my personal life is off-limits. And it's none of your damn business."

Her laughter was quiet as she tightened her arms over her chest. "I'd tell you what a jerk you sound like, but I'm too tired."

He studied her for a moment, taking in the dark circles under her eyes. Did she look a little paler than when they'd first started talking? When she yawned, he moved to her side. "Come on, you need sleep."

"I know. Sorry," she mumbled, turning back toward the table, where she'd left a sturdy backpack sitting in one of the chairs. She'd carried it in with her when they'd come inside, retrieving it from the shadows by the trellis.

"What's in the bag?" he asked, telling himself he wasn't disappointed that she'd been able to get the pack on her shoulder without losing her grip on her top, which she was still having to hold closed. But it was nothing but a big fat lie. He'd have probably given up a year of his life just for the chance to set eyes on her tits again. They might not be the biggest he'd ever seen, but they were definitely the most beautiful, not to mention the sweetest. There wasn't even a close second.

"Just a few things," she said, answering his question. "I left most of my stuff back at the motel I checked into this evening, before taking a taxi over here. Not that there's much. But I didn't want to be caught without anything if they found me."

"You've got clothes with you?"

"Yeah. I've got a clean pair of shorts and a shirt. My toothbrush. Hairbrush. A little cash."

He nodded, heading out of the kitchen, and she followed after him. "I'm sorry if I've been bitchy tonight," she said to his back. "I haven't slept much the past few days, and then that whole make-out session completely fried my brain. I can't stand to be left hanging."

Ryder flinched, hating the idea of her having sexual experience. Not that he had any claim on her. But he had no doubt that he'd go to his grave wanting to kill every bastard who was ever lucky enough to lay his hands on her.

When he started down the hallway toward the back of the house instead of the entrance, she said, "Uh, Scott? Aren't you taking me back to my motel?"

He turned around to face her, his brows pulled together in another frown. "I thought you wanted protection."

"I do. I guess I just thought that you'd stay with me there. At the motel."

Shaking his head again, he said, "You're staying here."

"Oh. Um, okay."

He showed her to the guest bedroom that sat across the hall from his. It had a double bed and its own bathroom, so at least he wouldn't have to think about her getting naked and wet in his shower. Careful to keep his eyes off her as she sat on the side of the bed, he told her to get some sleep and that he'd be in to wake her up early. Then he headed for the door.

"Scott. I—"

Ryder shut the door behind him without bothering to wait for what she wanted to say. He was half-terrified she'd come after him, knowing damn well his control was too shaky to withstand the temptation if she pushed him any more tonight. His stupid dick was still rock hard, and he wanted nothing more than to bury it so deep inside her she—

Fuck! I've got to stop thinking about it.

Since there wasn't a chance in hell he could sleep when he was this jacked up, he headed into his home office and sat down in front of his computer. Two hours later, he'd already hacked his way into a few government systems and had looked into everything they knew about Radovich and Lily's father. It wasn't much. The military was keeping Heller's death quiet until they had an answer about what had happened to him. They hadn't figured out yet that it was Rado—that the bastard was back from the dead—and for the moment Ryder planned to leave it that way. He didn't like the thought of how they might try to use Lily if they learned the truth about what had happened. Not that he wasn't thinking along the same lines, but only if he could keep her protected. The kind of brass who would kill for the chance to bag Yuri Radovich wouldn't be so concerned about her safety. But for the moment, as far as the military knew, she'd died on that boat along with her father. Heller's and the girlfriend's bodies had washed up on a Bahamian beach two days ago, but Lily's was assumed to still be lost at sea.

The government thought she was dead, but Rado knew that she was alive. Which meant one thing and one thing only.

The bastard was hunting for her.

THREE

THINKING THAT SHE'D JUST HEARD SOMEONE SAY HER NAME, Lily rolled over in the comfortable double bed and choked back a moan. Mmm, talk about waking up to a beautiful piece of eye candy. Ryder was sprawled back in the brown leather chair that sat in the far corner of the room, dressed in jeans and a gray T-shirt. He looked tired, but beautiful. The dark smudges under his eyes only added to the I'm-a-serious-badass image he projected so well. Of course, in Ryder's case it wasn't an image. He really *was* a serious badass.

"Did you sleep at all?" she asked him.

His dark eyes bored into hers. "I caught a few hours." His voice was low and morning-rough. If she had the choice, she knew she could be happy waking up to that voice every morning for the rest of her life. Too bad she had a better chance of winning the lottery.

"What were you doing all night?"

He scratched at the black stubble shadowing the hard line of his jaw. "I spent some time online."

Sitting up, she braced her back against the headboard. She'd slept in a thin tank top, and kept the sheet tucked up under her arms, covering her nipples. They'd gone hard the instant she'd set eyes on Ryder, but it wasn't like she wanted to hide from him. She wanted him. God, she wanted him. She just needed to wake up a bit more before she could throw off the nerves fluttering in her belly and put it all out there, nipples and all. "Were you looking into Rado?"

When he nodded, she asked, "What's your plan?"

She could have sworn he was fighting back a grin. "What makes you think I have a plan?"

She rolled her eyes. "I know you, Scott. I spent too many years of my life studying you. I know what your game face looks like."

Leaning forward in the chair, he braced his elbows on his parted knees, the position doing incredible things to his muscular arms and broad shoulders. "I think we let him know where you are, then sit and wait for him to fall into our lap."

Her jaw dropped so far she thought she probably looked like a landed trout. "Wait a minute. You *want* him to come to Moss Beach?"

His gaze was steady and direct, and deadly as hell. "We can waste weeks trying to track the bastard down so that I can make sure his ass is dealt with once and for all, or a few days waiting for him to make his move."

A few days. The more dangerous but faster option. And from the look on his face, it was obvious that he'd chosen it because he couldn't wait to get rid of her. She shouldn't have been surprised. He'd made no secret of the fact that he wasn't happy about being stuck with her. Oh, he might not have come right out and said it. But his facial expressions and body language had been easy to read. He didn't want her there.

Knotting the sheet in her hands, she worked to keep her voice calm as she said, "I came here looking for protection. Can't we just . . . I don't know. Alert the right people and let them go after Rado, while I stay here with you?"

He shook his head. "We both know how hard the son of a bitch is to kill, Lily. And until he's dead, you'll never be safe."

"And when he gets here? What then?"

"Then I kill him."

He said it so simply, as if he were talking about taking out the trash or grabbing some fast food.

"And his men? What are you going to do about the assholes he has working for him?" she pressed, knowing damn well that any chance she had of turning the fantasy that'd been playing in the back of her mind into a reality was getting slim. And it was such a good one, too. A raw, delicious fantasy where she and Scott Ryder lost themselves in each other before Rado found her and killed her. She didn't want to die, damn it—but if she had to go, she at least wanted as much time with Ryder as she could get before it happened. At the first sign of the terrorist, she planned to leave town, drawing the danger away from him. Just not until she'd gotten what she'd come for. But Ryder wanted Rado there *now*, leaving her no time at all.

Answering her question, he said, "If they try to hurt you, they die. But Rado's interest in you is personal. I'm guessing he's looking for some kind of payback against your father for sending the old unit after him. Once he's dead, his men will move on to greener pastures."

He dropped his gaze to her hands, which were still knotted in the top sheet, holding it tight to her chest. Her grip was so strong she figured her knuckles were probably turning white, but she couldn't relax her hold. When he lifted those dark eyes back to hers, she said, "I shouldn't have come here. I knew you were tough, that you could handle yourself, but I didn't think you'd want a showdown. You could get hurt." She darted her eyes to his scar, then quickly looked away. "You've already been hurt enough by this man. I don't want you in danger."

"We're not going to hide, Lily. I'm going to finish the job I started three years ago. I want that bastard in the ground." He paused for a second, studying her expression with those piercing eyes, before saying, "And don't even think about running."

She blinked. "What?"

"You heard me. If you think you can read me, then remember that I can read you even better." He paused again, his intense, heavy-lidded gaze making her feel as if he really could see right inside her, picking his way through her thoughts. With a slow shake of his head, he quietly said, "I don't know what plan you had in coming here, but it obviously wasn't this. You knew you'd be safe here, that I'd protect you if the shit hit the fan, but for some reason, you never planned on me going face-to-face with Rado."

"No. I—"

"Don't waste our time with lies." His expression was definitely veering toward a scowl. "Just know that if you try to run, you'll have both of us chasing you down—me *and* Radovich. And you won't like what happens if I find you first."

Her breath caught in her chest at the blatant warning in those low, husky words, but she knew she wasn't in any real danger from him. He wouldn't physically harm her—not like Rado would. No, Ryder was promising a different kind of punishment. One that made her heart pound and her pulse race, while she went warm and wet in places that were eagerly anticipating his possession. It was almost funny, the way he thought he was making some kind of threat, when she was more than willing to take whatever he wanted to dish out.

"If we do this," he added, "then we do it *my* way."

"Yeah, I know." The time for being shy was definitely over. Taking a deep breath, Lily deliberately let go of the sheet, watching his gaze drop as the white cotton slipped down to her waist. Her nipples pulled even tighter beneath the weight of his stare. "You're into control and all that, right?"

That muscle started to pulse in his jaw again. "I'm not talking about sex."

"I know *you* weren't."

His nostrils flared as he roughly exhaled. "Focus, Lily."

"Or what?"

Something hot and hard started to burn in that dark gaze as he slowly brought it back to her face. "You'll listen to me or I'll cuff your sweet little ass to that bed."

Refusing to back down, she drawled, "You can cuff it anyway, Deputy. I've always wanted to try a little bondage."

Ryder was on her before he'd even realized he was moving. Once second he was sitting in the chair across the room, and in the next he had her trapped beneath him in the center of the mattress, his hands manacling her delicate wrists. His eyes narrowed as he stared down at her triumphant expression. "You're pushing me, Little Lily."

She gazed up at him with wide eyes, her face flushed with excitement. "I'm not little, Scott. And if it'll get you pushing *into* me, then good. I'll just keep pushing. What do I have to lose?"

He shoved a knee between her legs, forcing them apart, and pressed against the crotch of her panties, letting her feel just how thick and hard he was. "You feel that?" he growled, his lungs heaving. "You still want me inside you?"

Instead of scaring her off, the look in her eyes got hotter . . . *softer*, as if she saw right inside him and liked what she saw. What the hell? It was like she understood his screwed up emotions even better than he did. "God, yes," she whispered. "I want it more than anything."

He made his tone as snide as possible. "You really think you can take it, baby girl?"

Her laugh was low and sweet, giving him chills. "Maybe the question is whether or not you can keep up with me. I mean, I'm younger, which means I've got more stamina. And I'm sure as hell not afraid of your dick, Scott—no matter how big it is."

He shook his head and glared. "You shouldn't talk like that."

"Why not?"

"For one, you're too damn young. And your fucking life is in danger. You need to stay focused and stop trying to get me in your pants."

She laughed a little harder, hugging his hips with her slender thighs. "Seriously, Scott. Do you even hear yourself? I'm twenty-five years old. And if my life's in danger, then shouldn't I be enjoying every moment of it while I still have the time?"

"Don't say that," he snapped, gripping her shoulders and shaking her. "Nothing's going to happen to you."

"You don't know that," Lily said softly, staring up at him. "I have every faith you can keep yourself alive—so long as you don't do something reckless—or I wouldn't have come here. But we both know the odds aren't in my favor. Not if he's decided I need to die."

And that right there was why she'd run to him. Because she refused to leave this world before she'd done everything she could to get her fill of this beautiful, somehow damaged, thoroughly exasperating man.

"You really think I'll let him touch you?" His face was right above hers now, his breath warm against her lips.

"*If* I stay, I won't blame you if you fail. We both know what he's like. You're my best shot, but a girl's gotta be realistic, right?"

His dark eyes glittered. "Damn it, Lily. I'm not going to let anything happen to you. Tell me you understand that."

"I'd rather tell you what I want to do to you," she shot back, knowing she was pushing him. But she couldn't stop. It was like the need inside of her had taken control of her mouth. "Or I could tell you about all the things I'm hoping you'll do to me."

"Is that really what this is all about? You came to me because you want to get fucked one last time before he finds you? Is that it? Was I the closest guy you could get to that you know?"

"No! I came here because I want *you*. Just you." Her voice shook with emotion. "I always have."

"You don't know what the hell you want," he argued, forcing the words through his clenched teeth. "You're acting like a spoiled little brat."

"Why? Because I'm not afraid to admit what I want? Does it freak you out that badly? Are you afraid I'm going to ruin you with my dirty mind?"

"I swear to God, Lily." Frustration thickened his words. "I've had enough of your smart-ass mouth."

"Then put something in it and shut me up," she flung back at him. "Come on, Scott. Quit wasting time!"

He didn't say anything more. He used actions instead of words. But there was no mistaking his meaning. One second Lily was trapped under him, and in the next he had her flipped to her front, braced on her knees, with her elbows on the bed and her ass in the air as he knelt beside her, holding her in place. When he ripped her panties down, pulling them to mid-thigh, she panted, "What are you doing?"

"Spanking your ass," he growled, quickly bringing one of his big hands down in a loud smack against her right cheek. Lily shrieked, startled and outraged by the pain, and more than a little confused by the pleasure that followed immediately on its heels. Did she like this? Did she want more? He didn't wait to ask. Within seconds he'd rained four more slaps across her bottom, alternating sides and making the sensitive skin burn, her body shivering as she tried to make sense of the strange sensations rushing through her.

Then he stopped, his breathing jagged and rough as he held still beside her, the heat of his body keeping her warm in the cool, air-conditioned air. He shuddered, making a low sound in his throat. The hand he'd used to spank her curved around her stinging flesh, gripping her in a hard, possessive hold, while the other pressed between her shoulders, keeping her in the provocative position. She panted harder, wondering what came next, when he dropped his forehead to her lower back.

"Scott? Wh-what are you doing?"

"I . . . *Fuck!* Shut up and let me think."

"Are you okay?" she whispered, which was odd. She was the one who'd just had her ass spanked. If anything, he should be asking *her* that question. But she could feel the brutal emotion gripping him, making his hard, powerful body shake.

"No," he finally admitted. "I'm not okay. I'm really fucking far from okay."

The hoarse, guttural sound of his voice made her melt, and she was keenly aware of the slick warmth of her juices slipping down her inner thighs. She was wet and empty and aching inside. What was he waiting for?

"Are you going to touch me?"

When he didn't respond, she arched her back a little deeper, swaying her bottom a bit, too desperate to care that she was practically begging for him. "Please, Scott. Do it."

His fingers tightened on her ass, and for a moment there was nothing but the heavy, breath-filled silence that surrounded them, pressing down on them, thick with secrets and things she didn't understand. Her lungs locked as his hand slowly started to slide lower. But his touch and weight were suddenly gone before he reached the drenched folds of her sex. There was a sharp, visceral growl, followed by the sound of one of his massive fists slamming into the wall behind the bed. She rolled over, crouching in the middle of the sheets, unable to believe he was walking out on her.

"Where are you going?" she demanded, watching him stalk across the room without once looking in her direction.

He stopped at the door, his big hands digging into the frame on either side, the power of his body so beautiful she wanted to throw herself at him. But it was what lay inside that had always fascinated her, trapping her heart before she was even old enough to understand what this kind of attachment meant. That it would ruin her for other men. Make her ache. Make her miserable.

"Get dressed," he muttered. "We're meeting Ben at his place in half an hour."

Then he was gone.

THE DRIVE TO the sheriff's house took little more than ten minutes. Ryder had been waiting for her when she'd finally come out of the guest room after getting ready, and by some unspoken agreement, neither of them had mentioned what had happened.

"Uh, Scott?" she murmured, staring through the windshield of his Jeep at the cars parked in the shared driveway of two beautiful beach houses that looked to be under a massive remodeling job that would make them a single house. "Is there some kind of party going on here?"

"Ben and his wife are throwing a birthday party for one of her sisters down on the beach later. He said people would probably show up early to help with the cooking and to get things ready."

Lily pulled her lower lip through her teeth. "Does he mind us being here?"

"Not at all," he said, not looking at her as he pulled his key from the ignition. "He invited us to the party, but I told him I thought it would be best if you kept a low profile for the moment."

"Thanks," she whispered, thinking the last thing she could probably handle right now was a party with a bunch of strangers.

They climbed out of the Jeep and made their way through the parked cars, then around the side of the house on the right, until they'd reached the crowded back patio. Standing on the fringes of the bustling group, Ryder pointed to a muscular, dark-haired guy who was sinfully good-looking. "The tall guy over there is Ben."

"That's who you're worried is going to play matchmaker?" she asked, barely able to hold in her laughter as she studied the man who was stringing a strand of small white lights across the opposite end of the patio. He was gorgeous, but looked tough as hell. "Honestly, Scott."

When she sent him a look that said she thought he was crazy, he smirked. "You want to feel my palm on your ass again?"

She was surprised he'd mentioned it, and more than a little surprised at how turned on she was by the idea. Heat sizzled through her as she murmured, "I might."

"Christ." He blew out a soft breath, and there was a crooked tilt to his mouth as he shook his head. "I walked right into that one, didn't I?"

"You certainly did," she said with a soft laugh, thinking he might actually be loosening up a little. Looking back at the sheriff, she asked, "Is it hard for you to take orders from a guy who isn't military?" On the drive over, he'd explained Ben Hudson's background as a Miami homicide detective, before the lawman had relocated to Moss Beach and taken on the role of county sheriff.

"Not at all," he murmured, nodding to the people who either smiled at them or gave them a little wave. They were definitely getting some curious looks, but everyone seemed friendly and welcoming. "Ben knows what he's doing," he added. "That's all that matters to me."

She smiled, thinking Ryder had always been that way. For such a badass alpha soldier who had been as lethal with a computer as he'd been with a knife, he'd never been one to play the macho asshole card. He'd taken his orders from her father without ever batting an eye, and he'd been loyal to the members of his team. He hadn't swaggered with attitude like so many of the elite soldiers.

"Hey, Ryder. You gonna introduce me to the lovely lady?"

Ryder mentally cursed as Michael Hudson, Ben's younger brother, walked toward him and Lily. Ben had obviously asked everyone to give them a bit of space, but Mike either hadn't gotten the message, or had simply decided to ignore it. Before he could tell the hotshot DEA agent to back off, Lily stuck her hand out and smiled. "Hi. I'm Lily Heller."

There was a wicked gleam in Mike's pale green eyes as he shook her hand. "Nice to meet you, Lily. I'm Mike Hudson. Ben's brother."

Though she'd had a change of clothes in the backpack she'd brought with her, she obviously hadn't had any makeup to put on. Her face was freshly scrubbed, her skin glowing and healthy, making her look even younger than she was. And incredibly innocent—even though Ryder knew she wasn't. Not after what had happened that morning. A virgin would have been screaming her head off at having her underwear ripped down and her sweet little ass smacked, instead of moaning and wiggling for more. His right hand flexed at his side, his palm burning with remembered sensation. Her rounded backside had been so smooth and soft. It'd taken every ounce of willpower he possessed not to push his hand lower, between her legs, and palm her hot little cunt. Even more to refrain from rolling her over and shoving her legs out flat at her sides so that he could get a good long look at her tender folds, before lowering his head and going at her like a man who'd been starving for too damn long.

"So how do you know this jackass?" Mike asked, interrupting the dangerous track of his thoughts. Last thing he needed was to get hard in front of all these fucking people. Ben would never let him live it down.

"Mike," he grunted, that single word holding a wealth of warning. Before Ryder could say anything more, Ben finally came over, slapping his brother on the back.

"Get lost, Mike. They're here on business."

Mike's pale gaze skimmed over the faded bruise on Lily's jaw. "Let me know if there's anything I can do," he said in a hard voice, before walking away.

Ben shot a warm look toward his wife, Reese, who was standing at one of the tables with her mother, both women busy putting flowers into little vases that'd been tied with ribbons. Then the sheriff turned and headed through a set of French doors, into the house, and Ryder and Lily followed after him. Ryder kept his hand against her lower back as they made their way through the house to Ben's home office. At the beginning of the summer, it had been a man's office, nice but rugged with a single desk. Now it sported a slightly smaller, feminine desk on the other side

of the room, where Reese worked. This room was hardly the only
change in Ben's life since he'd fallen head-over-ass for the sexy
little schoolteacher—but for some reason it made Ryder uncomfortable. He scowled as he looked around, noting the two mugs
sitting on the larger desk. One had lipstick on the rim, as if Reese
had been cuddled up in her husband's lap as they'd shared their
morning coffee. And then there were the fucking photos on the
walls and their desks. Wedding photos. Honeymoon photos. The
smiling, laughing couple with their arms wrapped around each
other. The looks on their faces happier than he'd ever thought
people could be. That it could happen to a tough son of a bitch
like Ben threw him. He didn't like being in this space, where
everything screamed couple and commitment and all the things
that scared the living shit out of him. And he sure as hell didn't
like being in here with Lily.

"You okay?" Ben asked him. "You look—"

"I'm fine," he grunted. "Just . . . worried." He almost flinched
when Lily turned her head and gave him a little smile, her eyes
flashing with emotions he couldn't deal with. And didn't want.
What the hell did she know anyway? She was too young. Too
trusting. Too fucking *everything*. He'd have to be an idiot to believe a single word that had come out of her mouth that morning.

Moving away from her, he threw himself into the chair over
by the wall, leaving her alone in front of the desk.

Ben frowned, looking between the two of them, before settling
his worried gaze on Lily. She was still standing, and he held out
his hand. "I'm afraid we didn't get properly introduced. I'm Ben."

"Lily," she said, shaking his hand. "I want to thank you for
taking the time to meet with us when you're so busy."

He gave her an easy smile. "Not a problem. I'm never too busy
for my friends."

Ryder stiffened, a little surprised by Ben's words. He hadn't really ever thought of him as being a friend. They worked together. Period. He didn't have friends. Or girlfriends. Hell, he was such a reclusive jerk, he probably wouldn't see his sister if she didn't make it a point to come down and visit.

Before he could sort out his thoughts, Ben asked Lily to take a seat, propped his hip on the edge of his desk, and caught Ryder's gaze. "Tell me what you need and I'll make it happen. But first, I want to know what's going on."

Though he'd given Ben a brief overview of the situation over the phone, he hadn't gone into any specifics. He did that now, explaining about Yuri Radovich, the op he and his fellow team members had carried out against Radovich three years ago that they'd mistakenly thought had resulted in the terrorist's death, and how Heller and his girlfriend had been killed. Then Ben asked Lily to explain how she'd managed to make it from the Caribbean to Florida, and Ryder listened with interest. His damn head had been so screwed up since last night he hadn't yet taken the time to ask her that question himself. Her story about paying some guy on a deep-sea fishing boat to smuggle her into the port so that there wouldn't be any records for Rado to trace gave him chills, considering how easy it would have been for some bastard to hurt her. When she was done, Ben looked at Ryder and asked, "Could Radovich's hit on Heller and his family be a personal strike against you?"

Lily sat up a little straighter in her chair, her confusion showing in the crease between her delicate brows. "What would an attack against my father have to do with Scott? As far as I know, they never spoke again after he left my father's unit."

Ryder shook his head a little, warning Ben off that particular track. He knew exactly what the guy was thinking—that Radovich thought there was a romantic connection between him and Lily and had tried to kill her because of it. No way in hell did he want his boss blurting out a bombshell like that. He'd never be able to convince Lily he wasn't interested if she suspected he might be lying to her. Idiot woman had decided she wanted a piece of him for some unknown reason, and until he'd dealt with Rado and sent her home, he needed to be careful not to give anything away. Not that he was doing that great a job of it. He'd already had her panties down around her knees once today, and it wasn't even lunchtime.

Picking up on Ryder's signal, Ben shrugged Lily's question off, saying it was nothing, then asked what he could do to help. Ryder rubbed his scar for a moment, knowing Ben probably wasn't going to like his plan. But he didn't have a lot of choice in the matter. He needed Radovich dealt with as soon as possible, because his control was only going to last so long. Sitting forward in his chair with his elbows on his knees, his hands clasped between them, he said, "I've talked to Lily, and we both believe that her best chance of survival is to draw Radovich to Moss Beach so that I can deal with him personally. I know Rado will be keeping tabs on the east coast for word about Lily. He's got guys who know their way around our statewide communication systems even better than we do. I was thinking that if you could put out a statewide alert for a man matching his description in connection with a local investigation, then it should be enough to snag his attention without setting off any red flags with the military, since they still don't know he's the one who made the hit. But the second Radovich realizes I'm a deputy in your department, he's going to know that Lily came to me for help."

Ben looked unconvinced. "Will he really think we're stupid enough to put out an alert like that and not expect him to find out about it?"

"It doesn't matter what he thinks. Even if he figures out it's a setup, he's still going to come after her. That's a given. Regardless of his reasons for wanting to kill her, he isn't the type of man who can allow a woman to get one over on him and let it go unanswered. He's too fucking arrogant for it."

"And you're both okay with this?" Ben asked, looking from one to the other.

Before she could say anything, Ryder grunted, "Yeah. We talked about it this morning."

Ben shot her an odd look, as if surprised to hear that she'd agreed to the plan. And Lily, damn her, hardly gave the impression that she was on board with the idea. She looked too pale, the tightness around her mouth a dead giveaway that she was on edge.

Rubbing the back of his neck, Ben said, "It's a hell of a risk, luring an international terrorist to our town, Ryder."

"I know. But I'll deal with the bastard when he shows. I don't expect the department to take this on."

"Christ," Ben muttered with a scowl. "No one's going to stand by and let you handle this on your own. But drawing him to your home isn't going to play out well if something goes wrong. I don't want you having to hit the road in order to fall off his radar and end up losing my best deputy."

"Nothing's going to go wrong. I made the mistake of leaving that asshole to die once. I won't do it again. This time I'm making sure he's in pieces before I walk away."

If Ben thought that was a bloodthirsty plan, he didn't show it. He simply asked, "And then what?"

Ryder was careful not to look in her direction. "Then I'll go back to work at the station and Lily can get back to her life in Virginia."

Ben sighed, cutting an almost sympathetic glance at Lily. Ryder didn't know what kind of expression she was wearing now, since he refused to look at her, but judging by the look on Ben's face it wasn't good. His boss looked like there was a lot he wanted to say, but knew better than to even try, and Ryder was grateful for his silence. He knew the next time he and Ben were alone he'd probably be getting an earful about God only knew what. But at least the guy was keeping his opinions to himself for the moment. The sheriff's only question was, "You going to stay in the county's safe house?"

"We have a safe house?" Ryder asked with surprise.

Ben grimaced. "Yeah, though the previous sheriff only used it as a place to house his latest mistress. I've slotted it for sale, since the county has no use for it. And I sure as hell have no need of the place. But it could come in handy in this situation. The security is tight, and there are cameras set up for outside surveillance."

"I'll think about it," he replied, moving back to his feet. "We should be okay staying at my place for the next day or so, but it might be a good idea by the time we're expecting Radovich."

Ben nodded his head in agreement. "Just let me know if you change your mind and want to head over earlier. I'll get someone from the station to drop the keys off at your place, and the house will be yours."

FOUR

GLAD TO BE GETTING THE HELL OUT OF THERE, RYDER CLIMBED into the Jeep, put the key in the ignition, and cranked the engine.

"Now what?" Lily asked, as she closed the Jeep's passenger door and buckled her seat belt.

Reversing out of the drive, he said, "We need to get your things from the motel."

"It won't take long, because I don't have much. When I ran, I barely had enough time to grab some money and clothes. The only reason I have my toiletries and birth control pills is because they were already in my pack. I didn't even have time to get my cell phone."

Birth control pills? *Fuck*. He wasn't touching that subject with a ten-foot pole.

When she'd rolled over on the bed that morning, after he'd spanked her, her panties had still been around her knees, but he deliberately hadn't looked. He'd known that staring at her glossy little bush and maybe even catching a glimpse of the pink folds between her legs was something he couldn't risk. If he had, it would have been nearly impossible to walk away. And if he'd known she might let him fuck her without a condom . . . *Christ.* He wouldn't have stood a chance in hell.

Three years might have passed since he'd last seen her, but the passage of time hadn't lessened the way he felt about her. In a different lifetime, he would have wanted to thoroughly imprint himself on the woman. To mark her. Ink his claim into her blood and bones, so that he could own every part of her. But that wasn't the fucking answer. Not in *this* lifetime. She was too damn young to know what she'd be signing up for with him. And he was too messed up to handle her. Trying to deal with her would drive him bat-shit crazy, and no doubt end up making her hate him within a month. Maybe even weeks. He'd want to tie her up and never let her go. Not for sex, though he definitely liked the idea of her bound and at his mercy. But just to keep her . . . *safe.* To keep her with him, so she couldn't ever slip away.

A healthy relationship required trust. Something Ryder knew he didn't and would *never* have in him. Not for her . . . and not for himself. And it wasn't because he didn't have it in him to stay faithful to a woman he loved and keep his dick in his pants. It was the sheer fact that he would never trust himself not to be a controlling, manipulative asshole.

That, and the fact that he'd be willing to destroy the goddamn world if it meant keeping her safe. If he ever doubted it, all he had to do was remember Minsk and the night his fucking face got ripped open. Then it became pretty fucking clear.

With the short conversation about her things at the motel over, he drove with the radio playing low, the windows down, enjoying the milder weather now that it was easing deeper into fall. He wanted to keep his mouth shut and just enjoy the calm while he kept his eye out for anyone following them. But he couldn't do it. There was something he had to say.

"Listen, about Mike." He scrubbed one hand over the top of his head, then dropped it back to the wheel. "Don't fall for his *I'm just a good ol' boy* routine. He goes through women even faster than Jace did." Jace had been a member of the old unit, and the biggest womanizer the state of Virginia had probably ever seen.

Though he kept his eyes on the road, he could feel the heat of her stare as she turned her head to look at him. "You're telling me this why?"

"I noticed the way he looked at you back at Ben's."

"Hmm. I didn't notice," she murmured, sounding uninterested and like she had something else on her mind. "He was nice, but he's not really my type."

Ryder snorted, finding that hard to believe. Mike was six-four, dark-haired, and green-eyed, with a face and body that probably stopped women in the street when they saw him. And there wasn't a single scar that he knew of on the cocky jackass.

She looked his way again. "What? You don't believe me?"

Rolling his shoulder, he said, "Come on, Lily. The guy's a fucking Adonis."

"Yeah?" She lifted her brows when he glanced at her. "You got the hots for him?"

He grunted something gritty under his breath. "No, but I've got eyes."

Lily bit her tongue, wanting to tell him that he might have eyes, but he still couldn't see what was right in front of his face. Not that it would do her any good. "Well, don't worry about Mike. I'm not going to embarrass you by throwing myself at him or anything. I doubt I'll ever even see him again."

He gave another masculine grunt, and they went back to not talking, until she said, "You don't think Radovich would do anything to your sister, do you?" She'd never met Ryder's sister, Shelby, but she'd read about her in his file. They had different mothers and hadn't grown up together, but when Shelby had been a teenager she'd tracked him down, determined to have a relationship with the brother she'd never even met. She sounded gutsy and loyal, and Lily had a feeling that she'd have really liked her if they'd ever gotten a chance to know each other. She went on, saying, "Some of the things Ben said have got me worrying about it."

"I don't think he'd target her." Stopping at a red light, he turned his head and caught her gaze. "But to be safe I called her in the middle of the night and told her to stay with friends until this is over. She wasn't happy about it, but I promised her it wouldn't be for long."

Oh. So getting rid of her quickly wasn't the only reason he'd sped up the time frame with Rado. Knowing that made her feel a little better. Not much, but a little.

"I also made calls to the other guys in the old unit."

"What did you tell them?"

"I kept it short and simple. Just let them know to watch their backs and keep their eyes open. I didn't mention Rado by name, but they know to be on high alert until I get back to them and give the all clear."

They reached the town's cheapest motel minutes later, parking the Jeep in the crowded lot at the side of the long, rectangular building, and then made their way through the front entrance. Lily was pulling the card key out of her pocket, when a woman's keening cries of pleasure echoed from the room across the hallway. "Wow. Someone sounds like they're having a good time," she murmured, sliding him a laughing look.

A grim smile twisted his mouth. "You just couldn't ignore it, could you?"

"Where's the fun in that?" She gave a soft laugh as she unlocked the door. They stepped into the room's narrow hallway, the bathroom on their right, the bed around the corner, out of sight. She shut the door behind him, then turned and leaned back against it.

"What?" he asked warily, studying the look on her face.

"Nothing." With a little grin, she said, "It's just that I always wanted to be in a sleazy motel room with you."

His expression tightened. "Stop talking shit like that."

"Sorry," she offered with a shrug. "You asked. I was just being honest."

He caught her arm as she started to move past him, forcing her to look up at him. "You really wanted me to fuck you in a cheap motel room?"

His rough voice was thick with disbelief, and Lily made sure to put as much conviction into her gaze as she could as she returned his stare. "Sorry to disillusion you, but despite my tender years, my Scott Ryder fantasies weren't all pink and sweet and idyllic. Yeah, I liked the idea of being held in your arms all night, your body inside mine, while you made love to me. But sometimes . . . sometimes I just wanted you to put me against a door and make me come so hard I screamed, while people out in the hallway could hear every sound."

He sucked in a sharp breath, the grip on her arm tightening. She thought he was going to push her away, but she suddenly found herself pinned against the bathroom door instead. Then he loomed over her, his face right above hers as he stared down at her. *Into* her.

With his chest rising and falling from his hard breaths, he

squeezed his eyes shut. "*Fuck*," he whispered, his voice tight and low.

"What's wrong, Scott? Did I shock you?"

His lashes lifted, and he glared from beneath his dark brows. "Shut up, Lily."

It was probably good advice. But she wasn't going to take it. "You know what? You've got a bad habit of bossing people around. If you want me to shut up, you're going to have to make me."

His hands speared into her hair, curving around her head as he tilted her face back. "Jesus! You just don't know when to fucking quit, do you?" he growled. And then his lips were on her lips, his mouth claiming hers in a hard, violent kiss that was deep and wet and screamingly good. As far as first kisses went, she would have been willing to bet every penny to her name that this one topped the scale. He knew how to do things with his mouth that should have been freaking illegal, the raw, devastating hunger she could taste on his lips and tongue making her whimper with need. He kept complete control, tasting every part of her, the way he breathed and groaned and held her tighter as he sucked on her tongue letting her know exactly how much he was enjoying it.

"Scott," she panted, when he let her come up for air. "I need you so—"

"Don't make me say it again. *Shut up*, Lily." Ryder licked his bottom lip, tasting her there, and went back for a deeper taste of her intoxicating mouth. He didn't want to hear what she needed. He just wanted to keep losing himself in her, pretending there wasn't a mountain of reasons why he should stay the fuck away from her. Moving one hand to her ass and the other across her back, he kept her against him as he turned and went down on his knees, then laid her on the carpeted floor. He'd followed her down, his mouth still eating at hers as if she were some kind of fucking necessity, like water or air. But he couldn't let her be something that he needed, and he had to make sure she understood that going in. So when he finally pulled back for a ragged breath, he looked her right in the eye and forced himself to say, "This is just sex. Do you understand that?"

"Whatever," she groaned, gripping his hair as she tried to yank him back to her. "Just don't stop. God, don't stop."

Stop? He couldn't have stopped if the cheap-as-shit ceiling crashed down on their heads. He'd wanted this for too damn long, and now that he had the feel and the taste of her under his mouth and hands, he couldn't get enough of it. The way she responded to him was so fucking hot, it only made him that much more desperate to have her, his cock hardening to the point of pain. Christ, his goddamn hands were shaking.

Shoving her shirt up, he pulled the cups of her bra down and straddled her hips on his knees. Then he stared down at her pale, pink-tipped breasts. Hard. "Jesus," he groaned, curving his hands under the tender mounds. "You're so fucking beautiful."

"You like them?" she whispered shakily.

"I fucking *love* them. Your tits are perfect, Lily. Fucking perfect." He lowered his head, rubbing his nose between the soft, firm mounds, then turned his head and blindly took one of her tight, pink nipples into his mouth and sucked on her, working the delicious peak with his tongue. He hadn't spent nearly enough time doing this when he'd had her against his front door the night before. There was no way to describe how goddamn incredible she tasted or smelled, her scent making him light-headed, while the taste of her skin just made him fucking hard as nails. At this rate he was going to do some kind of permanent damage to himself if he didn't get inside her, his head only getting lighter as what felt like every ounce of his blood rushed to his dick.

Using one hand to lift her breast to his mouth, Ryder ran the other down her side, loving the way she trembled when he swept the curve of her hip then pushed his hand between her legs, palming her through her shorts.

"I need to touch you," he panted, ripping at the button on her shorts then yanking them down with her panties. It wasn't easy, since he couldn't stop sucking on those firm, perfect tits long enough to move away, but he managed to get them past her knees. She helped him with the rest, working one foot free so that he could spread her legs wide and move between them. His hand went straight to her pussy, and this time there was nothing to keep him from stroking her bare skin, her tender folds slippery and warm beneath his callused fingertips.

"You're so fucking soft," he groaned against her breast, sinking a finger inside her. Then another. He nipped at her, then dragged his tongue across her shiny nipple. "Soft and tight and drenched."

"I want you. So much. I always have," Lily moaned, breathless, her hips arching against his hand, his long fingers driving her wild. "Now get your damn shirt off so I can look at you. I think I'll go crazy if I don't get to see how beautiful you are."

"Christ. Don't say that," he grunted, sitting up just long enough to pull his shirt over his head and toss it behind him before bracing himself back over her on one muscular arm, while his other hand reached between her legs again.

Staring up into his rugged features, Lily thought the expression on his face was so strange. He looked outrageously pissed, but . . . fascinated, as if he liked what he was doing but . . . but didn't *want* to like it.

"Are you always like this when you want a man?" he asked her, thrusting his slick fingers back inside her.

She shook her head, gasping as he reached even deeper, the base of his fingers stretching her tight flesh even wider.

His fingers instantly stilled, a small crease wedged between his brows. "You okay?"

"Yeah," she whispered. "It's just that you're stretching me. A lot."

"I know." He started rubbing her swollen, sensitive clit with the callused tip of his thumb. "Now come."

She blinked as he came down over her, the feel of his hard, muscular chest pressing against her breasts bringing another gasp to her lips. "What?"

"You heard me." His voice was a dark, dangerous rasp in her ear. "Come. Now. Let me feel it."

Before she could tell him that she didn't know how to orgasm on demand, he had his mouth back on her breasts, sucking and licking at her tight nipples until she could feel each rhythmic pull of his mouth between her legs, mirrored inside her sex and her clit. She was pulsing around his pumping fingers in a snug, wet clinch, the thrashing sound of her heartbeat roaring in her ears, growing steadily louder, until it all crashed down on her in a shocking, wrenching eruption of pleasure that had her sobbing and shouting, the muscles in her sex clamping around him so strongly he could barely move his fingers inside her. She had her nails buried in the hard muscles in his shoulders, her eyes squeezed tightly shut as she rode out the powerful waves, surging along with the crazy swells until she was finally floating in a calm, mellow lake of bliss. Her body felt steeped in heat, and she was so wet between her legs she could hear the slick sound it made when he eventually pulled his fingers free.

Seconds later, she heard him growl deep in his throat, the angry, guttural sound bringing her eyes open just in time to see him pulling one of the long fingers he'd had inside her out of his mouth. She cringed, wondering what was wrong with her, when he snarled, "You shouldn't be allowed to taste like this. It's fucking unreal."

Oh! Um, then what was the problem? She shook her head with confusion. "And that pisses you off why exactly?"

"Because now," he bit out, licking off the glistening juices that shone on his other finger, "the taste of your cunt is all I'll be able to think about."

She started to smile, but ended up gasping instead when he suddenly growled again . . . and shoved his face against the very place where his fingers had been. Her back arched as she felt his clever tongue hungrily licking between her drenched folds, and then pushing up inside her, unable to believe how wickedly good it felt. He was working her with a hot, delicious tongue-fuck, his hands digging into her thighs so tightly she knew she'd be bruised. But she didn't care. She just wanted to keep feeling this forever, the reality of having Ryder's mouth on her so much more mind-blowing than anything she'd ever imagined. It was heart-stopping. Would have ruined her for other men if he hadn't already done that all those years ago, without ever even laying a hand on her.

"I can't get enough of you," he groaned, suckling her clit as he shoved those two fingers back inside her, and Lily could feel that blinding, blissful madness start to overtake her all over again. She came screaming this time, hands gripping his hair, pumping herself against his face in a shameless need for more as he replaced his fingers with his tongue, moving it in and out of her. She shouted his name, holding nothing back from him. Not even the parts she knew he didn't want. That she doubted he even thought about, like her heart. But she wasn't going to let that stop her.

"Get inside me," she panted, struggling for breath as she blinked him into focus and watched him slowly lift his head from between her legs, his mouth wet with her juices. He flicked his tongue across his top lip, then the bottom one, so unbelievably sexy she felt a fresh wave of heat and need flood her body, melting her down. "*Please*, Scott. I can't wait. Don't make me wait. Just do it."

AS LILY'S HUSKY words echoed through his head, Ryder suddenly flinched. He felt like a bucket of ice water had just been thrown in his face. Jesus. What the hell had he done?

"We have to stop," he said in a low voice, knowing he had to get away from her. That instant. Before he took this someplace they couldn't go.

"Stop?" She blinked, looking confused. Not to mention completely adorable, with her shirt tucked up under her chin and her face all flushed from her orgasms. "Now?"

Hell yes now. Before he lost what little control he still had left. "We can't do this here. We've got to go, Lil."

"Go?" she whispered, bracing herself on her elbows as he sat back on his heels and reached for his shirt. She watched him pull it on, then shook her head, sending the strawberry blond waves spilling over her shoulders. "I thought we were having sex. You said, 'This is just *sex*.'"

His voice came out like a snarl. "We did."

"Did what?"

"Have sex," he muttered, careful not to look any lower than her face.

"Then did I miss something?" she asked slowly, starting to sound pissed. "Because I have a feeling I'd know if your dick was inside me. I seriously doubt that's something that would go unnoticed, even if you *weren't* huge. Which I could easily tell you are when you were grinding against me this morning!"

"You got oral sex," he grated, using the bottom of his shirt to wipe his mouth. "And you came *twice*. So why the hell are you complaining?"

Her eyes went wide, just before she suddenly scrambled away from him. She used the fall of her hair to hide her face as she quickly sorted out her panties and shorts. "Oral sex!" she muttered under her breath, lifting the cups of her bra before tugging down her shirt. "I can't believe you!"

He glared at her as they moved back to their feet, his dick so hard he knew he was going to be in hell until they finally made it back to his place, where he could grab a freezing-cold shower. Not that it would help. Now that he knew how fucking sweet she tasted, and how hot and wet her tight little pussy could get for him, he doubted anything but a long, hard, bed-breaking fuck would sort him out. Which meant he was seriously screwed, because he needed to keep his goddamn hands, as well as his dick, *off* her. Not *in* her!

Shoving his hair back from his brow, he stepped closer and got right in her face. Well, *over* her face, since he was so much taller than she was. "What is your problem?" he demanded. "It's not like I left you hanging. You came so hard you were screaming and damn near yanking my hair out!" Which he'd loved every second of, and wanted again. The sooner the better.

"Yes, your tongue is incredible and you made me come," she seethed, her green eyes glittering with fire, hands fisted at her sides. "That's not the point. The point is that I thought you were offering *more*. I thought I was getting the complete act, with you over me, holding me down, fucking my brains out!"

He scowled, determined not to let her know how much her words affected him. "Where the hell did you learn to talk like that?"

She looked ready to stomp her foot with frustration. "Like what? An adult? A woman? News flash, Scott: I grew up. A *long* time ago. You need to get your head out of your ass and realize I'm not that gangly seventeen-year-old you met all those years ago."

"I know you're not seventeen." His hooded gaze did a swift pass down her body, before locking back on hers. "And you're sure as hell not gangly."

"Then stop treating me like I need a time-out."

"I'm just trying to be . . . realistic."

This time Lily was the one who made a sound like a growl. "God, you are so frustrating!" She fought the urge to kick him in the shin, figuring she'd end up breaking a toe in her sandals, and forced herself to turn around instead. She was standing at the end of the small hallway now, and the instant she faced the room she had to reach out and brace her hand against the wall. "Oh, shit."

"Son of a bitch!" he snarled from just behind her, obviously staring over her head and getting his first look at her room as well. The next thing she knew he had her trapped between his back and the wall, protecting her with his tall body, a gleaming black 9mm gripped in his powerful hand. She blinked, shocked that she hadn't realized he had the gun tucked into the back of his jeans. He kept her behind him as he edged toward the side of the closet, kicking it open with his foot, making sure no one was hiding inside. He did the same with the bathroom, snapping for her to stay plastered to his back as he checked behind the curtains and under the bed. Only when he was certain the room was clear did he turn around and glare down into her eyes, the scar on his face turning white with his anger. "I swear to God, Lily. You make me lose my fucking mind." His deep voice was low and clipped. "I can't believe I was eating you out on the goddamn floor when there's a psycho killer on your ass!"

"You think it was Rado's men who trashed the room?"

He didn't answer the question, a muscle pulsing hard in his jaw as he looked away from her, taking in the destruction. The bed and pillows had been slashed, the pieces scattered all over the floor, along with the smashed drawers from the upturned dresser and nightstands. Whoever had done this wanted to scare her. It was textbook crime movie stuff, meant to incite panic and fear.

"Get what you need and do it quickly," he said in a flat voice. "We need to get out of here."

"Do you think they're still here?"

"I think they're probably watching the place. So we need to move. Now!" He slipped the gun into the back of his jeans again and grabbed the small, cheap duffel bag that she'd bought a few days ago, shoving her scattered clothes into it. She ran into the bathroom, grabbing the makeup she'd left on the counter, giving it to him to toss into the bag with her clothes. Then he threw the strap over his shoulder, grabbed her hand, and pulled her toward the door. "We're heading to the Jeep from the side exit and you're staying right behind me. Understood?"

She nodded at his back, trying to get control of her fear, knowing it wasn't going to help anything.

His voice was hard and rough as he shot her a sharp look over his shoulder. "Tell me you understand, Lily."

She huffed at his tone. "I understand. I'm not stupid."

"Stupid, no," he muttered, opening the door and carefully checking the corridor in both directions. "But you are definitely stubborn as hell."

She bit her tongue, knowing better than to argue with him as she followed him to the side exit. He kept checking to make sure they were alone, and despite the potential danger, she felt safe because she was with him. He crouched down, quietly telling her to do the same, as they made their way into the full parking lot. They stayed behind one of the rows of cars as they headed toward the Jeep, the lot thankfully empty of other people. She'd just started to breathe a little easier, thinking they were going to make it, when two thugs came out of nowhere. One second she was behind Ryder, his strong hand wrapped around her wrist, and in the next he'd shoved her to the ground, ordering her to hide under the SUV they were in front of as he dropped her bag and faced off against the two dark-haired assholes.

She didn't hide. She was too terrified for his safety to do more than crouch by the SUV's bumper, ready to help him if she could, but worried that she'd only be in his way. It'd been so long since she'd seen him fight—she'd always loved to spy on his sparring sessions when she'd been younger—and she briefly wondered if it would be like she remembered . . . or if civilian living would have lessened his skill and intensity. But she'd been stupid to question his abilities for even that brief second. He wasn't as good as he'd been, he was even *better*, his body moving with a powerful, lethal grace as he immediately went on the offensive. He smashed his elbow into one guy's face, blood spurting from the man's crushed nose as he flipped the thug over his shoulder and slammed his booted foot into the jaw of the other one. Then the guy with the gushing nose fired a wayward shot from the gun he'd yanked off his ankle, making her scream, but Ryder was in full control. He didn't even have to pull his own weapon. He simply spun, grabbed the gun, and tore it from the man's hand while slamming his knee into his groin. As the guy doubled over, snarling something in a Slavic language, Ryder punched him in the face, knocking him out just as the other one jumped on his back. Within seconds he had the man flipped over his head and sprawled across the hot asphalt. With a well-placed kick into the bastard's face, Ryder left him in the same shape as his partner, both of the idiots bleeding and unconscious.

Shoving the thug's gun into her bag, Ryder threw the strap back over his shoulder and took a death grip on her hand, jerking her to her feet and hustling her toward the Jeep. He didn't waste any time getting her inside, then made his way around the front, tossed her bag in the back, and climbed behind the wheel.

"Now what?" she asked, gripping the seat belt with both hands as she watched him crank the engine.

"Rado has obviously figured out where you're at," he said, not even winded from the fight, though he flexed his right hand as if it was sore, before curling it around the steering wheel. "That means he most likely knows you're here with me. We have to assume that my place is being watched."

Her grip on the seat belt tightened. "Which means what?"

His expression was grim as he turned his head and looked out the back window, peeling out of the parking space so fast the tires squealed in protest. "It means we can't go back there," he grunted, giving her a hard look before accelerating out of the lot. "So I'm taking you to that safe house."

FIVE

AS RYDER STEERED THE JEEP THROUGH TOWN, LILY LISTENED
to him talk to Ben on his phone. He told the sheriff what had
happened, then arranged to have a patrol car sent to the motel,
though he doubted Rado's men would still be there. She knew if
she hadn't been with him that he would have taken the time to
question and arrest them himself. Hell, if they'd tried to hurt her,
instead of jumping him, they would have ended up dead. But he'd
left them because he'd wanted to get her out of there as quickly
as possible, his protective instincts making her heart beat just that
tiny bit faster, even though she was still upset that he'd ended
things in the motel room before making love to her. The way she
saw it, if a man wasn't willing to have sex with you after going
down on you, then the odds were high that he just didn't want
you. That hurt. So much that she couldn't think of a single thing
to say to him after he'd ended the call, her arms wrapped tight
around her middle as she tried to put on a brave face.

But it wasn't easy when she felt like a freaking idiot for running to him with her whole *I need to sleep with Ryder before I die* plan. What on earth had she been thinking? The guy had made it clear that he didn't want to get down and dirty with her. Yeah, he'd made her come, but maybe that'd just been because he felt bad for not wanting her the way she wanted him. Which just made her pathetic. She wrapped her arms around herself a little bit tighter and stared out the window.

"The safe house is in the Westbrook neighborhood, on the north side of town," he murmured, breaking the silence. "I have to swing by the station to get the keys, but that should only take a minute. Ben's making arrangements for some extra security at the house, but we should beat them there."

Without looking at him, she asked, "Who's he sending over?"

He lifted his shoulder in a shrug, repeatedly checking the rearview mirror to make sure no one was following them. "I don't know. But once they get there, I'm going to head back over to my place to pick up a few things."

"Won't that be dangerous?"

He shook his head. "Not if I go in on my own. I'll be quick, and I know how to get in without being seen. I'll also grab the stuff that you left in the guest room while I'm there." As if he expected her to argue, he added, "But I won't be gone long."

"Don't worry about it," she murmured, figuring he was itching to get away from her. "Just do what you need to do. But be careful."

She could feel the questioning force of his gaze as he turned his head to glance at her, before looking back at the road. But he didn't say anything, and neither did she.

Thirty minutes later, they were pulling into the driveway of a Spanish-style, single-story house at the edge of a well-to-do neighborhood. Lily wasn't sure what she'd been expecting, but she could understand Ben wanting to unload this place off the city's budget if there wasn't any need for it. Ryder drove up the flower-lined driveway, parking around the side of the house, and they made their way in through the side door using the keys he'd picked up on the way there. They took the time to do a walk-through, familiarizing themselves with the floor plan, and Lily told him she would like to take the smallest of the three bedrooms, so long as it was okay with him. She'd decided she liked its bathroom the best because of the gray and white tiles that covered the floor and the walls. They were similar to the tiles in the bathroom she had in her apartment back in Virginia, and she was desperate for anything that reminded her of home.

Picking her bag up from where Ryder had set it down by the sectional sofa in the living room, she said, "If you don't need me for anything, I'm going to go ahead and grab a shower."

"Another one?" he asked, pushing his hands in his front pockets as they eyed each other across the room. Her hair had still been damp when they'd left his house that morning, so he knew she'd taken one before getting dressed.

Deciding she wasn't going to tiptoe around the issue, she gave him an honest answer. "My bare ass was on that grungy motel room carpet. I'll feel a lot better when I've scoured myself with some soap and hot water."

His gaze got a little sharper, as well as his tone. "You didn't seem to care at the time."

Lily snorted. "Trust me, once the glow faded and I realized what a liar you are, it's all I've been thinking about."

Before Ryder could argue his side of things, she left the room, closing the bedroom door behind her. He sighed, scrubbing a hand over his eyes, a frustrated curse on his lips. Too wound up to sit down, he paced the length of the room a few times, trying to figure out what the hell he was going to do about her. He still hadn't come up with an answer when someone knocked on the front door. Rather than check the security cameras in the control room, he walked over and looked through the peephole, another gritty curse on his lips when he saw Mike Hudson standing out on the doorstep.

"What the hell are you doing here?" he growled, after jerking the door open.

"I'm your second set of hands," Mike replied, a crooked grin kicking up the edge of his mouth.

Ryder's eyes widened. "You are fucking shitting me."

The jackass laughed as he stepped past him into the house, carrying several shopping bags in each hand, the strap of a duffel bag thrown over his shoulder. "'Fraid not, super soldier."

"I'm killing your brother." He shut the door and locked it before turning to face the grinning pretty boy.

Setting the bags down in the tiled entryway, Mike's tone was wry as he said, "This isn't exactly how I wanted to spend my days off, so suck it up and be thankful that I said yes. You could have ended up with Alex."

Ryder winced. Ben's older brother was a good guy, but even more quiet and brooding than he was. The two of them together would have probably driven Lily crazy within an hour.

Then again, he was pretty sure that Alex wouldn't hit on her, since that wasn't his style.

As if he could read his mind, Mike laughed. "Before you suggest a trade, Alex is out of town on one of his P.I. cases. So I'm afraid you're stuck with me. But there are groceries in a few of these," he said, nodding toward the bags on the floor, "and I'll even make dinner tonight. Nothing fancy, but I can do a mean Mexican spread. There's lunch and breakfast stuff, too."

Ryder crossed his arms over his chest, holding back another wince when he realized he and Lily still hadn't eaten that day. Shit. He couldn't believe he'd forgotten to feed her. Pissed that he obviously hadn't been thinking as clearly as he'd thought he was, he asked, "And what's with all the other crap you've brought with you?"

Mike flashed his dimples. "I picked up a few things for Lily."

"What kind of things?" He darted a suspicious look at the bags.

"I just stopped by a few stores in town and grabbed her some stuff. Jeans and tops. Things like that. Figured she wouldn't have much, what with being on the run and all. And Reese sent over some books and movies that she thought she might enjoy."

He grunted in response, wanting to tell Mike to take his "stuff" and shove it up his ass. But he knew Lily probably needed some more things to wear, especially since most of the clothing she'd had back at the motel was likely to be in bad shape after all that destruction. He just wished he'd thought of it himself.

When a half hour had gone by and she still hadn't come out of her room, he went and knocked on her door, telling her that Mike was there. She came out dressed in jeans and a tight tank, her friendly smile for Mike setting his teeth on edge. Then Mike gave her the stuff he'd bought for her, and she actually hugged the jackass, making Ryder want to smash Mike's perfect face in with his fist. After that, he'd figured he'd be in a tense, pissed-off mood for the rest of the day, but he eventually mellowed out when he realized she was treating Mike the same way she'd treated the guys in her dad's unit—one of those friendly, big brother, asexual ways. He'd been the only one of Heller's Hellions she hadn't cut up with easily, and he'd never let himself think about why, knowing the answer could have been damn dangerous to his control.

Either she'd been scared of him, or she'd wanted him, and he hadn't wanted to know which it was at the time.

After they ate some sandwiches and chips, he made the quick trip over to his place for their things, the fact that she was alone with Mike motivating him to move even faster. He talked to Ben again on the phone while he was gone, giving him hell about the Mike situation, which had made Ben laugh, before they got down to the serious stuff. Ben told him that the thugs he'd left in the parking lot had been gone when the deputies arrived. The sheriff had all the available deputies in the county searching the town for any sign of Rado and his crew, and they hoped it wouldn't be long before they had his location.

When Ryder made it back to the safe house, it felt good to see Lily's obvious relief, though he tried not to let it show. But from the wry look on Mike's face, he knew he'd done a shit job of it. The next few hours were spent going over all the security systems in the house, and he explained to Lily that Ben had deputies canvassing the town, searching for any signs of Radovich and his men.

Around six, the two of them helped Mike make dinner, filling the house with the spicy scents of cumin and cilantro. The more she and Mike cut up with each other, the quieter Ryder got, beginning to feel like the proverbial third wheel. Especially when they discovered that they loved the same movies and started jawing about actors and screenwriters. But he suffered in silence, determined not to complain, knowing it would just make him look like a jealous loser. Unfortunately, his patience didn't last past the beginning of the meal. Lily carried their cold Coronas over to the table in the breakfast nook, taking the seat by the window, while Ryder brought over their plates. When he set her rice and tacos down in front of her, she looked up at him with a

deadpan expression and asked, "Do you have anything here besides Mexican food?"

He sent her a quizzical look, remembering it was her favorite,
while Mike snorted on the other side of the table and said, "Lips
would be fine."

Lily giggled. Mike smiled. And Ryder lost the tenuous hold
on his temper. "What the hell is so funny?"

Before Lily could explain, Mike shouted, "Line!" and she
ended up laughing so hard that tears filled her eyes.

"I swear to God," Ryder bit out. "What the fuck is going on?"

"They're just movie quotes," she gasped, trying to stop laughing. "From *The Three Amigos*."

He closed his eyes for a moment, exhaling a rough breath,
then shoved his hand back through his hair and scowled. "Never
heard of it," he muttered, feeling like an idiot as he dropped into
his chair.

Lily blinked. "Ohmygod! Steve Martin. Martin Short. Chevy
Chase. El Guapo and the 'Look up here' scene. Have you really
never seen it? Are you serious?"

His response was dry. "As a heart attack."

With a sympathetic shake of her head, she reached over and
laid her hand on top of his. "We'll have to fix this. As soon as
we're done with this Rado nightmare, I'm buying a copy so we
can watch it."

He looked at her hand, making her aware of what she'd said
and done, then lifted his gaze back to hers and slowly arched a
brow. She looked away as she pulled her hand back, reaching for
her beer and quickly changing the subject. Ryder remained silent
as he ate his food, irritated with himself as he listened to her and
Mike talk about their families and where they'd grown up.

"And your mom?" Mike asked, after wiping his face with his napkin. "Where is she?"

Pushing the rice on her plate around with her fork, she said, "She died when I was five."

Mike winced. "Damn, I'm sorry."

"It's all right." She gave him a little smile. "It was a long time ago."

"So were you one of those teens who gave her old man gray hair?"

"In some respects, probably. But he was a great dad. I'm going to miss the hell out of him."

Ryder fisted his hand on the tabletop, fighting the impulse to reach over and pull her onto his lap, where he could hold her close and comfort her.

"Jesus. I'm sorry. Again," Mike murmured, looking more than a little pissed at himself as he leaned back in his chair. "I wasn't thinking. You just lost him, and here I am bringing him up. I'm an ass."

Shaking her head, she said, "No, it's okay. He wouldn't have wanted everyone acting all maudlin." She was putting on a brave face. But the pain in her voice was unmistakable. "It actually feels good to talk about him."

"You were close?"

She took another drink of her beer, then gave a soft laugh. "Yeah. I probably drove him crazy at times with all the nutty stuff I would do"—she flashed a look at Ryder that he didn't quite know what to make of, then turned her gaze back to Mike—"but I settled down once I moved out. I don't feel the need to push the limits anymore."

Ryder had a feeling she was trying to explain something to

him, but Mike's next question snagged his attention before he could figure out what it was. "And what about men?"

Her head went back as she gave another laugh, this one richer and deeper. "What about them?"

Mike shot Ryder a knowing look as he leaned forward and braced his crossed arms on the table. Then he grinned at Lily as he asked, "Any significant others?"

Ryder tensed in anticipation of her response, but Lily just smirked and turned the tables on Mike. "Any in your life?"

The idiot flashed his dimples. "That would be ladies in my case, not men. And the answer is not yet. But I wouldn't turn my back on her if I found her," he admitted, grabbing his Corona again and tilting the bottle up to his lips. He gave Ryder another quick look that set his teeth on edge, and he suddenly wondered if Ben had sent his brother there with the express instructions to irritate the crap out of him.

"So what about you?" Mike asked her.

Ryder held his breath and kept his gaze on the table. But he was watching her from the corner of his eye as he waited for her to answer the question.

Tucking a strand of hair behind her ear, she said, "No one . . . significant. I've kept pretty busy with work and school, so it feels as if my time hasn't really been my own until now."

"What do you do?"

"I studied art history at school, which my dad didn't think was at all practical, so I also majored in graphic design. I've been doing some freelance work the past few years and have been making good money. I'd taken off until January so that I could go on this boat trip with my dad, visiting a bunch of different places, but when we got back I was planning to open my own business." With a little shrug, she added, "I guess that's still the plan, once this whole . . . *situation* is over."

While they continued to chat, Ryder lost himself in his own thoughts, only half listening to the conversation as it steered toward Mike's work. He couldn't let go of the way Lily had brushed off Mike's question about boyfriends, wondering whom she'd dated after he'd left. If it turned out to be any of the guys from his old unit, he figured he'd probably end up killing them. Or at least tracking them down and making it clear why they'd be smart to *never* go near her again. There'd been so many times, over the years, when he'd been tempted to put his hacking skills to good use and keep electronic tabs on her from afar. But he'd been fully aware of his own weakness. He never would have been able to handle reading about her with another man.

But it didn't mean he wasn't curious as hell about what she'd been up to.

After they cleaned up the kitchen, Lily thanked Mike for an awesome dinner then told them both goodnight, saying that she wanted to read for a while before crashing. Ryder bit the inside of his cheek as he watched her walk away, knowing it would only have led to trouble if she'd stayed. Mike was heading off to better familiarize himself with the surveillance equipment in the control room, which meant he and Lily would have been on their own. Considering what had happened when they'd been alone in her motel room, it was smart to keep some distance between them. But that didn't mean he had to like it.

Knowing he wouldn't be able to sleep if he tried, he changed into a pair of sweatpants and used the house's fitness room for a grueling workout on weights. He then ran five miles on the treadmill, pushing himself to go faster than his usual pace. But it didn't help take his mind off Lily and the reason they were hiding out there. He was still jacked up on restless energy as he grabbed a shower in the bathroom attached to the bedroom he'd taken, which was right across the hall from Lily's. He did his damnedest to stay away from her, but after two hours of fighting the inevitable, he finally gave in with a hoarse curse and crossed the hallway. Mike was taking the first watch, which meant he had until 4 a.m. to fucking lose himself in her. And since staying away appeared beyond his abilities, he planned to use every minute of the time he had.

He didn't bother to knock, not willing to risk her telling him to go away. And she hadn't locked the door. He opened it, keeping his grip on the handle as he walked in, then pushed it shut behind him, flipping the lock. His sharp gaze had found her surprised the second he'd opened the door, and he didn't look away as he took a few steps toward the bed, his heart hammering in his chest like a heavy bass drum.

Christ. He'd been so sure he could keep this from happening, but he'd been an idiot. She'd barely been back in his life for twenty-four hours, and he was already here. In her room. He opened his mouth, closed it, and opened it again. Then he finally just said, "Fuck it."

"What?"

"I said 'Fuck it.' I'm not going to be able to keep my hands off you. I know I should, but it's not gonna happen. So fuck it."

Lily blinked as she set aside the book she'd been reading, unable to believe what he'd just said. She was so excited she wanted to squeal, but was terrified of ruining the moment. He was standing there dressed in nothing more than a well-worn pair of blue jeans that hung low on his hips, his body so gorgeous she was pretty sure she'd started drooling the second she set eyes on him. Broad shouldered. Long legged. Ripped and cut and lean, bringing to mind ancient warriors who fought to the death. She hated the scars that covered his tanned skin, but only because she knew that each mark held a history of violence and pain behind it. They didn't detract from his beauty. If anything, they only made him more gorgeous in her eyes, since they were proof of how incredible he was. How brave and selfless and willing to put himself in harm's way to protect others. God, if she'd been thinking clearly after her father's murder, she would have figured out that Ryder would never let her get away from him once he knew her life was in danger. To do so would have gone against every natural instinct he possessed.

"Is that true?" she whispered, finally finding her voice again. "You can't keep your hands off me?"

"Not unless you tell me no. You understand what I'm saying? You can always tell me no and I'll leave you the hell alone."

Pushing the covers back, she scrambled onto her knees. "No. I mean . . . that's not what I want. I don't want you to leave me alone."

"Be sure, Lily. Because it isn't going to be nice and easy. I've waited too long for it. And the same rules apply." His hands flexed at his sides, his breathing getting deeper as he dragged that intensely erotic gaze down her body, then slowly up to her face again. His expression was raw-honed and deliciously male, full of primitive hunger and intent. "Just sex. That's all I can give you."

"Okay." It wasn't what she wanted, but when it came to this man she'd take what she could get.

His gaze got a little sharper. "You even know what that means?"

Her laugh was husky. "I'm not a starry-eyed virgin, Scott. I understand *just sex*."

She could have sworn he'd flinched when she said the word *virgin*. "I don't want to talk about . . . that," he practically croaked, sounding like a boulder had lodged in his throat.

"Why?" she asked, her own gaze starting to get a little narrow. "You think I'm . . . what? Tarnished? A slut? Because after some of the things I heard Mike say about your reputation today, that would be pretty freaking rich coming from you."

"I hardly expected you to live like a nun," he growled, making a cutting motion with his hand as he stepped closer. "I left. You had every right to sleep with whatever guys you wanted. But that doesn't mean I don't want to kill them."

"Then I'll be sure to keep the names to myself," she offered with a quiet snort.

Something hard and male flashed in his eyes, his voice little more than a throaty whisper. "I could always fuck them out of you, Lil."

Her pulse quickened. "You can certainly try."

"Maybe I will," he said, undoing the top button on his jeans.

Lily bit her lip, stunned by how freaking sexy he looked standing there glowering at her, his muscles bunched beneath his golden skin, his abs rippling as he came another step closer . . . and then another. His jeans were hanging even lower on his hips, the soft denim pulled taut by the massive erection it was trying to contain. He was right at the foot of the bed now, but she held out her hands, stopping him from coming any closer. "Wait!"

He'd started to undo the next button on his jeans, but his fingers stilled, his dark gaze locked hard on hers, waiting for her to speak.

Bracing herself for his answer, she asked, "Are you here because of Mike?"

His head jerked back, his straight brows drawn together in confusion. "What? Why the hell would you ask me that?"

"Because you were jealous," she said daringly, searching his expression. "Is that why you're here? Are you trying to rub it in his face that we're together? To prove a point?"

He took a few hard, deep breaths, keeping her locked in his glittering stare. Then he growled, "I'm here because I couldn't stay away. I don't give a fuck about Mike. I just give a fuck about you."

"Good. Then get rid of those jeans," she said breathlessly, eyeing him hungrily as she moved her legs out from under her and whipped her tank off over her head.

He did just that, and the sight damn near stopped her heart. He swiftly shoved his jeans down, kicking them away, then turned to face her. With his hands fisted at his sides, he let her get a good long look. And, God, did she look. His erection sprang up against his ridged abs, hard and brutal and beautiful, with black hair curling at the base and two heavy testicles hanging low that were in perfect proportion to the rest of him.

It took her a moment to get her tongue working, but she finally managed to say, "Holy hell, you're gorgeous."

He immediately scowled. "Christ, Lily. You don't have to lie."

She shot him a stunned look. "You think I'm lying?"

"I'm no fucking oil painting," he muttered, working his jaw. "I'm scarred inside and out."

"You think I care about your scars? I hate that you were hurt, but they don't change how I see you."

He grunted, obviously deciding he was done talking. He crawled onto the foot of the bed, yanked her ankles between his knees and reached for her panties, ripping them down her legs and tossing them over the side of the bed. Then he ran his big hands down the insides of her trembling thighs, curved them around her knees, and shoved her legs apart, holding them that way as he knelt between them. And after that he just stopped . . . and stared, his chest rising and falling with the jagged rhythm of his breaths.

Resting back on her elbows, her face flushed with embarrassment to be so exposed, she finally asked, "What are you doing?"

He didn't bother looking up as he answered the question, his heavy-lidded gaze fastened on the glistening pink folds of her sex. "I didn't take the time to get a good long look at your pussy at the motel," he said tightly. "Been regretting that ever since."

She swallowed, her face burning even hotter as she felt her body respond to his sexy admission with a warm rush of moisture. She was swelling and softening like a ripe piece of fruit, her insides aching and empty, desperate for him to get on with it and take her. "Oh, God, hurry. Please. I can't wait."

"I know, baby. I'm desperate, too. But I have to get you ready." He let go of one of her knees and slipped two fingers through her drenched slit, separating the puffy folds, then swirled the callused tips of his fingers around her clit.

"Now," she snapped, falling to her back. "I mean it, Scott. I need you now!"

A low, gritty laugh rumbled in his chest as he came down over her, working those two big fingers into her opening. He gave a hard, wet suck to each of her nipples, then lifted higher. "Go on, Lil. Screech at me some more," he whispered in her ear, nipping at the lobe. "Tell me you want me to fuck your tight little pussy."

"I do," she moaned, running her hands down his sleek, muscular back. "I want you to fuck me."

"Say it." He licked the side of her throat, pumping his fingers into her, then rubbing the moisture on them around her opening. "Say it exactly how I said it."

She writhed, wanting him inside her so badly she was ready to scream. "Fine! I want you to fuck my tight little pussy. Now, damn it!"

He gave another one of those low, sexy laughs, and the instant she felt his broad, hot cockhead touching her vulva, her hips jerked up to take him in. But he held himself back, not letting her have it. "Do I need a condom?" he whispered in her ear, bracing himself on his elbows.

"What?"

"I'm clean. I get checked regularly, and I always, *always* use latex. But you said you were on the Pill. So I'm asking if you want me to wear a condom."

"No. No condom. I want to feel you inside me, skin on skin. Every hard, thick inch of you."

His breath left his lungs in a shuddering rush, and he reached down, positioning the flushed head of his cock at her opening. He rubbed it around a little, getting it wet with her lube, and driving her wild in the process. Her skin was hot, tingly, her breaths coming in short, sharp pants that should have been embarrassing, considering he wasn't even inside her yet. But she didn't care. She just wanted him. Needed him so badly she was going out of her mind.

"Don't move!" he grated, when he finally started to push himself in. "Stay still!"

She gasped for air, burning up inside. "Why?"

He groaned, the thick sound rough and male. "Because if you don't, this is going to be over before we even get started."

"But I can't stay still," she moaned, gripping his hips as she tried to pull him deeper inside her.

"You *will*, damn it." He captured her wrists and pulled them over her head. "You're tight as a fucking fist, Lily. I don't want to hurt you."

"You won't," she whispered, feeling desperate, knowing she only had one shot at getting this right. "Do it, Scott. Damn it, just do it. Please. I need you." She knew she was begging, repeating herself. But she couldn't help it. She meant every word. She'd never meant anything more.

He shuddered as he pressed forward, starting to work against her snug resistance as he bore down on her with his weight. Knowing she had to have the timing perfect, Lily waited until he'd pulled back and started pushing forward again before making her move. Lifting her head, she set her teeth into the tight tendon between his neck and shoulder and bit down just as she wound her legs around his hips and slammed her feet into his ass. He roared, jerking hard from the erotic bite, and rammed himself into her with so much force it made her scream. But his shout was even louder.

"What the FUCK, Lily?"

She gasped from the sting of pain as he wrenched back, pulling his cock completely out of her. He shook his head as he looked down, staring at his dick in disbelief, and Lily prayed the best night of her life wasn't about to end in disaster.

SIX

WITH HER BREATH HELD TIGHT IN HER LUNGS, LILY WAITED for the explosion . . . but it never came. Instead, Ryder simply looked up at her and said, "There's blood on my dick." He didn't sound exactly angry. But he didn't sound particularly thrilled with the situation, either.

"I'm sorry," she whispered, aware of the heat rushing beneath her skin, burning in her face. "I was hoping that wouldn't happen. I mean, not at my age."

She could feel his hands shaking as he gripped her thighs, keeping her legs spread apart. He looked from her face, down to her swollen, tender entrance, then up to her face again. "What the fuck, Lily? How in God's name are you still a virgin? You're twenty-five years old." His voice was getting harsher with each word. "What the fuck is going on?"

Swiping at the stupid tears she could feel leaking from her eyes, she said, "Look, I know it's stupid. Just drop it. *Please*."

Ignoring her plea, he reached out and gripped her chin, forcing her to look at him. "Did something happen? Did someone hurt you?"

She sniffed and gave a pained laugh. Oh, God. Yes, she'd been hurt. But not like he meant. He'd hurt her when he left. But she couldn't just blurt that out. Throwing her heart at this guy would send him running from her bed faster than anything.

"No," she lied, chewing on her lower lip. "No one hurt me, Scott. I've just been waiting for the right time."

"And *this* is the right time?" His voice was incredulous, his thick lashes so low she couldn't read the look in his eyes.

"Um, well . . . you know how it is. I might not have a lot of time left."

"Oh, hell. *Don't!*" he forced out through his gritted teeth, bracing himself on his bent arms as he came down over her. "Don't even say that. If you fucked me because you think it's your last chance, I'll—"

"No," she whispered, reaching up to cup his scarred cheek in her hand. "That's not why. I've wanted this forever. You *know* that. I know you do. Even if you don't want to admit it, you knew I wanted you all those years ago. I always did."

He groaned, burying his face in the curve of her throat. "Jesus. You make me so fucking crazy, Lily."

"Yeah, well. Back atcha."

He gave a low, raw laugh, then lifted his head and stared deep into her eyes. "I'm so damn angry at you for not telling me. I could have made it . . . easier."

"I know. I'm sorry. Yell at me later. Just don't leave me. *Please.*"

He opened his mouth, but choked off whatever he'd been about to say the instant he saw the fresh tears in her eyes. "Okay, all right. I'm here," he rasped, pushing her hair back from her face, the look in his hot gaze stealing her breath. She'd never seen a man look at a woman with so much blistering heat and possessiveness. She felt scorched, the fact that it was Ryder who was looking at her like that making her heart feel like it was about to burst from excitement.

For so long. She'd wanted this moment for so damn long, and now she was finally going to have it.

He leaned down, rubbing his lips against hers, the gentle caress mirroring the careful way he started nudging his thick shaft back inside her body. She was sore enough that it burned, but she didn't care, the emotional depth of the moment battering any discomfort she might have felt into obscurity. There was only Ryder and the incredible feel of his heavy penetration as he slowly rocked and nudged and worked his way back in until she had almost every inch of him packed up deep inside her. All the eager little muscles in her sex convulsed around him, holding him tighter, and his breath hissed through his teeth, his body shaking as he struggled to hold still, giving her time to get used to him.

"You okay?" he asked hoarsely.

"Mmm," she moaned, spreading her legs a little wider as she arched her back. He must have liked it because he made a guttural sound in the back of his throat as he started giving her easy strokes that slowly worked him in and out. But while it was easier for her, the muscles in his magnificent body were beyond rigid, carved like steel beneath his hot skin, and she could tell exactly how much it was costing him to keep his control. He was still being careful not to go too deep. Not to be too rough. And she wasn't having it.

"Stop holding back on me," she panted, gripping the powerful muscles in his back, their bodies sliding against each other as their skin misted with sweat.

He grunted, burying his face in the curve of her throat again.
"You're so slick and hot. I'm trying to be careful, but fuck, you
don't make it easy."

"Me? You're the one doing everything. I'm just lying here."

It was a low, pained laugh that vibrated in his chest this time.
"Yeah. But you're lying beneath me all soft and gorgeous, blowing my damn mind."

His words only made her more desperate. "I want it harder. I
mean it, Scott. Let go."

"Christ, Lil. You're gonna be the fucking death of me," he
groaned in her ear, his voice slurred with pleasure as he began
quickening his pace. She moaned, squeezing her hands between
them so that she could feel the rippling of his abs as he fucked
her with that incredible cock, and the cracks in his control started
to show. His strokes became harder, deeper, his hips slamming
into hers with each penetrating lunge, followed by the sexy grind
against her clit before he pulled back and did it again . . . and
again. She clutched at him, coming undone, the raw, powerful
way he moved driving her wild.

He lifted his head, a hard glint in his dark eyes as he exhaled
a harsh breath. "I've never felt anything this good in my entire
life. Nothing that even came close."

She blinked up at him, knowing that everything she felt had
to be showing on her flushed face, burning in her eyes like a
hot, shimmering message. He groaned and held her head in his
hands, then lowered his mouth to hers and kissed her deeply, hungrily, his tongue thrusting and stroking, touching her teeth and
the inner surface of her lips, then tangling with her own. She
melted, sighing into the pleasure, seduced by the tenderness she
could taste in his breathtaking kiss. And thrilled by the way it

mixed with the raw lust as he moved one of his hands down to her knee, lifting it higher, wider, so that he could get even deeper inside her. He fed sexy growls into her mouth as his rhythm picked up, his thrusts so hard they started to shake the bed . . . along with the very foundations of her soul.

She was changing, evolving . . . becoming something lush and warm and full of sensation. She felt transformed, and knew her stupid heart was getting into dangerous territory. As hard-assed as she'd tried to be about the experience, there was no way for her to separate the emotion of the act from the physical. She was hyperaware with every cell of her body that this was *Ryder* between her legs, buried inside her, blowing her mind. The man who owned her without even knowing it. Who didn't want her forever. Just for now. For this blinding moment. She had no guarantee there would even be a second time, and so she surrendered completely, knowing she needed to glean as much from the experience as she could. Secure the memories in a box in her mind that she could protect forever . . . or for however long she had. Memories that no one could ever take away from her. She sobbed at the thought, clinging to him, kissing him back with everything that she felt and feared and ached for, and he went wild, his pounding rhythm shoving her into a devastating orgasm that made her thrash and scream. He swallowed her raw cries with his mouth, drinking them in, then tossed back his head and gave a guttural roar as his own release slammed through him, his cock pulsing and jerking, spurting hot bursts of cum inside her. She kept climaxing, milking his steely shaft with her cushiony inner walls, and they strained together in that tangled, intimate knot until the violent shudders had eased into twitches, their lungs no longer heaving for breath.

Lily closed her eyes and held him tighter, knowing this had been right and perfect and necessary.

And that she'd never be the same again.

RYDER SHOOK HIS head, trying to make sense of what had just happened. When he'd come, it had been unlike anything he'd ever experienced. Yeah, he'd been with more than his fair share of women, and he'd started young. But nothing had ever prepared him for this. For Lily. She was the blow he couldn't recover from. One incredible fuck and she'd somehow taken his memories of other women and burned them to the ground until they were nothing but scattered pieces of ash floating around in his head. The only thing that was solid and real and vibrant in the twisted landscape of his reality was the intoxicating woman trapped beneath him. She was a goddamn live wire of hunger and pleasure and emotion every fucking time he touched her.

He didn't know how he hadn't figured it out immediately last night when he'd had her against his door. That she was the woman in his arms. He'd never felt the way he did with her with anyone else in the world. Which just proved that deep down he'd known it was Lily all along. What a stupid prick, trying to convince himself that he hadn't. He could be such a goddamn idiot at times.

Just look at his fuckup tonight. Not realizing she was a virgin. He didn't even know how to wrap his mind around the fact that he was the only jackass who'd ever filled her with his cock. But he liked it. Liked knowing that no one else had ever known her the way he did. Better not to dwell on it for too long or he might just start beating his chest like a caveman. But now that his head had cleared he wanted some answers. And he wanted them now.

He wasn't as hard as he'd been before he'd blown like a fucking geyser, but he was still firm. Keeping himself buried inside her, Ryder slid his arms beneath her and rolled to his back, then settled his hands on her hips, holding her in place. As she braced her soft palms against his chest and pushed up a little, her silky hair a wild, beautiful mess around her face, he said, "I want some answers, Lily. I want to know how a woman like you could still be a virgin at twenty-five."

Her disgruntled expression was beyond adorable. "I'm not sure what you mean by *a woman like me*."

Rubbing his hands over her hips, loving how soft she was, he said, "Sexy as all get out. A goddamn walking wet dream. What the fuck is going on?"

Her gaze skittered to the side. "I was hoping you wouldn't notice. Not because I wanted to lie to you," she said in a rush, lowering that worried gaze back to his. "I was just hoping to avoid the freak-out."

"I'm not going to freak out," he murmured, biting back a grin. "I'm a grown man, Lil. I don't freak out."

She didn't look like she believed him.

Keeping his tone deliberately calm, he said, "If you'd told me before we got started, I would have done things to make it easier for you." At least he'd have tried. He sure as hell wouldn't have driven himself inside her like a jackhammer before making her come a few times.

"I didn't want easier," she confessed in a low voice, a frown weaving between her slender brows as she held his heavy-lidded stare. "I just wanted *you*. And now you're going to run."

"I'm not going to run," he told her, his cock already getting harder, stretching her tender little pussy wider.

Her eyes went bright at the feel of him getting bigger. "You're not?"

"No. Because then I wouldn't be able to do *this*," he whispered, leaning up to take one of those candy-pink nipples into his mouth as he lifted her hips a little, then jerked her back down on him. Her soft cry of pleasure only made him harder, the drenched heat of her plush, fist-tight little cunt the most perfect thing in the world he'd ever felt. She was full of the cum he'd blasted into her, steeped in her own slick juices, clasping him like a leather glove that pulsed in time to her heartbeat. He moved to her other breast, sucking and licking at the succulent peak, undone by the heady taste of her skin. Then he pulled back, locking his narrow gaze with hers.

"If you're not going to tell me why you stayed a virgin, then at least tell me why you're on the Pill." He curved his hands around her ass as she leaned forward, putting her pussy at the perfect angle for his deepening thrusts. With his knees bent and his feet braced on the bed, he held her in place and pumped up into her, filling her again and again with his thick rod, her virginal body somehow taking every broad inch of him when most women couldn't.

"Because I didn't know," she murmured, closing her eyes. When she opened them again she looked like a woman who was thoroughly enjoying a long, grinding fuck. Rosy mouth and cheeks. Creamy, glistening skin. Glowing eyes beneath the heavy weight of her lashes. She was so goddamn beautiful it hurt just to look at her.

"You didn't know what, Lil?"

His sharp gaze followed her tongue as she wet her lips and moaned, "When I might see you again."

Oh, God. The instant the telling words slipped past her lips, Lily panicked. *Shit.* She couldn't believe she'd just said that to him. To Ryder, the most emotion-wary man in the world. Worried he was going to toss her aside and leave her, she sat straight up, and they both gasped as the position shoved him even deeper inside her.

His jaw was tight. So was his grip on her ass. "Damn it, Lil. Are you okay?" He studied her expression with a worried scowl.

"Yeah. You're just . . . um, really far inside me. And there's a *lot* of you."

His fingers flexed, a hoarse catch of breath at the back of his throat when her body gave a greedy pulse, squeezing his shaft. He closed his eyes for a moment, then slowly opened them. His gaze was somehow even hotter than before, telling her exactly how much he enjoyed the way she felt around him.

"I'm sorry I didn't tell you it was my first time," she whispered. "I just didn't want to scare you off. If you'd known, you wouldn't have touched me."

"I *shouldn't* have touched you." He worked his jaw for a moment, then muttered, "But it wouldn't have stopped me."

"Really?"

"Yeah, really," he breathed out, sliding his hands to her hips again and giving them a firm squeeze.

She couldn't help but smile. "Good," she told him, reaching for his right hand. She held it with both of hers, lifting it to her lips, and pressed a soft kiss to the knuckles he'd bruised fighting Rado's thugs that morning in the parking lot. He groaned and pulled his hand free, curling both hands around her breasts, his thumbs rubbing her nipples. He made her feel so incredible; she wanted to make him feel that way, too. And while she didn't have a lot of hands-on experience, she'd read enough to have some interesting ideas.

Placing her hands on the solid slabs of his chest, Lily shifted her legs so that she could brace herself on the balls of her feet.

Then she spread her knees and started riding him harder as she lifted herself up and down on the thick, scorching inches of his cock. His eyes widened, and she let a slow smile curve her mouth. She watched him lower his gaze, the lust carved into his rugged features impossible to miss, and when she looked down she knew why. The position was erotic as hell, making it easy to see the way her tight, tender entrance was stretched to its limit around his brutal width, the vein-ridged shaft gleaming with moisture every time she lifted, before driving herself back down in a move that hurt but was too good to stop.

"You sure as hell don't fuck like a virgin, Lily."

She fluttered her lashes at him. "That's because I've done every dirty thing you could imagine in my head with you more times than you could count. If imagination were experience, I'd be the slag of the universe."

He laughed, and she gasped as she felt that husky sound move through his body and up into hers, another slow smile curling her lips. "Do that again," she all but purred.

He snorted, looking a little embarrassed. "I can't laugh on command."

"Then I'll help," she said, bracing herself on her knees again so that she could tickle his ribs. His body shuddered beneath her as another deep burst of laughter rumbled up from his chest, the happy sound making her feel ridiculously pleased with herself. He gave a playful growl as he grabbed her wrists and rolled them over, trapping her beneath him as he reversed their positions. For a moment she thought he was going to tickle her back in retaliation, but he reached for the tank top she'd tossed to the far side of the bed instead.

Panting with excitement, Lily watched the muscles in his arms move beneath his golden skin as he easily ripped the tank into several strips of cotton. Within seconds he had her arms over her head, wrists bound together with one of the thin strips of material. Tying the ends around one of the wooden slats in the headboard, he secured her wrists to the bed, making it impossible for her to move away. God, having a naked Scott Ryder between her legs while she was bound and at his mercy was even sexier than she'd dreamed it would be.

He stared down at her with an outrageously wicked look. "I have to admit, I love the feel of your hands on me. But there's something to be said for how beautiful you look like this." She shivered, and he cocked his head a bit to the side. "Scared?"

"No. I couldn't do this with someone else. But I trust you. It makes me hot, knowing you can do whatever you want to me."

"Anything at all."

"That's what I want. I want you to do it all."

His nostrils flared as he pulled in a sharp breath, and his mouth went hard. "Don't do that, Lily. I can think of a hell of a lot of things that would probably freak out a girl like you."

"Yeah? Like what?"

Very slowly, he reached down and rubbed his thumb around the taut skin the broad root of his cock was stretching wide, getting it wet. Then he pulled out about halfway and ran his thumb from her vulva down to the puckered entrance of her anus, pressing against it with the slightest amount of pressure. "What if I put my dick in you here?" he asked her. "Fucked you deep and hard right up this tight little ass?"

She knew her eyes had gone wide with shock. "You like anal sex?"

A sexy smirk tilted his lips. "I like the thought of doing everything with you, Lil. Every raunchy, dirty, explicitly sexual thing you can think of. There isn't any part of you that I don't want to violate and own. So, yeah, I like anal sex. I'll especially like it with you."

"I've, um, never done it before."

He laughed, then looked a little surprised, as if he didn't know what to make of his own reaction. "Seeing as how you were a virgin, I kind of figured you hadn't. But I won't go there tonight," he said, pulling his hand from between her legs as he surged back in, giving her every inch. "I'm not that much of a bastard."

"Then what are you going to do with me?" she asked, liking the way it felt when she pulled a little at her bound wrists.

"Brace your feet on my shoulders, Lily."

She shivered but did as he said, the result leaving her in a position that had her completely open to him. Once again, he could see every intimate, erotic detail, from the glistening juices that were gleaming around the thick base of his cock to the sensitive knot of her hard, pink clit.

"It feels really intense like this." She bit her lip as he withdrew almost to the tip, then shoved himself back inside that swollen little hole. She gasped, thinking that it felt a bit odd to be so exposed when she was unable to cover herself with her hands. But what really threw her was the way he lifted his gaze and locked it with hers, his dark eyes making her feel like he could see right inside of her. Like he could uncover all her secret emotions and dreams that needed to remain hidden if she wanted the chance to keep enjoying him. "We, um, need to turn the light off or something."

"Like hell we do," he grunted, grabbing her behind her knees and pushing them out even wider as he moved over her. "I like you like this. I fucking love it. Don't you dare try to hide from me."

Tendrils of hair stuck to her damp cheek as she shook her head. "I'm not. I just . . ."

His hot stare drilled even deeper into hers. "Do you trust me, Lily?"

"What? Of course I do!"

"Then get over being shy," he bit out, leaning down and taking her mouth in a greedy, explosive kiss that was so freaking hot it probably killed a few of her brain cells. "You wanted this," he said against her lips, thrusting faster . . . *harder*, the heavy lunges slamming his cock impossibly deep. "So now you've got to deal with it. With *me*."

She didn't argue, because there was no hiding how desperately she kissed him back . . . or how turned on she was. She knew he could feel it in the way her tight sex rippled around his massive shaft. She was getting even wetter . . . slicker, a hot, scorching glow burning deep inside her, pumping through her veins. When she came the eruption of ecstasy was so intense she almost passed out, and he was right there with her, his thick cock jerking inside her with powerful bursts as he growled into her mouth, swallowing her cries.

"Jesus, Lil. I think you killed me," he groaned, reaching up to untie the knot securing her wrists once their bodies had finally calmed and they'd caught their breath. He turned off the light and collapsed beside her, burying his face in the curve of her throat as he threw one of his long legs over hers, his fingers tenderly rubbing her wrists as if to ease any ache she might be feeling.

Oh, wow. This was almost as incredible as the sex. The feel and the weight of him holding her. The hot, masculine scent of his skin and the even sound of his breathing as he relaxed. Thank God she'd come here because she would have been seriously pissed if she'd missed out on this. On *him*. She drifted into sleep, mellow and soft, muscles like taffy that'd been warmed in the sun. She remembered him getting up at some point and gently cleaning her between her legs with a warm washcloth, before climbing back into bed with her. Then, later, she woke up cold, wondering why she didn't have his warmth. Maybe he'd gotten up to go to the bathroom. Or to check on Mike. She burrowed under the covers, wanting to wait for him to get back, but drifting into sleep again. But she was tense as thoughts of Radovich kept working their way through her mind, and the nightmares wouldn't leave her alone.

The next thing Lily knew, she was sitting up in bed, her throat hoarse from screaming, and Ryder was rushing into the dark room dressed in his jeans, the door shutting behind him. He quickly flicked the light on low and climbed onto the bed, his back braced against the headboard. Then he pulled her shaking body onto his lap, and held her against his chest. "Jesus, Lil. What were you dreaming about, baby? You must have had a nightmare."

"Nothing," she gasped. "It's nothing."

His arms tightened. "Was it about that night on the boat?"

She squeezed her eyes shut. "I don't want to talk about—"

"Too bad," he grunted, cutting her off. "It's time you tell me. I need to know how you got away that night."

She wanted to argue, to refuse, but she was cuddled naked in his arms, her head resting back on his right biceps, the look in his dark eyes when she lifted her lashes making it clear that this was important to him. He lifted his free hand, pushing her hair back from her face, and the tender touch was her undoing. Forcing the words from her tight throat, she said, "I don't remember a lot from when Rado was talking to my father. That monster and his men were hurting him, torturing him, and I was screaming, fighting, trying to reach him as they held me back. Then Rado sent me off with one of his men until he was ready to deal with me, telling the guy to clean me up so I would be ready for him and the others. So the man . . . he took me down to my state-room." Her face burned as she gave a hard swallow. "And then I played him."

His brows were drawn together in a V, a muscle pulsing in his scarred cheek. "What do you mean?"

She wet her lips, trying to keep her voice steady as she lowered her gaze to his chin, not wanting to see the look in his beautiful eyes when she explained. "I came on to him, acting like I . . . I wanted him over the others. Told him that I'd run away with him if he helped me. That I had a lot of money and would make it worth his while. That I'd be willing to do whatever he wanted, as long as it was just him. So he, um, took the bait and started to kiss me. I hated it, wanting to throw up. But I kissed him back until I knew he was focused on me and not worrying about what I might do."

She could feel the tension creeping into his muscles. "Did he rape you?" he asked in a low, deadly voice.

"He would have. But when he broke the kiss to pull off his shirt, I grabbed his balls and twisted so hard they probably don't work right anymore."

She took a quick peek at his face and caught the twitch at the corner of his mouth. "Good girl," he murmured, rubbing the pad of his thumb beneath her eye. She hadn't even realized that she was quietly crying until he lifted his thumb to his mouth, tasting her tears. Her breath caught as she struggled to remember what she'd been saying.

"What'd you do after that, Lil?"

"Um, I grabbed what I could, stuck it into the waterproof kayaking pack I still use, and snuck out of my room. I made my way to the deck and slipped over the railing, into the water. When I started swimming away, I heard something that made me look back. They were dumping my dad's and Nancy's bodies over the side of the boat."

"Jesus," he hissed, pressing his lips to her forehead. "I'm sorry, baby. I'm so damn sorry. I know I should have told you that before, but things have been . . . *Shit*, I'm just an ass. And I'm sorry." He pulled his head back so that he could catch her gaze again, his expression confused. "But why didn't you want to tell me?"

"I didn't want you to think . . . I don't know. I felt stupid. You would have kicked his ass, while I had to use a ridiculous deception to get free. I guess I just didn't want you to think I was pathetic. I mean, you weren't exactly friendly when I got here."

"You're not pathetic," he said fervently. "You're amazing. You saved your ass when most people would have been catatonic with fear. That took balls and guts and more courage than I can even imagine. I'm proud as hell of you."

The tightness in her chest eased, and she blinked up at him. "Yeah?"

"You bet your sweet little ass, yeah."

"But there was a moment, I don't know how long it lasted, where I started to think my plan wouldn't work. I've never been so scared in my life, Scott. And I felt so horrible, for being afraid of what might happen to me, when my dad and Nancy had already suffered so much."

"No, baby," he rasped, pulling her against his chest. "That's called survival instinct and there's no stopping it. I know for a fact that your dad would have been so damn proud of you."

She tucked her head under his chin and wrapped her arms around his lean torso, hugging him. She thought she probably could have stayed like that for the rest of the night and enjoyed the best sleep of her life, until she remembered that she'd been alone when she'd awakened from her nightmare. "You'd gone back to your room, hadn't you?"

His body stiffened against hers. "Yeah."

Forcing herself to pull out of his arms, she climbed off his lap. "I'm fine, Scott. You can head back to your own bed now. I'm sorry for bothering you."

"Lily, I just—"

"Really, it's okay," she said, cutting him off. "I just need to get some sleep. I'll see you in the morning, okay?"

"Shit," he muttered under his breath, moving to his feet. But he didn't leave her. Instead, he took off his jeans and turned off the light.

"What are you doing?" she asked, when he climbed back onto the bed, pulled the covers over them, and yanked her against his chest, tangling his legs with hers.

"Just shut up and let me hold you," he said into her hair, tucking her head beneath his chin again. "I haven't been able to sleep worth a damn tonight anyway."

She was still hurt that he'd left her, but didn't argue or resist, simply wanting as much time with him as she could get. Lying quietly in his arms, she thought he'd already fallen asleep when his deep voice rumbled above her head in the darkness. "Did you know that you're the only person I know who calls me Scott?"

"Not in my thoughts."

"Huh?"

"I *think* of you as Ryder," she explained. "But I purposefully started using your first name when talking to you a long time ago so that you might notice me. I wanted to be different from all the other girls you knew."

Running his big hand down her back, he said, "You didn't need to do that to get me to notice you, Lil. You were firmly stuck in my head from the first moment I ever saw you, even though you were too damn young for a guy my age."

"Well, I'm a big girl now. So you don't have to feel like a pervert anymore," she teased, cuddling a little closer to his mouthwatering bod as she hitched her leg over his hip.

She could hear the smile in his voice as he said, "Considering some of the things I'd like to do to you, I think the pervert thing is probably still valid." His tone was wry.

"Oh yeah? What kind of things?"

"Things that would be too much for your sore little pussy right now," he rumbled, sliding his hand between her legs and cupping her puffy folds. He slipped his fingertips around her vulva, which was already hot and slick. "God, I love how wet you get for me. But damn, you're really swollen, Lil. I went at you pretty hard tonight."

She moaned low in her throat. "I'm okay."

"Well, let's make it better than okay."

Even though she knew how incredible his mouth was, she was actually sore enough that she didn't think she would be able to fully appreciate his efforts when he pushed her to her back and started kissing his way down the front of her body. But she'd underestimated him and her need for him. Her craving for the way he could make her feel. Her body melted into a pool of hot liquid as he held her open with his thumbs and took his time, licking her slowly, thoroughly, *hungrily*. The hard, husky sounds he made in the back of his throat, along with the feel of his hands as he gripped the insides of her thighs, keeping her pressed open, made it clear that he was really enjoying himself. Even when she started to come, he kept at her, licking and sucking on the tender opening of her body, eating her out in every sense of the word until she was boneless and replete, too steeped in satisfaction to even open her eyes.

"What now?" she asked when he placed a lingering kiss to her still softly pulsing clit, then moved back up beside her.

"What do you mean?" There was a definite edge in his voice, as if he was worried about where she was going with the question.

She trailed her fingertips down the hard ridges on his sexy-as-sin stomach. "Don't I get a turn?"

"You can have your turn later," he said, clearly relieved she'd been talking about giving him head, and not what was happening between them. He grabbed her hand and flattened it against his chest, over the heavy beat of his heart. Then he pulled her close and pressed a gentle kiss to the top of her head. "Right now, just get some sleep. I'll be here until I have to go and take over the watch for Mike. I won't leave you again. I promise."

With those beautiful words drifting through her head, Lily closed her eyes and drifted away.

SEVEN

THE NEXT DAY PROVED TO BE HELL FOR RYDER. SHEER FUCK-
ing hell. He'd wanted to wake Lily up slow and easy, with his dick
already buried deep inside her, where he knew she would be soft
and wet . . . soaking him, hugging him. Had wanted to squeeze
himself in, forcing that mouthwatering cunt to give way for him,
and then ride her with gentle nudges, like a lapping sea, until she'd
finally opened her eyes and stared up at him. There would have
been a small, sexy smile on her pink lips. And it would have been
his signal to fuck her harder, until they were pounding away like
a storm. Hot and raw, with sweat flying and her short nails digging into his back, urging him on. It was a hell of a fantasy. But
he hadn't been able to play it out, since he'd had to leave her to
take over for Mike in the early hours of the morning.

Like a bad sitcom, his luck hadn't improved as the day progressed. Once everyone was up and moving around, he'd kept
trying to snag a moment alone with her but shit just kept getting
in his way. First there were the calls from Ben, giving him frus-

trating updates on the search for Radovich that was so far going
nowhere. When he'd finally gotten off the phone with the sheriff
and tracked Lily down in the living room, where she was reading,
Mike had walked into the room announcing that lunch was ready.
Getting desperate, Ryder had cornered her in the kitchen when
they'd finished eating and managed to steal a hungry, mouthwatering kiss from her. She'd tasted delicious, and the innocent blush
on her cheeks when he'd finally pulled away to suck in some
much-needed oxygen had only cranked up his need to fuck her.
But before they'd even made it out of the kitchen, there was another interruption when Reese showed up at the front door with
her friend Brit. The women had come over to keep Lily company
for the afternoon, and while Ryder appreciated the friendly ges-
ture, he'd still wanted to wring their damn necks for getting in
his way.

Listening to the women chattering away in the living room,
he'd hunkered down with Mike in the control room and focused
his mind on the Radovich problem. He knew Mike had to be
aware of what had happened between him and Lily during the
night, considering how loudly she'd been screaming. But Mike
had been smart enough not to say anything about it, which was
a relief. She might be gutsy as hell in some ways, but Ryder wasn't
sure how much teasing she could take about the two of them
fucking each other's brains out. Especially when it was just a
temporary thing.

A scowl wove its way between his brows as that last thought
twisted through his mind, same as it'd been doing all damn day.
He hated the cramp in his gut that came every time he thought
about the fact that what they had wasn't permanent. He had no
doubt that the end would . . . suck. For both of them. But it wasn't
going to keep him from getting as much of her as he could until

the Rado situation was over and she could haul her little ass back
to Virginia.

*Where I'll never get to see her. Or talk to her. Or hear her
laugh.*

Muttering a guttural curse under his breath, he pushed away
from the desk in the control room, breathing a sigh of relief when
he heard Reese and Brit saying their good-byes. The women had
even stayed to help clean up after dinner, and Ryder had tried to
work out his frustration in the fitness room, then grabbed a
shower while everyone had coffee. But now they were finally
leaving, Mike was taking the first watch again, and Ryder couldn't
wait to get Lily alone.

With a comfortable pair of jeans hanging low on his hips, he
waited in the hallway for Lily to head to her room, anticipation
making his heart pound like a bitch when she turned the corner.
She gave him a shy, sweet smile the second she saw him, and his
damn dick nearly burst through the denim.

"Jesus. I didn't think they were ever gonna leave." He grabbed
her by the waist, jerking her against him, and buried his face in
the curve of her throat. "I can still taste you in my mouth, Lil. I
can't get it out of my head. It's kept me hard the *entire* fucking day."

Her arms wrapped around his neck, and he could hear the
smile in her voice as she crooned, "Aw. Poor baby. That can't have
been comfortable."

"You're telling me," he muttered, herding her into her room
and locking the door behind them. It took him only a handful of
seconds to get rid of her tank top and lacy bra, and then he lifted
her against the front of his body, his face buried between her
perfect tits as he carried her to the bed. "I need help, Lily. I need
you to help me."

Her touch was gentle as she sifted her fingers through the damp locks of his hair. "Not that I'm complaining, but what exactly has gotten into you?"

"What's gotten into me?" He was already leaning over her and pulling down the zipper on her jeans, his shaking hands making the task anything but easy. "How about the fact that I'm dying to get my tongue back *into* you? It's damn near the only thing I can think about, which is seriously fucked, seeing as how I'm meant to be thinking about how to keep you alive."

"You want to go down on me again?" she whispered, still touching his hair, petting him like a wild animal. Which was exactly how he felt with her. Wild and savage and completely out of control.

"Again?" He wrenched her panties down with her jeans, pulled them off her slender legs, then tossed them over his shoulder, his lungs working even harder as he took in the beautiful sight of her spread out naked before him. "I never wanted to stop in the first place. But you were tired last night and needed to get some sleep."

A warm blush started to burn beneath her creamy skin, her bright eyes glowing in a way that made her look impossibly happy, and it pierced something deep in his chest. "You really like it that much?" she asked him, scooting back a little to make room for him as he climbed onto the bed with her.

Loving the way her breath quickened as he crawled over her, he said, "You have the sweetest little cunt I've ever tasted and I just want to keep my face buried in it. So yeah, baby, I definitely like it." He flashed her a sharp smile. "I fucking love it."

She gave him a teasing look through her lashes, her tone coy. "And is your tongue the only thing you were hoping to get back inside me, Deputy? 'Cause I was kinda hoping we could do more."

"I'd love that, too, but we can't," he said wistfully. He'd noticed her wincing a few times when they'd been clearing the table after dinner, and when he thought about how hard they'd gone at it the night before, it hadn't been difficult to figure out why.

Her expression fell. "What? Why not?"

He gave her a knowing look. "Because you're probably sore as hell, Lil."

Oh . . . She was, but Lily wasn't going to let *that* stop her when there was no telling how much longer they had together. "It doesn't matter."

His response was gruff. "It matters to *me*."

Before she could argue, he shoved his hand between her legs, his long fingers slipping through her swollen folds, opening her. He pushed two into her, working them deep, pumping into her tight, wet heat before pulling out. Then he lifted his hand to his mouth and sucked the glistening digits clean. "Fuck," he groaned. "I swear you taste even sweeter today. How is that possible?"

She pushed against his chest, making him roll onto his back. Kneeling beside him, she started yanking at the buttons on the fly of his jeans. "No more of that until I get to mess with your mind the same way you're always messing with mine."

He went so still she didn't even think he was breathing. "You want my cock in your mouth?" The husky rumble in his voice left no doubt that he liked the idea. *A lot.*

"That's exactly what I want."

He raked a hand back through his hair and grimaced, as if the idea caused him pain. "Fine," he growled, lifting his hips to help her as she struggled to pull down his jeans, stripping him bare. "But it'll probably kill me."

Lily started to scowl, until she realized he was teasing her. "I might not have a lot of practice, but surely I can't be *that* bad at it," she said, throwing his jeans over the side of the bed.

He seemed to be having a little trouble breathing as she situated herself between his long, powerful legs, and his eyes were getting heavy. "I have no doubt it'll be the best I've ever had. But my heart might not take it."

She snorted, pressing her forehead to his muscular thigh as she took him in hand. "You'll survive."

"You think I'm joking, but I'm not." He pulled in a deep breath, then slowly let it out. "Seriously, Lil. You have no idea how far this is going to push me."

"Come on. I know you, Scott." And thanks to some of the comments she had heard Mike make, she knew he had a helluva reputation in this little beach community as a guy who liked to fuck but not commit. "You've probably had more head than any other man I've ever known."

SHIT. **EVER SINCE** he'd walked away from her, Ryder had tried screwing Lily Heller out of his memory in a never-ending stream of women. But it hadn't worked, and there'd always been a part of him that felt like hell for even trying. As if he were betraying her somehow. Of course, he'd justified his actions with the belief that she probably had her choice of handsome men whom she willingly shared her body with. Only, that hadn't been the case. Oh, he knew she'd had the opportunity, and that she'd dated, but after last night it was obvious she'd never let anything get too serious between her and another man. He, on the other hand, had slept with more women than he could remember, and it made him cringe. They might not have meant anything to him, but it didn't change the fact that he'd fucked them. If Lily had done the same, he'd want to hunt down every man who'd lost himself in her beautiful little body and make him hurt for it.

Not that he had the right to feel that way. All he'd offered her was sex. It seemed like so little in comparison to what they could have had if he wasn't so screwed up inside. But at least he could offer her a little honesty to go along with it.

Lifting himself onto his elbows, Ryder gave her a sharp look. "I don't give a fuck how many mouths I might have been in. They weren't yours."

She lifted her brows. "And I'm supposed to think that makes a difference?"

His jaw tightened. "Think what you want. But I'm telling you the truth."

She didn't say anything at first. Just stared back at him with those big green eyes. "I guess I better make it count, then," she finally murmured, the husky words followed by a slow lap of her tongue over the very tip of him. Then she took the heavy head inside her mouth, sucking on it, and Ryder felt every drop of blood drain from his brain.

"*Damn it*," he gasped.

She pulled back, keeping her lips against the broad, flushed crown as she asked, "Good damn it? Or bad damn it?"

He pressed the heels of his palms into his eyes as he fell back to the bed, his chest shaking with a gritty burst of laughter. "Uh, that was a *I think I just saw stars* damn it."

"I can live with that." Then the crazy woman set about driving him out of his ever-loving mind.

"Oh, God. Go slow," he panted, reaching down and digging his fingers into her hair, curving them around her head. "Make it last. I don't want this to be over too soon."

She sucked him a little deeper, and he cursed, his back arching as if he'd been jolted with a sharp burst of electricity.

"Fuck!" he snarled, when his legs started to shake, the base of his spine tingling. It was crashing down on him, *hard*, and he couldn't hold it much longer. "I said *slow*, Lily!"

Her soft curls whipped against his thighs as she shook her head. "No. Just let go. I want to feel it."

And she got exactly what she wanted. The instant she sucked him deep again, Lily felt his incredible power blast against her as he slammed over the edge, coming in hot, violent bursts. His flavor was incredible, driving her hunger higher, pushing her craving for him to a place she hadn't even known existed.

"Wow," she whispered, when she finally pulled back and looked up at him. "That was really hot."

"Yeah." Ryder blinked, not even sure what he was saying. He lowered one hand, rubbing his thumb against the corner of her swollen lips, where a drop of his cum was glistening. He could feel his expression tighten, the way she was smiling at him the most beautiful thing he'd ever seen.

"What?" she asked, her head tilting a bit to the side as she studied him in that way that always let her see too much. But in this moment he had nothing to hide. She'd ripped him wide open.

"You." He shook his head, his voice shaking a little, too. "You're so fucking sexy."

A shy laugh slipped from her lips. "Naw. I'm just kneeling here."

He touched his thumb to her bottom lip, rubbing the tip across her white teeth. "You were doing a hell of a lot more than that. And now it's my turn," he said, quickly grabbing her and pinning her beneath him as he reversed their positions.

"You're obsessed!" Lily squealed, laughing as he kissed his way down her torso, until he had his broad shoulders wedged between her legs.

He muffled his laughter against her inner thigh. "You complaining?"

"Hardly. It's just that—"

He cut her off. "Based on the moaning and the screaming you did last night, and in the motel before that"—he lifted his head a little and winked at her—"I kind of thought you like it when I go down on you."

She blinked at him across the trembling length of her body, thinking he was the most gorgeous man in existence, with that hungry look on his face and his mouth already damp from the way he'd rubbed his lips across her tingling sex before looking at her. "Of course I like it," she panted. "If I liked it any more, it'd probably kill me. *My* heart wouldn't be able to take it."

He laughed, a crooked grin on his lips as he kept his eyes locked on hers and stuck his tongue out, giving her clit a slow, deliberate lick. "Mmm," he hummed, pressing his lips to the sensitive bundle of nerves. "I promise not to kill you. So just shut up and let me do my thing."

And, God, was he good at it. As his eyes slid closed and he tilted his head a bit to the side, he went kind of wild on her, leaving no part of her untouched and untasted, the sounds he made only making her burn hotter. Then he slowed, moving his tongue inch by inch, taking his time, making sure she was feeling every second of it. Cranking the tension to an unbearable level. She could see his right biceps flexing as his arm moved faster and faster, and knew he was touching himself while he went down on her. It was sexy as hell, and she wished she had mirrored doors on the closet so that she could watch him in action.

He brought her off so many times she lost count, the breathtaking orgasms melting into each other until she couldn't tell them apart. He was groaning now, breathing hard, his clever tongue rubbing across her pulsing entrance, and she knew he was getting close. Wanting to be wicked and turn him on, she reached down and touched her finger to his tongue, feeling it move against her drenched flesh, and he gave a shocked, guttural growl that she understood perfectly: *He thought her touching him like that, when he was doing what he was doing, was hot as hell . . . and he was about to shoot his load.*

"In my mouth!" she burst out, suddenly pushing against his shoulders.

He lifted his head, blinking, his dark eyes nearly black with passion and lust and achingly emotional things that made her heart skip a beat. "What?"

"I want you in my mouth again," she said in a rush, already scrambling around so that she could put her mouth on him as he moved to his side, looking dazed, his huge fist still pumping his shaft. She licked her lips, then took that dark, gleaming crown between them, moaning at his hot taste, letting him do the rest. Seconds later, he exploded with a harsh shout, blasting in a series of heavy spurts against the back of her throat, his body shuddering from the violent force of his release.

"Christ," he groaned, "you really *are* going to be the death of me."

She smiled as she scooted up beside him, both of them still breathing a little heavy as they lay on their sides facing each other. He stared back at her with an arrested expression on his face, and then slowly, as if he was waiting for her to tell him no, he pushed his hands into her hair and brought her closer as he shifted forward, touching his mouth to hers. She was shocked, wondering if he would actually go through with it—slide his tongue into her mouth after coming in it—when he did. And there was nothing half-assed about the kiss, either. His hands tightened around her head, and he kissed her harder, clearly getting off on tasting himself inside her.

"Never done this"—his voice was low, rough, his lips rubbing against hers—"but I like the way you taste with a part of me inside you, Lil."

She licked his lower lip, which was still sticky with her juices. "Me, too. We taste good together."

"Mmm. We're good together in lots of ways."

He froze, and Lily knew he immediately regretted the words. He was probably beating himself up inside for even thinking them.

Pulling back a little, she reached up and pushed her fingers through his thick, glossy locks. And then she said to hell with everything else, and finally asked the question that had been burning inside her for three long, heartbreaking years. "Why did you leave?"

Rolling to his back, he draped a powerful arm over his eyes and winced. "I don't want to talk about it, Lily."

She absorbed that for a moment, hating it but knowing that she had to accept it. She couldn't make him trust her and open up. But she needed *something*, no matter how small. "Then tell me something else. Anything. Tell me what you did after you left. Why you never called or wrote. Why we never heard from you again."

"It's nothing you need to know or hear." He exhaled a ragged breath, then lowered his arm and turned his head to look at her. "There's a lot you don't need to know or hear. Just enjoy the moment."

She blinked, unable to believe that was his response. "Please, don't do that. Don't treat me like I'm stupid. I'm not a child."

His voice was cold. "And I don't touch you like one."

"But that's how you treat me," she told him, determined not to shout. For once, she didn't want their conversation to spiral into a pointless argument. She just wanted answers. Just needed to know why things had turned out the way they had. "I don't need to be coddled, Scott. I just need to be . . ."

"What?"

She gazed at a distant point on the wall over his shoulder, shaking her head. "Never mind."

"No. Say it."

She forced her gaze back to his. "You want to know why I waited for you?" she asked, sniffing as she swiped at the hot tears that filled her eyes. "Why I couldn't lose myself with another man? Why I can be the way I am with you? It's because I love you, Scott. I'm in love with you. I have been . . . for a long time. For what feels like forever."

He sat up, giving her his back as he threw his legs over the side of the bed. With his elbows braced on his knees, he hung his head forward, his voice little more than a graveled whisper. "You think you know me, but you don't."

She moved to her knees behind him, pressing her hand to the center of his back. "I know I love you."

"Christ, Lily. Don't do this," he groaned, dropping his head into his hands.

She could feel him pulling away from her, closing himself off, and it made her want to scream. And cry. And pray for a way to reach him. "Is this because of your mother? Because of something that happened when you were growing up? Please, just talk to me. I'm begging you."

He flinched, and the powerful muscles beneath his warm skin went rigid. "There's nothing to talk about. Just try to get some sleep."

Letting her hand fall, she shook her head, her heart splintering. "Would it kill you to just open up and tell me something?"

"It might," he muttered.

"God. What happened to you?" she whispered brokenly. "I tell you I love you and you can't even talk to me? I . . . I deserve more than that, Scott."

She was right. She did. And the knowledge made him want to fucking roar with frustration. He knew he needed to get up and leave, but he found himself turning toward her instead. She'd started to move away from him, crawling to the far side of the bed, and he reached for her, shoving one arm under her hips and then yanking her against him as he knelt behind her. She gasped, bracing herself on her elbows, her sweet little ass pressed against his groin. But she didn't say anything. Didn't tell him to fuck off. Already granite hard, Ryder fit his cock to her delicate entrance, a low, guttural sound ripping from his throat as he clutched her hips and rammed himself deep. Her plush, slick sheath fit him like a glove, and he had to suck in a few desperate breaths to keep from shooting off then and there. Then he started to move, the rhythm urgent and raw, and before he knew it he was giving her every part of him. She was too small and he was built too big for this kind of fucking between them, but there didn't seem to be any other way.

With their breathless moans filling the air and the sweat flying, Ryder gave it to her like he'd never allowed himself to do with any other woman. He gave her everything inside him. *Everything.* All the gut-churning hunger and want and need. Because it was all hers. Anything he'd ever thought he'd known about lust or pleasure was nothing compared with this one searing moment, her inner muscles convulsing around him as she came in a wild, beautiful rush, her hot little cunt milking him with each tight, breathtaking spasm. He gritted his teeth, never wanting it to end. Wanting it to go on forever. But it was crashing down on him, and his head went back with a guttural shout as he shuddered and pumped inside her, blasting her with hot, heavy shots of cum, then collapsed over her, his forehead pressed between her trembling shoulders, her own climax still shivering through her.

He hoped like hell that he hadn't hurt her. And wished to God that he knew how to stay away from her.

"Of course you deserve better," he eventually rasped in her ear, when he could finally find his voice. "That's what I've been trying to make you understand, right from the start."

Her hands fisted in the sheets as he pulled his cock from her tight clasp. "I want *you*."

"Christ, Lily. You sure as *fuck* deserve better than that." And with those hoarse words standing between them, Ryder got up, yanked on his jeans, and walked away.

EIGHT

THE FOLLOWING DAY CRAWLED BY IN TENSE, STIFLED INCRE-
ments that saw Lily spending most of her time alone. Mike slept
the first part of the day, since he'd been on night duty again, then
was busy with some computer work Ryder had given him. And
Ryder just basically ignored her, holing himself up in the control
room the entire day. Whenever she'd gone in to try and ask him
a question, he'd been on the phone, acknowledging her with a
brief nod and then acting as if she wasn't even there. She finally
went back to her room and laid down for a nap, exhausted from
lack of sleep and the constant stressing about . . . well, about
everything. Rado. Her life. And the stubborn ex-soldier turned
deputy who was slowly driving her out of her mind. She fell into
a deep, restless sleep, and when she finally opened her eyes the
sun was no longer shining against the room's curtained window.

She got up and changed into one of the new outfits Mike had
bought for her, needing something to cheer her mood a bit. The
skirt was short and denim, with a gauzy short-sleeved blouse that

made her feel flirty and feminine. She hoped Ryder choked on his own tongue when he saw it because she wasn't going to let him just bulldoze his way into her bed again. Not without something seriously changing. She didn't think it would be possible for a person to want someone more than she wanted him, but she couldn't stand to keep ramming headfirst into those walls he kept throwing up between them.

She'd known, going in, that he wasn't thinking in terms of forever. But, damn it, he could at least trust her enough to talk to her and let her in a little. For crying out loud, she'd told him she loved him! It's not like there was anything a person could say that was more trusting and emotionally vulnerable than that. She'd laid her heart on the line and let him know it was his for the taking, if he wanted it.

Unfortunately, he'd made it pretty clear that he didn't.

"Hey, Mike. Is Scott in the control room?" she asked, when she found the DEA agent sitting alone on the sofa in the living room, watching a ball game on the television.

Mike looked her way, shoved a hand back through his hair, and then his gaze quickly skittered away. "No, he's, uh . . . out."

She didn't know why, but something that felt a little like pain started to coil through her belly. She had a bad feeling. Such a bad freaking feeling, and she started breathing a little faster. Had he gone after Rado? Was he off doing something dangerous that could get him hurt or killed? "Out? Out where?"

"I don't really know," he murmured, before he changed the subject. "I thought I'd make us some dinner. You like pesto?"

"Mike, where's Scott?" She knew he wouldn't just leave her with Mike and not come back. No matter how frustrated he might be with her, or angry, he wouldn't bail on her when Rado was still out there. She believed that with every fiber of her being. "What's he doing?"

Scrubbing his hand over the sexy five-o'clock shadow on his jaw, Mike said, "I'm not sure, Lil. All I know is that he said he'd be at the Palm for a few hours."

She pressed a hand to her stomach, her nerves jumping. "The Palm? What is that? A bar? A club?"

Mike looked uncomfortable as hell. "It's just a hangout in town."

Her voice was starting to get a little brittle. "He left us to go and hang out at a bar? Or a nightclub? Which is it, Mike?"

"Lily, let it go. Please."

"Like hell." She didn't want to think about what this meant—but that didn't mean she hadn't already figured it out. Some things were easy to see without a lot of thinking, and this was unfortunately one of them. She just didn't understand why she hadn't realized before. Why she hadn't anticipated it. But then, there'd been a part of her still foolishly hoping that if she ever worked up the nerve to tell Ryder how she felt, he'd fall in line with her dreams and love her back.

God, she really was a naïve little fool. She should have known that he'd run. And from the sound of it, he was determined to—

No, she didn't want to think about it. Not unless she had to. Unless she saw it with her own two eyes and knew, without any doubt, what choice he'd made.

Looking at Mike, she said, "I need you to drive me over there."

His eyes went wide. "What? *Why?*"

"I need to go there. To talk to him. Can you please take me?"

"Fuck, no!" Mike grunted, moving to his feet.

"Then I'm calling a taxi," she muttered, starting to turn away, but Mike reached out and grabbed her arm, pulling her back around.

"You're not calling a damn taxi! There's a fucking terrorist gunning for you, Lily, and Ryder and Ben haven't been able to find where he's hiding. Ryder spent hours on the computer today searching for any cyber links to the guy, and Ben's had every damn deputy in the department scouring the town. Until we know what the hell this bastard is doing, you're not leaving this house."

They wasted another ten minutes arguing, but in the end Mike drove her to the nightclub in his truck, the silence in the cab charged with tension. He seemed pissed at himself for giving in and doing what she wanted, though she hadn't left him much choice. He'd even tried to call Ryder, but Ryder wasn't answering his cell phone, which only made her more anxious. Was he okay? Or was he purposefully avoiding Mike because he wanted to avoid *her*?

A quarter of an hour later, Lily was standing in the already crowded club, her ears ringing from the blaring music, while her eyes burned with tears, and she had her answer. It'd taken her only a handful of seconds to spot Ryder, and now she knew that she'd been right about the bad feeling she'd had. But Ryder wasn't out doing something dangerous. He was too busy feeling up the woman sitting on his lap to worry about catching a terrorist. Lily couldn't see his face behind the woman's waves of strawberry blond hair, but she knew it was him. She recognized his long, jean-clad legs and black boots, the strong forearms and hands that were wrapped around the woman's waist, and the shaggy locks of hair that were visible as he nuzzled his way up the side of her throat. With a small choked sound, Lily pressed a hand against the searing pain in her chest. It was unlike anything she'd ever known, as if a white-hot poker had been stabbed right through the center of her heart.

"Who is she?" she croaked when Mike placed his hand on her shoulder, her voice thick with the tears that were already running down her face.

"I don't know." He sounded as surprised as she was to find Ryder sitting at one of the tables on the edge of the dance floor with some unknown woman in his lap. From the edge of her vision, she watched Mike pull a hand down his face, then slowly shake his head. "Fuck. I shouldn't have brought you here."

"No. This is good. I needed to see this." The last time Ryder had walked out on her, she'd cried for nearly two weeks, then spent three years missing him and hating him and trying to convince herself that she didn't love him, without ever letting another man touch her. Tonight, there was no way in hell she was going to be so pathetic.

Not wanting to give herself time to think about what she was doing, she quickly turned and put her hands on Mike's chest, pushing them up and over his broad shoulders, then around the back of his neck as she tried to pull him down to her.

Mike tensed against her. "What the hell are you doing, Lily?"

"Please, don't tell me no," she said in a rush, going up on her tiptoes. He was even taller than Ryder, which made reaching his mouth anything but easy. "I need this. I can't lose it in front of him. I need this to ground me."

"Shit, he's going to fucking kill me," he growled. But he didn't push her away. He was already pulling her closer.

"Help me," she whispered, knowing he probably couldn't hear the soft plea over the music. But he was staring at her mouth so intently, she was sure he could read the words on her lips. "*Please*."

He groaned deep in his chest, leaning down and giving her

exactly what she wanted. And he was good, too. Better than good. If her heart didn't already belong to someone else, Lily knew Mike Hudson could have rocked her world. But she'd met him too damn late.

Needing to push the pain to a place where she couldn't feel it, she kissed Mike harder, thrilled with his response when he grabbed her ass and jerked her up against him, lifting her off the floor. She felt bad for using him—and knew damn well that it was wrong. But she couldn't make herself stop. She wanted Ryder to see this and know that he hadn't broken her. That she could take his childish shit and throw it right back in his face.

Only . . . she was acting like a child, too.

Hating herself for being such an idiot, Lily pulled back, knowing she needed to apologize to Mike. But she didn't get the chance. All of a sudden Ryder's strong, masculine arm was wrapping around her waist, yanking her away from Mike and plastering her against the front of his body. Then he lowered his head, and his voice was a furious hiss in her ear. "What *the fuck* are you doing?"

Struggling against his hold, she yelled, "Why should you care?"

His arm tightened. "Damn it, Lily."

"Let go of me!" she screamed, prompting him to drag her through the growing crowd of customers and out the back door of the club. She had no idea where his date had run off to, but Mike followed after them with a grim look on his handsome face.

"I wouldn't play with him if I were you." Ryder's voice was like cold steel, completely devoid of emotion. But he was vibrating behind her, his arm wrapped so tightly around her middle she could barely draw a breath, his other arm now banding across her chest to hold her arms in place so she couldn't hit him. "Mike's idea of fun is *way* out of your comfort zone."

"I don't have a comfort zone anymore, thanks to you," she snapped, her voice cracking at the end.

"He'll hurt you."

"Not as badly as you have!" she flung back at him.

He sucked in a sharp breath, and she renewed her struggles, finally managing to break away from him. It was galling to know she'd only succeeded because he'd let her. They were standing in the far corner of the club's back parking lot, close to his Jeep, the night illuminated with the flickering orange glow of a tall light post. The pain in her chest was raw and burning, but she forced it down, determined to see this through and salvage what shreds of her pride she still could.

Looking at Mike, who had stopped a few yards away from them, she said, "I want to go home now."

RYDER GROWLED WITH impatience, thinking it would be a cold day in hell before he let her leave with Mike. "You're not going anywhere until we've talked."

She turned her head and glared at him. "I have nothing to say to you. And I don't want to hear anything that might come out of your lying mouth."

"I haven't lied to you. Not once," he argued, forcing the frustrated words through his clenched teeth. "And you *are* going to listen to me."

She curled her lip at him, trembling with fury. "I don't have to do anything where you're concerned. You didn't even have the balls to talk to me before hooking up with another woman. Do you know how juvenile that is? You are such a jackass!"

"Damn it, Lily. It's not what you think!"

"I don't care what it is. I just want you to leave me alone!"

"That's not gonna happen," he muttered, wiping his hand over his mouth as he struggled to get a hold of his temper and figure out what the fuck he should do. A cold, slick sweat slipped down his spine as he realized just how screwed up things had gotten. From the moment he'd left Lily at the safe house, he hadn't been able to shake the feeling that he should have talked to her before heading off, instead of sneaking out while she'd napped. But he'd been reeling, spinning, feeling like he'd been hit upside the head with a two-by-four. That morning, when he'd opened his eyes, the words she'd said to him the night before had come at him like a fucking wrecking ball, flattening his chest, making it impossible to breathe.

On top of that, he hadn't been able to stop thinking about the danger she was in. He knew Rado was up to something—he just didn't know what. Not a single one of the asshole's thugs had checked out Ryder's house. The bastard was lying low, like a snake in the grass just waiting to strike. He was frustrated by the lack of progress he and the others had made in their search for him, and so he'd reacted like a fucking idiot and gone ahead with what had obviously been a stupid plan. One that had backfired so badly he wanted to beat the living shit out of something. That "something" being the man who was standing off to the side watching them. The man who'd had his tongue down Lily's throat and her sweet little ass in his hands.

"What the hell are you even doing here?" he demanded, taking a step toward her.

"What's the big deal? You left me at the safe—"

"With protection," he growled, cutting her off. "What are you doing here with Mike?"

She crossed her arms over her chest and narrowed her eyes. "Same thing you were from the looks of it."

"I told him to watch you," he bit out, suddenly gripping her shoulders. "Not fuck you!"

"Well, thanks to your little stunt, who I sleep with is no longer any of your business," she shouted up at him. "If I want to go to bed with him, then I'll damn well go to bed with him!"

"The fuck you will!" he bellowed, turning and slamming his fist into the side of his Jeep. He silently cursed himself as pain radiated up his arm. When he turned toward her again she was blinking at him in astonishment. He knew his face was a rigid mask of anger, his lips parted for the hard breaths rushing from his chest. He wasn't just mad, he was furious. But she wasn't afraid of him. She looked more than ready to keep on giving him hell, knowing damn well that he'd never do anything to physically hurt her.

Lifting her chin, she said, "You can't tell me what to do, Scott. You *lost* that right."

"It's not gonna happen, Lily." He felt a muscle pulsing in the hard line of his jaw. "He never gets to lay a fucking finger on you."

Unable to believe his freaking audacity, Lily fought the urge to stomp her foot and scream. "Hello? Are you listening? You don't get to make those decisions for me."

From the corner of her eye, she caught a flash of Mike's dark expression as Ryder came even closer. So close that she had to tilt her head back to hold his blistering glare. "Let me make this clear for you, Lily. You let him touch you, he dies."

"You can't kill every man who touches me!"

"I'll be the *only* man touching you!"

"Why?" she shot back, jabbing her finger into his rock-solid chest. "You don't even want me!"

"Not want you?" he grunted. He gave his head a hard shake, looking as if he was having trouble believing what she'd said.

"Christ, woman. I want you so fucking bad it's driving me out of my goddamn mind. I want you so much I can't fucking think straight half the time!" he roared, and then his mouth was on hers, his hands on her body, and Lily suddenly found herself on her back on the hood of the black Porsche that was parked beside his Jeep. The skirt she was wearing made it easy for him as he shoved her legs apart and pushed between them, kissing her even harder as she tried to resist. But it was impossible. She loved his mouth and his taste too much. Damn it, even hurt and pissed off at him, she still *loved him*, contrary, confusing son of a bitch that he was.

"We can't do this," she hissed, breaking away from the kiss to gasp for air. "We're not alone out here. Mike is with us."

He locked his sharp gaze with hers, breathing in rough, uneven bursts. "Did you know he's into threesomes? And I'm not talking girl-on-girl action. I'm talking two men pounding into a woman at the same time."

"Yeah? Sounds interesting," she drawled, knowing it would only make him angrier.

He leaned down and put his lips against her ear. "Keep pushing me and I'll fuck you right here, Lily. I'll bare that beautiful little pussy between your legs and let him watch it swallow every inch of *my* cock until he gets the picture," he threatened in a guttural rasp. "No other man touches you!"

She was so outraged she could barely speak. "So you can screw around but I can't?"

"I wasn't screwing around!"

"You're such a liar!" she seethed, putting her hands between them so that she could shove at his chest. But she only succeeded in getting him to lift his head.

His eyes were narrowed to hot, glittering slits. "I didn't fuck her. I didn't even kiss her on the lips. Just her neck. Which is more than you can say."

"I kissed him because I was pissed off! I've never been angrier with anyone than I am with you right now!"

"You didn't look like you were hating it!" he shouted, straightening his arms. "You looked ready to screw him on the fucking dance floor!"

Seeing red, Lily slapped him with as much force as she could while lying beneath him, struggling like crazy as he caught her wrists and slammed them down on the hood of the Porsche. "You don't get to judge me," she yelled, glaring into his hard-set face when he looked back down at her. "If I want to kiss another man, I'll kiss another man. I'll do whatever I want with him!"

"The hell you will!"

"You can't stop me!"

"You wanna bet, Lil? Because this is *mine*," he growled, letting go of her wrists so that he could rear back and shove her skirt up to her waist. She gasped, too shocked to try to stop him when he ripped her panties off, no doubt giving Mike an embarrassing shot of her intimate bits before Ryder suddenly shoved his face against her. He went at her slick flesh like a man who'd been starved for years, using his lips and tongue and teeth. He thrust his tongue into her snug opening, fucking her with it, and she dug her nails into his broad shoulders, screaming from the onslaught of sensation. Hot, wet, melting her down into a molten glow. Her skin misted with sweat, mouth open, lungs gasping for air as she shivered and cried out. She knew she should shove him away and tell him to fuck off, but she couldn't. Instead, she braced her feet on the Porsche's hood and shoved herself against his mouth, trapped by her own desperate desire. By her need and want and all the unforgivably stupid shit that was going to land her in a world of heartbreak. He was meant to be her treat. She wasn't supposed to get hung up and serious about him. Just mutual sexual gratification to finally scratch her itch and get him out of her system, before she either died or he walked away. Instead, she'd gone and admitted she was in love with the arrogant, know-everything, have-it-his-way jackass. And now look at her. God, she was so easy when it came to Scott Ryder it was embarrassing!

When she'd finally stopped sobbing and screaming from the violent force of her release, he pressed his forehead to her stomach, his hands keeping a firm grip on her waist. She blinked up at the stars in the nighttime sky, then glanced a little off to her left, and her eyes connected with Mike's burning gaze before he quickly looked away, scanning the parking lot with a strained expression. *Ohmygod*. She was so embarrassed she thought she might pass out.

"Scott, let me go," she whispered, surprised by the ravaged sound of her voice.

He lifted his head, his expression as hard as the gritty "No" that left his lips.

"I'm so pissed at you," she snapped, bracing herself on her elbows. "I'm even more pissed at you for making me come!"

"Yeah, I know." He ran his tongue over his lower lip, licking the glistening juices she'd left there. "Be pissed, Lil. But it isn't going to change anything. I'm just going to shove my tongue up your cunt again and make you come until you're ready to give me what I want."

"You sadistic son of a bitch! What is that?"

He scooted down a little to lick her tight, throbbing clit, and she actually whimpered. Keeping his lips against her, he locked his heavy-lidded gaze with hers and said, "I'll tell you what it is when I've gotten it. In the meantime, I want my tongue back inside you. I want to feel your juicy little pussy coming all over my face. So go ahead and keep yelling at me, Lily. It just makes me want to go down on you even more. I could eat your sweet little cunt out all night long and never get tired."

Oh, God. If she didn't put a stop to this now, she was lost. She loved him too much to win against him. But he was already going at her again, and she was powerless against the waves that slammed into her, her second climax hitting her so fast he didn't even have to work for it. It swelled through her like a storm, the hot, vital throb of pleasure leaving her utterly destroyed.

And completely at his mercy.

FORCING HIMSELF TO stop licking her before she got too sensitive, Ryder rested his forehead against her stomach again as he tried to catch his breath, his body burning with need. His cock was so hard he was a little surprised the jeans had managed to contain him. When he could finally breathe without worrying he was going to blow his load, he turned his head and looked at Mike.

"Point taken," Mike drawled with a tight smile, pushing his hands in his front pockets. "Now maybe you should tell her the truth about what you're doing here, before she decides to smash your nuts in."

"You figured it out?" he asked, pulling her skirt down for her before he straightened and took a step back.

He caught Mike's nod when he looked his way again. "It took me a moment, but I've got it. I had to think about the hair and build. She was the right height. Had the right coloring."

From the corner of his eye, he saw Lily frown as she hopped off the Porsche's hood, and knew she was wondering what the hell Mike was talking about. "What did you figure out?" she asked Mike. But Mike just looked at him, waiting for him to explain.

Locking his gaze on Lily's strained face, Ryder finally forced out the truth, knowing that if he didn't do it now he was going to lose her forever. "It wasn't what you thought."

"Don't try to—"

He gripped her chin, cutting her off. "You're going to listen to me, so shut up and focus."

She glared, but didn't say anything.

"I was *not* on a date with that woman. I was trying to pull off an op."

She actually laughed as she jerked her chin from his grip. "Oh, God. You must think I'm so stupid if you expect me to believe that."

With a fierce scowl, he said, "I admit that it wasn't my smartest idea, and I was wrong not to tell you. But I've been out of my mind worrying about you. So cut me some fucking slack."

"You honestly expect me to believe it was an op? You were licking her neck!"

"It was an act. I needed it to look real." Exhaling a rough breath, he shoved his hair back from his brow. "It's the truth, Lil. I was trying to draw Rado out with a decoy."

"A decoy?"

His voice was raw. "I wanted him to think she was you and make a move on us. I want this shit to be over."

Lily pulled her bottom lip through her teeth, wanting to believe him so badly that she was afraid to. "I thought *I* was meant to be the bait."

"Yeah, that was the idea. To get him here. But when it came to putting you out in the open, I couldn't do it. I couldn't stomach the thought of putting you in danger like that. It nearly killed me just to think about it."

"So that woman. Who is she? A cop?"

He jerked his chin down in a stiff nod. "A deputy who works in one of the neighboring counties. She's trained to handle these types of situations. If Rado and his men had tried to jump us when we left here and headed down to the beach for a walk, she would have been able to take care of herself, giving me the opportunity to take him out."

"And now?"

"It doesn't matter," he muttered. "They obviously haven't caught wind that I'm here. But if they had, I would have screwed the plan to hell when I went after you."

"You could have just told me, Scott."

He tightened his jaw, and she could see the truth in his eyes, even though he didn't say a damn thing.

A bitter laugh fell quietly from her lips. "But you were still reeling from what I said last night, weren't you? You saw this as a way to push me away. You said you only kissed her neck, but just how far would you have been willing to go for your deception?"

"I . . ." He glanced at Mike, then back to her. "Do we have to do this in front of him?"

Lily smirked. "Why not? This is hardly the time to get shy."

Ryder cursed under his breath, then cut another lethal look toward Mike. But the jackass didn't retreat. Instead, he looked at Lily and asked, "Do you need me to stay?"

Shaking her head, she said, "It's okay, Mike. I'm sorry for dragging you into this. Go and enjoy your night."

"You sure you're going to be okay?"

She gave him a watery smile. "I'll be fine. Thanks for your, um . . . help tonight."

Ryder scowled at the crooked grin Mike gave her in return. "You and I will talk tomorrow," he snarled at the smiling jackass.

Mike shot him a wry look. "Whatever you say, man. I'll just wait until you've bundled her up safely in the Jeep, then follow you back to the safe house." Lifting his brows, he added, "Someone's got to be on watch tonight, right?"

He wanted to argue, but knew he needed the bastard's help. He jerked his chin in silent agreement, then looked back at Lily. "Come on. I'm taking you home."

She shook her head again. "That isn't my home, Scott. *None* of this is mine. I don't belong here."

"Just get in the damn Jeep," he grunted, knowing that whatever else was said between them that night, it needed to be done in private.

NINE

THE DRIVE BACK TO THE SAFE HOUSE WAS SHORT, BUT LONG enough for Lily to work through some things in her head. She listened while Ryder phoned the female deputy who'd been in his lap, telling her the op was over and that she could head on home. Then he phoned Ben and told him the plan had fallen through and that he'd be in touch tomorrow. She was surprised to learn that the sheriff had known about the op, but then Ben must have been the one who gave the female deputy the okay to take part. She'd also learned that a backup team of deputies had been waiting in a car just down the road from the club.

Thank God they hadn't been parked in the back lot. It was embarrassing enough, what had happened in front of Mike. She could only be grateful she hadn't lost her mind in front of a group of strangers.

Once they were inside the house, Ryder followed her back to her room and shut the door behind him.

"I'm done," she said, her arms crossed over her chest as she turned to face him. "We're talking *now*. Either you tell me why you left three years ago or I'm leaving."

His expression was hard, but she could have sworn there was a touch of fear in his dark eyes. "If you did, you'd be signing your own death warrant."

"I'm still so upset right now I don't even care."

He worked his jaw as he started to pace in front of her, looking as though he was trying hard to figure out what he should say. "I've tried before to protect people who didn't give a shit and failed," he finally told her. "I couldn't go through that with you."

"Are you talking about Rado?"

He slanted her a grim look. "No. I'm talking about before. By the time I met you, you were a risk I couldn't afford."

"I don't understand." She frowned with confusion. "What makes you think I would have been a risk?"

He stopped in front of her, bracing his hands on his hips, and gave a harsh laugh. "Jesus, Lil. Everything you did back then was a risk."

"Now wait a damn minute," she said hotly, unable to believe he was throwing this in her face. "That's not fair, Scott. I pushed my limits to help . . . to help deal with the things I was feeling. You got to run all over the world, blowing things up. Living on the edge. Getting away from everything. *I* didn't. I needed something to take my stupid mind off how badly I wanted you! Then you left, and I . . ."

"You what?" he grunted, when her voice trailed away.

"I . . . changed." And she had. She'd been broken when he'd left. Crushed. She'd barely wanted to crawl out of bed and go to work, much less go climbing up the side of a mountain or jumping out of an airplane. Shaking off the remembered pain, she looked at him and said, "What happened on that last op in Minsk? What pushed you away from me?"

At first, Lily didn't think he was going to answer her. Then he started pacing again, shoving his hands back through his hair, his voice tight as he said, "I made some bad calls that got soldiers killed because I knew Radovich was a threat to your family, which meant he was a threat to you. And I wasn't willing to live with that." When he looked her way again, she flinched under the raw force of his gaze. "When I realized I was ready to detonate enough explosives to kill an entire city block of innocent people in order to make sure he could never harm you, I knew it was time I let you go. That I got the hell away from you."

Her heart was beating so fast that it hurt, and she swallowed hard. "But you didn't do it, Scott. *Wanting* to do something and actually going through with it are two entirely different things. You *know* that."

He blew out a rough breath, his tall, muscular body vibing with a vicious tension as he continued to pace. "But I almost did. Christ, Lily, you have no idea how badly I wanted to, just so I'd know that bastard could never get to you."

She couldn't stop herself from taking a step toward him. "And you don't think I would have felt the same way about protecting you?"

He stopped pacing and shook his head. "Most women aren't like that."

"Well, I'm not *most* goddamn women," she shot back, her voice cracking with emotion. "I'm the one who wanted you more than life!"

He flinched, then fisted his hands at his sides and bellowed, "You were a fucking child!"

"I wasn't," she argued, swiping at the stupid tears on her face.

"You were just too blind to see it. But take a good look at me now. Tell me if you still think I'm a little girl."

His hot gaze slid up and down her body. "After the things I've done to you, you know I don't. You wanted me to fuck you and I have."

Her laugh was brittle, filled with pain and the longing for things she knew she wasn't ever going to get. "I didn't just want to fuck you. I wanted to *belong* to you. I wanted to make a life with you. Have a family with you. Grow old with you. And you left without even saying a single word to me!"

"And you don't think I'm sorry for that? That it hasn't torn me apart every fucking day I've been away from you?"

"I . . . I don't know," she said, shaking her head. "How could I know? You give me nothing."

"I couldn't!" he roared, swiping his hand through the air. "Fuck, Lily. Listen to what I'm telling you. What I want doesn't matter. The problem is that the two of us together would be like a goddamn natural disaster. We're talking storm of the century!"

"No, that's not true. I think it's all a matter of perspective, Scott. As well as trust. And just for the record, I happen to love storms. They're . . . exciting. And beautiful." She took another step toward him. "If you have the right person by your side, there's nothing in a storm that can hurt you. Except *them*. They hold a power over you. One you end up giving over to them whether you want to or not. Even knowing they might destroy you with it."

He screwed his eyes shut, looking pained, then slowly opened them. "Damn it, Lily. I didn't want to hurt you."

She sniffed. "And yet, that's what you always end up doing."

"I know." His shoulders fell as he watched the tears spilling down her cheeks, his tortured voice little more than a croak.

"Christ, Lil, I'm sorry. I've fucked up so many times with you. I just . . . I thought I was doing the right thing."

"By breaking my heart three years ago? And then, tonight, using your stupid decoy idea as a way to push me away?"

His corded throat worked as he swallowed. "Yes. But when I saw Mike put his hands on you"—he ground his jaw—"I wanted to kill him. I still do."

"Yeah, well, you don't have that right. Only someone who loves me has the right to kill for me."

"I have *every* right when it comes to you," he scraped out, closing the distance between them. He speared his fingers into her hair, holding her head in his rough hands, and put his face right over hers. "You're *mine*. Every beautiful, stubborn, mouth-watering inch of you. You may not believe me, but you *mean* something to me, Lily. A hell of a lot more than any other woman ever has." His voice dropped, and he pressed his forehead to hers. "It's scaring the shit out of me, baby. We're talking pure fucking terror."

"Her perfume," she muttered, turning her head to the side, afraid to let his words into the tenderness of her heart. They could do so much damage in there. "You still smell like her."

"I can fix that." He took his gun from the back of his jeans, set it on the bedside table, then picked her up and carried her into the bathroom. Seconds later they were both naked and she was against the shower's tiled wall, the water misting against her face as Ryder lowered his head and took her tight nipple into the scorching heat of his mouth. With her heartbeat roaring in her ears, she watched the erotic play of his mouth as it skimmed over her flesh. Watched the glistening drops of water cling to his thick lashes, the lush detail the perfect complement to his rugged, outrageous beauty. He was mesmerizing her, steam collecting around their bodies like a primordial mist as his lips found hers, the drugging, head-spinning kisses clouding her mind.

But the feel of his hands suddenly gripping her ass, lifting her off her feet, his hips pushing between her thighs, demanding she make room for him, jerked her back to the moment. His cock was heavy and urgently hard against her cleft, and she knew from the coiling in his muscles that he was only seconds away from burying himself deep.

"Don't come in me," she gasped, watching him from beneath her lashes. "Not tonight."

His sensual mouth flattened into a hard line. "Why?"

"Because that's something that only lovers should do. Not two people who are just fucking each other."

Pushing her wet hair back from her face with his hand, he said, "I've *fucked* a lot of women, Lily. More than I care to admit. I've fucked them without even knowing a damn thing about them. Without caring, except for what I could get out of them. So *don't*, for one goddamn second, look at me and tell me that when I'm buried inside you it's nothing more than fucking. You might not know the difference but *I* do."

The next thing she knew he was carrying her out of the shower, back into the bedroom, and tossing her into the middle of the mattress. Then he stared down at her from the side of the bed, dripping with water, his lean muscles coiled with power beneath the tight stretch of his skin. "Open your legs for me."

"No. I need to—"

"Open your fucking legs, Lily." His deep voice resonated with a sharp bite of command that only made her wetter. "Do it now or I'm spanking your ass."

"Like hell you are," she snapped, rolling over. She tried to crawl away, thinking she could scramble off the other side, but he was too fast. He came down over her hard, flattening her against the damp sheets.

"I know I should let you go, but I can't," he groaned, before doing his best to blow her freaking mind. His mouth was on her everywhere, pressing kisses down her spine, before he turned her over and licked his way from her navel up to her chest. He made thick, sexy sounds under his breath as he moved from one breast to the other, leaving both nipples shiny and throbbing, before moving higher, covering her with his strength and his heat. His hips settled against hers, his heavy shaft rubbing through the drenched folds of her sex. Then he reached down between them, fitting the broad crown against her opening, and started that slow, thick push inside. His hands found her wrists, holding them against the bed, his weight braced on his elbows . . . and his face close to hers. "You feel so fucking *good*, Lil. I can't get enough of you. Of touching you. Of feeling you trapped beneath me."

She arched, shivering as he started to ride her with grinding, devastating thrusts, unable to believe how quickly he could melt her down. Make her ache. Her pulse raced, body clenching, her head thrashing as a lush, shattering burst of pleasure slammed into her so hard she screamed like someone in pain, sobbing and crying. When she'd finally quieted, she realized he'd been waiting for her to calm before letting himself experience his own release. Looking savagely gorgeous, he gritted his teeth and shoved himself deep, holding there as he came, and Lily knew this was why he'd waited. He'd wanted her to feel every exquisite throb and pulse of his magnificent cock as he blasted inside her, filling her up. When he finally drew back, pulling his shaft from her greedy clasp, he braced himself on a straight arm at her side, his other hand pressed against her inner thigh, and stared between her legs.

"What are you doing?" she whispered.

"Watching my cum drip out of you." He ran his fingertips over her drenched vulva and lower, where she could feel his semen sliding down, then looked up at her from under his lashes. "I could never get tired of seeing that. It's so fucking beautiful." He took a deep breath, and his voice got even huskier. "I want all of you, Lily."

"I've given you everything," she breathed.

"Almost." His teeth nipped her earlobe as he came down on top of her, one hand braced by her head while the other curved around her hip to grab her ass. With his fingertips slipping into the crease, rubbing against the sensitive flesh there, he said, "I want it all. Every part of you."

Although it wasn't something that she had ever thought she would experience, Lily surrendered completely, trusting him to take care of her and bring her pleasure in an act that was far more erotic than anything she'd ever imagined she would engage in. He used her baby oil to lube his cock, then positioned her on her hands and knees as he knelt behind her. She gripped the slats in the headboard with white knuckles, not really knowing what to expect. She'd enjoyed his thumb touching her there—but his erection penetrating the tight hole might be another matter entirely. She braced herself, but he wasn't in any rush, soothing her with his touch and his seductive words as he told her how much he wanted her, needed her, owned her. He said she was *his* again and again, his voice turning guttural as he finally started to work that massive, vein-ridged shaft inside her. She panted, gasping, eyes squeezed shut against the muted glow of light spilling in from the bathroom. She hadn't expected the pleasure to be quite so strong, and she trembled, shaking, sounds crawling up from her throat that spurred him on, letting him know without words that she was enjoying herself.

"You are so fucking incredible, Lil." He pulled her up so that his mouth was at her ear, and filled one hand with her breast, pinching her nipple, while the other burrowed between her legs, stroking her clit. He was all the way in now, and he held her against him like that as he started to move, pumping into her with slow, thick lunges that made her desperate for more. He moved the fingers on her clit to her vulva, pushing them inside her with a greedy, sharp-edged hunger, as if he wanted to be everywhere at once.

"Give me your mouth," he growled, and she turned her head, crying out as his tongue thrust past her lips. He was filling every part of her, and it was too much, pushing her over the edge. She came hard and wet and long, sobbing into his mouth. He kissed her more aggressively than he ever had before, then started fucking her harder as he curved her forward, back down to the bed, and followed her over. With a harsh shout, he buried his face in the curve of her throat and rammed himself deep, pulsing inside her in a long, shuddering climax that left them both wrecked. When he finally stirred and carefully pulled out, he lifted her into his arms and carried her back into the shower, soothing her sore body with the hot water and steam, carefully washing and caring for her. As his rough fingers gently touched the puckered entrance where he'd been buried, he softly growled, "No one but me," in her ear, then moved his fingers to her swollen vulva, touching her there as well. "I mean that, Lily. Only me. You're *mine*."

She nodded weakly, too limp to even be embarrassed by anything that they'd done. It had felt right. And the raw, aggressive way that he'd staked his claim on her had felt right, too.

"I can handle you, Scott. I will be whatever you need. You just have to be honest with me."

"All I need is you," he told her, and it was true. With Lily, the games he played for control didn't matter. There were no rules with her. No boundaries. He just wanted to consume her in every possible way and make himself a permanent part of her life. Make a *new* life with her. One that didn't have any ties to the past. One that looked, for once, to the future. He just didn't know how to make that happen. How to fix what was wrong with him, so that he could be what *she* needed.

They finally dragged themselves from the shower, and he dried her with a towel, before carrying her back into the bedroom. He stripped off the damp sheets, tossed some dry blankets over the mattress, and then they got into bed. She cuddled against him in the darkness, with her back to his chest, his arms wrapped tight around her. Though her breathing was slow and even, he knew she hadn't yet fallen asleep. He hadn't planned on making the confession, but he suddenly heard himself saying, "My mom was a junkie." He had to swallow against the knot in his throat, but forced himself to keep going. "Not party drugs. The hard stuff. The kind that left you drooling on the kitchen floor, while your kid tried his best to drag you to bed. On the nights you actually made it home."

"That couldn't have been easy," she said quietly, lifting his hand to her lips and softly kissing his battered knuckles.

"It sucked. I never knew when I was going to find her passed out in her vomit or screwing some dealer on the kitchen table or no longer breathing. She finally OD'd when I was sixteen, and I . . . I decided from that point on that I never wanted anyone to mean anything to me. That I didn't want to feel responsible for keeping someone I cared about alive."

When he fell silent, she didn't push him for anything more. She simply rolled over in his arms, cupped his face in her hands, and tenderly kissed his mouth. Something hot and vibrant and tender rushed through him, his hands pressing against her back, locking her against him as he deepened the kiss, slipping his tongue between her lips, her sweet taste somehow washing away the bitterness of his past and replacing it with something that felt strangely like . . . *hope.*

They kissed for what felt like hours, neither pushing the intimacy to the next level, as if they just wanted to stay lost in the moment, until exhaustion finally claimed them. They slept in a tangled knot, his palm resting against the center of her chest, as if he could hold the rhythm of her heart in his hand. He slipped his other hand under her hair and curled it around her nape, as if he could hold *her* forever.

But their time was already running out.

TEN

RYDER WASN'T SURE WHAT IT WAS THAT HAD WOKEN HIM. He'd heard something, but it hadn't been loud. Maybe a creak in the hallway or the rasp of a door being opened. But it'd been enough to catch his attention.

He woke Lily up as he pulled out of her arms, throwing his legs over the side of the bed, careful not to make a sound.

"Scott?" she whispered groggily, lifting up on her elbow.

"Shh."

"What's going on?"

Though he didn't have any proof, he listened to what his gut was telling him. If he was wrong, then he'd let her and Mike have a good laugh at his expense about it later. But he wasn't going to second-guess his instincts. Not when Lily's life was on the line. "It's Rado," he told her. "He's here."

He heard her stifled gasp, but she was too smart to cry out. They both got to their feet and silently dressed. He pulled his cell phone from his back pocket, only to find that the battery had died on him. *Shit*. And there wasn't a landline in the room. Grabbing his gun from the bedside table, he checked the clip, then curled the fingers of his free hand around Lily's wrist and motioned for her to stay behind him as he made his way over to the door. There was a soft scrape of sound as he started to pull the door open, his hand now gripping her arm as he positioned her against the wall. If someone was in the hallway, he didn't want them getting a clear shot at Lily when he opened the door.

Forcing himself to stay loose and calm, Ryder took a quick look around the edge of the doorway. The hallway was clear in both directions, the low glow of a light in the living room relieving the shadows. He listened for any sounds, but the house was silent, and he wondered where Mike was. If Rado and his men had found the safe house, the odds were high that they'd followed them from the club, which meant they already knew about Mike. It also meant they'd probably been watching him and Lily in the parking lot, and his gut cramped, his lips pulling back from his teeth as he choked back a snarl. He should have never put her in that position, damn it. He'd let his jealousy overrule his common sense, and had failed to protect her. Jesus. He was such a fucking jackass!

And this is not the time for this shit. Not if I want to keep her alive.

Taking a deep breath, Ryder shoved the fury back and focused instead on the problem at hand. He was about to let go of Lily's arm and step into the hallway, when he heard a deep voice say, "Drop the gun and kick it over to me or I shoot her."

Fuck! The gritty, accented words had come from across the hall, where Yuri Radovich was now standing in the open doorway to Ryder's room, gun in hand. The sound he'd heard had probably been when his door was opened, and he thanked God the asshole had chosen to search that room first.

"You can't shoot her if you don't have a shot," Ryder replied, tightening his grip on Lily's arm. But the monster wasn't fooled. With a low laugh, Rado eyed the position of Ryder's body and the visible portion of his arm, then shifted his aim. If he fired the powerful 9mm now, the bullet would go right through the wall and into Lily.

Son of a fucking bitch.

As if she could read his mind, Lily said, *"Don't."* Her low voice vibrated with anger. "Don't you dare do it, Scott. You know he's going to kill me anyway. Don't you dare give him your weapon and leave yourself unprotected!"

"Smart girl, your Lily. But do you really want to stand there and watch her bleed out, knowing you could have prolonged the moment?" Radovich murmured. "Maybe have even given the men who will no doubt be rushing to your rescue a chance to get here in time? We disabled several of the alarm systems you had in place. But who knows if we got them all, eh?"

The bastard was right. He had to buy them more time. Dropping his gun to the floor, Ryder kicked it across the hall, Lily's shocked gasp echoing in his ears as he watched Radovich squat down to retrieve the weapon.

With a gun in each hand now, Radovich moved forward, nearing the doorway to Lily's room, and Ryder yanked her behind him, using his body as a shield as he backed away from the door. With Radovich standing in the semi-lit hallway, he had a clearer view of the terrorist, and the man was just as ugly as he remembered. Tall and bulky with an oily head of thinning hair and jowls like a bulldog, he had a crooked nose that sported red veins from too much vodka over too many years. He smelled like sweat and smoke and something sour, the combination enough to turn your stomach if you took too many deep breaths.

"I know what you were trying to do at the club tonight, Mr. Ryder," Rado drawled with a gloating smile, his Slavic accent adding a guttural edge to his words. "You wanted to draw me out. And it worked." His smiled widened. "Just not quite the way you wanted, eh?"

"You came alone?"

"Of course not. My men are dealing with the sheriff's brother as we speak. So I'm afraid he won't be much help to you this evening."

Ryder shoved any worry about Mike to the back of his mind, knowing he couldn't let it get to him. Not now, when he had to find a way to get Lily through this alive. Stalling, hoping like hell that Mike had gotten the chance to call Ben, he asked, "How did you know where to find her?"

Rado's heavy-lidded eyes glittered with triumph. "Given what I know about *you*, I thought it a safe bet that she would run here for help. Who better to protect her than the man who would die for her?"

"What do you know about me?" he demanded, the hairs on the back of his neck rising as dread slithered through him like a knife. "What the hell are you talking about?"

Radovich glanced at the right side of his face, then smirked. "The night I gave you that pretty scar, Mr. Ryder. The night you and your men destroyed nearly everything I'd built before you were captured. You made your feelings regarding the girl painfully obvious."

He shook his head, trying to remember, to understand what the jackass was talking about. He remembered Rado's threats . . . but not what he'd said in response. Only what he'd been willing to do in order to stop him.

Obviously relishing the sound of his own voice, Rado said, "I was enjoying myself that night, telling you about your friends who had already died, then promising you that I would take out Heller and everyone that you had ever cared about in this world. That's when you came at me like a rabid dog, screaming the name *Lily* as you tried to kill me. You had so many injuries you could barely stand, but you kept coming, somehow staying on your feet, swearing that you would gut me before ever letting me touch her. When you were close enough I slashed your face. I just wish I had taken the time to kill you then, instead of leaving you half-dead on the floor to deal with later. I'd wanted more time to properly see to your torture."

Ryder tried to remember, but his memories were hazy. He just recalled being driven beyond sanity by Rado's threats, knowing he needed to kill the bastard before the terrorist harmed Lily. He'd been fueled by raw emotion, rather than tactical skill, and it had nearly cost him his life. In his blind rage, he'd allowed the bastard to cut him. But like Radovich had just said, he'd been left alone when something had drawn the terrorist and his men to another part of the building. When Ryder had finally pulled himself back to his feet, he'd almost done the unthinkable and blown up the entire city block using the explosives that were stored in the room just to ensure that the bastard was killed. But then Rado had returned. And he'd been alone. Knowing he had only moments before the rest of Rado's men arrived, Ryder had shoved the knife that'd been hidden in the sole of his left boot right through Radovich's heart. The terrorist had collapsed, blood pooling beneath him as more bubbled on his lips, and Ryder had escaped out the second-story window, managing to make it to the safety of his team's mobile command center by sheer force of will.

He'd never realized what he'd revealed in those telling moments that he and Radovich had faced off against each other.

Even after Lily had run to him, he'd been thinking the terrorist
wanted her because of Heller. But it'd been because of *him*.

Son of a bitch. He couldn't deal with this now. Had to somehow shove it down with all the other shit he would have to face
once this fucker was no longer breathing. It didn't matter that
Rado had the guns. He wasn't going to let this bastard win. If he
had to give his own life to save Lily's then he would. He had no
qualms about dying to keep her alive. But if it came to that, he
was taking the jackass with him.

"And what now?" he asked, curling his lip in a sneer. "Are
you really such a pussy that you're going to just shoot me?"

Radovich lifted his bushy brows. "What do you suggest?"

His voice was low and controlled. "Put the gun down and
fight me, man to man."

"Last time we did that, you didn't fare so well," Rado drawled,
eyeing his scar.

Ryder gave him a sharp smile. "Then what are you afraid of?"

Color rose in the terrorist's face and his eyes narrowed. "I'm
not afraid, Mr. Ryder. But I'm also not stupid."

Going straight for the bastard's ego, he shook his head and
laughed. "I know a pussy when I smell one, Radovich. What's
the problem? Are the years catching up to you? You just don't
have the balls to fight me now, do you?"

Radovich came a step closer, radiating cold, deadly rage. "I
think, instead, I will enjoy putting bullets in your most vulnerable body parts, one by one, to make up for the shit you forced
me to live through after stabbing me in the heart. I spent nearly
six months in a coma, then another three in recovery. Almost a
year went by before I could climb out of bed and deal with the
scum that had tried to take over my crew while I was healing.
And finally, when I was once again at the top, I knew it was time

to come after the man who had tried so hard to destroy me." Rado's gaze slid to Lily, and his eyes gleamed with malice as they came back to Ryder. "But first," he snarled, spittle spraying from his wide lips, "I wanted to take away everything that had ever meant anything to him. I wanted to start with what meant *most*. Which is why I plan on leaving you alive just long enough for you to watch me take your woman, ripping her into pieces, before I finally take your *life*!"

"Better yet, asshole, why don't you just drop the guns?" Mike rasped, the barrel of his 9mm pressed against the back of Rado's head. "Drop them and kick them over to Ryder. Now! Before I decide these walls will look more lively with your fucking pea-sized brain splattered all over them."

The pistols made a heavy clunking sound as they hit the floor, Rado's kick skidding them toward Ryder, who stopped them with his foot. "Take it," he said to Lily, after picking up both weapons and holding Rado's out to her.

Slipping his own gun into the back of his jeans, he shot a glance at Mike, thankful as hell to see him. "The others?" he asked, wondering about the terrorist's men.

Mike's voice was flat, his gaze hooded. "Dead."

Cracking his knuckles, Ryder said, "Hear that, Rado? Your dumbass goons failed. It's just me and you now."

"Scott," Lily whispered, touching the back of his arm. "You don't have to do this."

He looked at Mike. "Get her out of here."

"No!" She moved to the far side of the room, holding her hands out in front of her, as if she could stop Mike from grabbing her. But she was looking at Ryder as she said, "Please, don't make me leave you."

Mike forced a furious-looking Radovich into the bedroom

ahead of him, his gun still pointed at the fucker as Mike made his way over to Lily. But he didn't try to force her out. He simply positioned her in the open doorway, and put his body in front of hers, making it clear that he would protect her with his life. Satisfied that she was safe, Ryder turned his attention to the man he was going to enjoy the hell out of killing. "Now we deal with this in a fair fight, you ugly son of a bitch."

He would have been lying if he'd said he thought it would be easy. He knew from the intel he'd collected on Radovich that the terrorist had grown up on the streets in one of the poorest cities in Eastern Europe, where he'd had to battle daily for survival. The man also had nearly three inches on Ryder and outweighed him by a good fifty pounds, with a right hook that felt like a fucking wrecking ball. But Ryder had speed and training on his side, and the bone-deep determination to wipe the floor with the asshole for what he'd done to Lily and her family. They traded a dozen punches, landing hammering blows to the other's ribs, kidneys, and face. A stream of red poured from the terrorist's nose, while Ryder's lip was busted open, his tongue tasting the sharp, metallic tang of his own blood. He could tell Radovich was tiring, his fondness for vodka taking its toll on his stamina, and Ryder moved his head from side to side while retaining his fighting stance, anticipating the bastard's next move. When Rado suddenly rushed him, trying to take him to the floor, Ryder spun to the side and rammed his knee into Rado's belly, doubling him over. He followed with a swift uppercut to his chin that snapped his head back, then a powerful right hook to his jaw that sent the asshole crashing to the floor. Radovich groaned, looking dazed, not even trying to get up.

Taking his gun from the back of his jeans, Ryder aimed the barrel at the center of Rado's greasy forehead. Then he lifted his gaze and looked at Lily, who was peeking around Mike's arm. "Go to my room."

Tears filled her eyes, her gaze darting to the scar on his cheek. "I don't want to leave you with him," she whispered, the words thick with fear.

"I know. But I need you to do this for me, Lil. And I don't need an argument. Please. Just go."

She frowned, but nodded. She didn't look back as she made the short walk across the hallway, then closed the door to his bedroom behind her.

"I'll wait in the hallway," Mike said, making it clear that he didn't object to what was about to happen.

When they were alone, Ryder looked back down at Radovich. "You can't shoot a man who's already down," the terrorist said with a gritty laugh.

A cold smile twisted Ryder's mouth. "That just shows how little you know me."

"You're a lawman. A soldier," Rado sneered in his thick accent. "Your honor ties your hands and makes you weak. Your mercy makes you pathetic."

"You came after my woman and you think I'm going to show you fucking mercy, you miserable piece of shit?"

Radovich wiped at the blood on his face, his upper body twisted to the side as he braced himself on an elbow. "You don't have any choice," he muttered.

"If the choice is between my honor and her safety," Ryder said in a low, deadly voice, "then it isn't any choice at all."

As if he was finally starting to get the picture, the terrorist's eyes widened. "Are you serious? You're going to let a little snatch decide your actions?"

"She's my fucking heart, you stupid prick. And you're nothing more than a dead man." He lowered his aim, then fired, shooting the bastard straight through the heart, killing him instantly. But he put a second bullet through Rado's forehead, and would have kept firing if not for the fact that Lily was waiting for him.

Stepping over Radovich's stinking body, Ryder intended to find her and just . . . hold her, but Ben and a small army of deputies suddenly arrived and almost two hours had gone by before Ryder finally made his way to his bedroom. He found her inside, talking on the phone, making arrangements for what sounded like a car service to take her to the airport.

"Lily? What's going on?" he demanded, shutting the door to the room behind him.

She set the phone down on the bedside table, then turned to face him. Her face was tense and pale. "Now that Radovich is dead," she said quietly, wrapping her arms around her middle, "I . . . um, called one of my friends in Virginia. She's bought me a plane ticket home and paid for a car to pick me up. I just needed to give the driver the address."

"What the fuck? You're just gonna up and leave?" he scraped out, while inside he was thinking *No, don't do this. Don't make me lose you. Not now* . . .

She sniffed, then took a deep breath before saying, "I've had some time to think while I was waiting for you, and I . . . I know you well enough to know that what he said about you being the reason he came after me is only going to push you away from me again. I can't go through that," she whispered, swiping at her tears with her fingertips. "Not again. I have to get out before it happens."

"That doesn't make any fucking sense!"

Her mouth trembled. "I'm sorry, Scott. I just . . . I know we won't be able to get through this without something strong holding us together. Without something that's permanent and lasting. I know . . . I know you care about me. But that's not going to be enough."

Christ. This was such a fuckup, and he didn't know whether to be pissed that she had so little faith in him . . . or if he should just kick his own ass for failing to make his feelings for her clear. "You think I *care* about you? Like the same way I'd *care* about my elderly neighbors or a pal at work?" He moved closer, hating the pain he could see shimmering in her beautiful eyes. But, damn it, he was hurting, too. "After last night, is that honestly what you think, Lily?"

She bit her lower lip, and her gaze slid away. "I don't want to fight with you."

Bitterness sharpened his voice. "Then you should have thought of that before trying to sneak out on me."

Her head snapped back in his direction and her eyes went wide. "I wasn't sneaking anywhere. I was going to talk to you before I left."

"Yeah? Then call back and cancel that damn car."

"Scott, I—"

"There's a hell of a lot we need to say to each other," he growled, cutting her off, "and we can't do it here. At least come back to my house with me. You owe me that much."

She sucked in a sharp breath, then reluctantly nodded, calling the car service to say that she'd be in touch with a new address and pickup time as soon as possible. Working his jaw, Ryder grabbed their bags—a deputy had brought hers from across the hall earlier—then followed her out of the room. They came across Ben in the living room, which was still crowded with deputies, and Ryder told him he was taking Lily home. Ben nodded, casting a worried look at her pale face, no doubt thinking she was upset because of what had happened with Rado, and Ryder didn't correct him. But he knew Lily well enough to understand that even though she'd been concerned for his safety, she was as thankful as he was that Radovich had finally been dealt with, once and for all.

They made their way out to the Jeep after finding Mike and thanking him, and the drive to his house was quietly tense, the air heavy with the weight of everything that needed to be said. No matter how many ways he turned it over in his head, Ryder knew that the crux of the matter was the fact that she trusted him. Since coming back into his life, she'd trusted him with her body, with her heart, and with her well-being. It was far past time that he trusted her, too. And maybe, just maybe, he needed to trust that together they were right where they were meant to be.

Fuck, there was no maybe about it. He was *meant* to be by this woman's side. Today. Tomorrow. For fucking eternity. And there was nothing he was going to let stand in his way. Not fear. Not his past. And sure as fuck not his desire to protect her. It was what he'd been made for. If he was crazy and overly protective at times, Lily would handle him. Hell, that's what she did best.

After all this time, he finally got it. He'd always felt like he was getting it wrong with Lily because he hadn't done what he should have done the second she was legal. Which was claim her sweet little ass by putting a ring on her finger, his name after hers, and make sure his fucking stamp of ownership was on every inch of her. And he didn't feel like a possessive ass for wanting it, because he expected her to claim him in the same fucking way.

The sun was only just coming up as he parked the Jeep in his driveway and climbed out, not bothering with their bags, just wanting to get her inside as quickly as possible. She followed him up the walkway and he opened the front door, letting her go inside first. Then he went in and locked the door behind him. If he could have barricaded the damn thing to keep her there with him, he would have. He couldn't stand the thought of her leaving him. Of not going to sleep every night with her soft little body in his arms, and waking up to her beautiful smile.

"What do you think of Moss Beach?" he asked, tossing his keys onto the small table that sat at the end of his sofa.

She was standing a few feet away, arms crossed over her middle again, and her expression made it clear that she thought it was a strange question. "Um, I haven't gotten out much. But what I've seen is beautiful. And I like the people you work with. The friends you have here."

He lifted a hand, rubbing the back of his neck. "It's a good place to build a life. Raise a family. All that normal shit I know nothing about, but that I'm, uh, hoping you'll show me."

She stared back at him, her breaths starting to come a little faster. "What are you saying, Scott? Spell it out for me."

Yeah, it was about damn time that he did that, wasn't it?

He knew that he was going to spend a long time being pissed at himself for not telling her how he felt all those years ago when he'd had the chance. He'd fucking choked, but he wasn't going to choke now. He scrubbed his hand over his mouth, then dropped it back to his side, looked her right in the eye, and said, "I love you."

Ohmygod. Lily's throat shook, melting, her eyes instantly filling with tears. "Wh-what did you say?"

He took a step toward her, looking as if he very much wanted to grab hold of her. "I love you, and I'm not the kind of man who does things in half measures. So I hope you know what this means. I don't just love you—I fucking *live and breathe* you, Lil. You are in every part of me. And I'm done running. I can't do anything now but grab hold of you so hard and tight you can't ever get away."

"I don't want to get away," she told him, breathless, unable to believe this was actually happening. "I just want *you*."

His smile was slow and sweet and sexy. "Then it sounds like we're finally on the same page. About fucking time, too. Don't you think?"

"I can't think," she gasped, barely able to breathe through her happiness. "You're smiling and that always blows my mind."

He laughed one of those rich, husky rumbles that made her toes curl, and the next thing Lily knew she was in his arms and he was kissing the hell out of her. Then they were ripping each other's clothes off, and he was taking her down to the sofa, growling that he was too desperate to get inside her to make it to a bed. She smiled and told him that she couldn't care less about a bed . . . and he could get inside her *whenever* and *wherever* he wanted, because she could never get enough of him. He came down over her, his big, beautiful body caging her in, and the way he took her mouth made it clear that he *loved* what she'd said.

"Sweetest fucking pussy in the world," he groaned when he slid inside her, a sexy lock of hair falling over his brow as he started to move. The muscles in his shoulders and arms flexed with his incredible strength, his mouthwatering abs rippling beneath his skin with each driving, deliberate stroke.

Straightening his arms, he looked down, then brought that heavy-lidded gaze back to hers. "Watch it go in, Lil. Look at us together. You're so pretty and pink, your swollen little entrance stretched so tight around me, barely able to take me. But you're slicking me up so nice and hot, you just suck me right in."

"Oh, God," she gasped, lifting her head from the sofa cushion so she could watch.

A deep, guttural growl rumbled in his chest. "You have no idea how incredible it feels when I pull out, all those plush little muscles inside you fighting to hold on to me. And then the slow thrust, forcing my way back in. You have no idea how it feels to know that you're *mine*. If you knew, baby, then you never would have thought I could let you walk away." His gaze sharpened, and his voice got rougher, the raw edge telling her how much he liked what they were doing. "I'll never get enough, Lily. No matter how many times I have you, I'll just want you more."

"*Scott*," she moaned, writhing from the blissful sensation of having him so hard and deep inside her. A part of her.

"I love you." He punctuated each rough word with an even harder thrust, slamming into her with thick, grinding lunges that sent her crashing over the edge. She screamed his name, arching, shuddering, her mouth open as she gasped and cried and tried to breathe through the wrenching pleasure, her body convulsing in sharp, heavy jolts that pulled her tighter and tighter around him.

"*I don't want to lose you*," he snarled under his breath.

"You won't. I'll always be here. Always," she promised, her words pushing him over the edge. His hips jerked against her as he let out a guttural shout, his arms banding around her as his cock spurted hot, heavy blasts of cum into her, filling her up until she was drenched in him. A grin curled her lips when she realized they were definitely going to be dealing with a BIG wet spot on the sofa.

"You're not getting away from me. *Ever*," he groaned when he could finally lift himself onto his elbows and look her in the eye.

"I'm not trying to get away. All I've ever wanted was to get closer. Even when I was telling myself that you would break my heart, I couldn't stay away from you." She grinned, and gave a dreamy sigh, knowing she must look like a besotted idiot and not even caring. "God, I've been waiting for so long."

He rubbed his thumb against her cheek, his dark eyes showing her every incredible emotion that was burning inside him. "For what, Lil?"

"For this. For you to make me yours."

"It was inevitable," he told her, his deep voice husky and low. "There's no other woman in the world who could ever fit me the way you do. Inside *and* out. You were meant to be mine."

She shot him a playful smirk. "I'm glad you finally figured it out."

"I might be slow, but I get there in the end. And you're going to enjoy how I make it up to you, baby. I promise."

There was a wicked smile on his lips, a scorching look of hunger in his dark eyes as he started to harden inside her, and Lily looked forward to his efforts. Almost as much as she looked forward to their future. She had her man, his heart, and she knew that from this point on her life would be filled with pleasure and laughter and more love than any woman could ever possibly deserve.

And she was going to cherish every beautiful, breathtaking moment.

ABOUT THE AUTHOR

Rhyannon Byrd is an avid, longtime fan of romance and the author of more than twenty erotic and paranormal titles. She has been nominated for three RT Reviewers' Choice awards, including best shapeshifter romance, and her books have been translated into nine languages. After having spent years enjoying the glorious sunshine of the American South and Southwest, Rhyannon now lives in the beautiful, but often chilly, English countryside with her husband and family.